THE
KILLING OF
OLGA KLIMT

THE KILLING OF OLGA KLIMT

R.T. RAICHEV

The
Mystery
Press

This is a work of fiction.
All the characters are imaginary and bear no relation to
any living person.
R. T. Raichev

Original cover photograph: © iStockphoto.com

First published 2014

The Mystery Press is an imprint of The History Press
The Mill, Brimscombe Port
Stroud, Gloucestershire, GL5 2QG
www.thehistorypress.co.uk

British Library Cataloguing in Publication Data.
A catalogue record for this book is available from the British Library.

ISBN 978 0 7509 5830 1

Typesetting and origination by Thomas Bohm, User design
Printed in Great Britain

To Nick Hay, aficionado, friend and critic extraordinaire.

Also for Chitra, master of the mot juste*!*

'Well, there will be a Victim, of course. And Clues.
And Suspects. All rather conventional – you know, the Vamp
and the Blackmailer and the Young Lovers and the Sinister
Butler and so on …'

Agatha Christie, *Dead Man's Folly*

CONTENTS

1

VERTIGO

If I can't have her, no one else will.

I imagine this is one of the thoughts passing through Mr Eresby's mind at this very moment. Mr Eresby, you see, is in the grip of considerable mental turmoil – what I believe alienists term 'unrelieved anguish'. Mr Eresby's hands are clenched into fists. He keeps shaking his head. His shoulders are hunched forward. His movement can only be described as 'jerky'.

I am walking some distance behind him. I have been following Mr Eresby for the past – let me see – ten, no, twelve, minutes.

Left, right, left, right. Though all I am presented with is the back of Mr Eresby's head, I am sure his expression is still dazed, the corners of his mouth pulled down, his complexion exceedingly pale, his eyes 'unseeing'. They say exercise has a beneficial effect on the nervous system, but, in my opinion, it is too soon for any tangible changes for the better to have started manifesting themselves.

The situation is incomprehensible and, frankly, quite absurd. Mr Eresby ('Charlie' to his intimates) is young, rich and handsome and he can have any girl he wants; yet it is Olga Klimt on whom he has set his heart. No other girl will do. He says he can't live without her. He says, rather extravagantly, that he'd rather die. I read somewhere that emotional problems of such extreme nature invariably go back to one's childhood and have something to do with one's relations with one's parents. I wonder if that is true.

Mr Eresby's papa, of Eresby's Biscuits fame and fortune, has been dead twenty-two years, so Mr Eresby has no recollection of him, though his mama is still very much with us. She is a very interesting woman, 'unconventional', perhaps is the best word to describe her, and she cares deeply for Mr Eresby, even if she tends to treat him as though he were a boy of ten. Maybe *that's* the problem? Perhaps at this point I should mention that relations between me and the former Mrs Eresby – Lady Collingwood, as she now is – are excellent. Lady Collingwood regards me in a most favourable light. Indeed she thinks, if I may be excused the cliché, the world of me. She is convinced that I am an exceptional, if not unique, human being. Well, she is right. I *am* unique.

It is thanks to Lady Collingwood that I obtained my position with Mr Eresby. Lady Collingwood telephones me once a week and we have a 'chat'. She listens carefully to what I have to say. My opinions matter to her. It pains me that Lord Collingwood does not seem to share the high regard in which his wife holds me. Apparently Lord Collingwood has expressed concern about the influence I exercise over her and on two occasions at least has referred to me, somewhat fancifully, as playing Rasputin to Lady Collingwood's Russian Empress. He has also said I am 'the sort of fellow who should be tarred and feathered or, failing that, flung over a precipice'.

I would have preferred to have had my specialness confirmed, not deprecated, and having pondered the matter, I have reached the conclusion that Lord Collingwood should be punished. Not at the moment, since I have so many other things on my mind, but at some point in the not too distant future. I am not the kind of person who takes slights and slurs lightly. I do not forget easily either. Tarred and feathered indeed!

Left, right, left, right. My young master needs a haircut. I make a mental note to remind him. His hair is getting too long at the back.

I am sure Mr Eresby knows I am following him but he hasn't yet acknowledged my presence. I dab at my forehead with my handkerchief. I loosen my tie a quarter of an inch. It is the sixth of September, but it could have been the height of summer. London is 'blowsy' with heat.

I see Mr Eresby nod to himself. I observe his fists tighten. He seems to have come to some decision. What decision exactly? To end it all? To kill himself? No, to kill Olga, and *then* kill himself? This may sound ludicrously melodramatic, but isn't that what forlorn lovers do?

(Attempting to read Mr Eresby's mind is something of a hobby of mine, what bobsleighing, collecting Victorian pornography, borzoi-breeding or rearranging the furniture is for some.)

Sloane Square is now behind us. We are walking along the kind of well-bred street my master sometimes professes to despise. Symons Street. We pass by a delicatessen that looks like a mini Fortnum & Mason's, a post office with two traditional pillar boxes of gleaming red outside, an exclusive florist's, a small bookshop catering for esoteric tastes. My eye catches some of the titles of books displayed in the window: *Carnivorous Butterflies*, *The Androgynous Virgin*, *Combating Loneliness via Commercial Transactions*.

A chair in the Lowenstein antique-shop window claims my attention. It is upholstered in smooth black velvet; it has high-stepping legs and a noble straight back; it stands alone in arrogant elegance. For a second I halt. It would be perfect for my room, I think.

Left, right, left, right. My master moves like a clockwork toy soldier. I don't believe he has any definite destination in mind, but he seems determined to keep walking. The heat is becoming quite unbearable. When will this purposeless wandering cease?

Bedaux must be pleased about what happened, Charlie thought. Bedaux didn't like Olga. Bedaux had never said so, but Charlie had seen him look at her contemptuously. But what did it matter what Bedaux thought? Blast Bedaux. Bedaux could go to blazes.

I can't live without her, he thought. I love her. I have never loved anyone before. She is the first and she will be the last. I'll never love again. I can't imagine not seeing her, not hearing her voice, not holding her in my arms. I can't imagine not kissing her. I can't imagine anyone else kissing her. I'll go mad if I see her kissing someone else. I'll kill him. I'll kill her. I'll kill myself.

The night before Charlie had had a dream. It was after nightfall and he was in some small town which looked Germanic. Looking up he had seen two moons in the sky. A clock moon above a solemn black courthouse and the real moon that was slowly rising in vanilla whiteness from the dark east. He had woken up feeling happy. Never for a moment had it occurred to him that this would turn out to be the most dreadful day of his life.

I am sorry, Charlie, but I am thinking and I decide that we don't see each other any more. No, I can't tell you why not. I am sorry. Please, do not call me ever again. I don't want to see you. I am sorry. It is difficult, I know, but it is all over. I am going. You won't find me at Philomel Cottage. Don't start looking for me, because you'll never find me. It is all over.

That was what Olga had said to him on the phone. She hadn't given a word of explanation. She hadn't offered him any reason. Just when he thought nothing could possibly go wrong between them! It had been a shock. He had felt sick. He had felt faint. He had rung back at once, he had kept calling her, but she never answered.

There was somebody else, there must be. That was the obvious reason. The thought had always been there, if he had to be honest, at the back of his mind, *the fear*. Olga had mentioned a former boyfriend once, someone in Lithuania. Perhaps the former boyfriend had reappeared. The former boyfriend had come to England. Yes. That was it. That's what must have happened. The former boyfriend had claimed Olga back. Perhaps the former boyfriend was a better lover than he would ever be?

How sordid it all was. Good riddance to bad rubbish. He was a fool to care. She wasn't worth it.

I hate her, Charles whispered. I detest her. I despise her. Wayward and feckless, fickle beyond belief. Lying whore. Mercenary slut. I hate her.

No, that was not true – *he loved her*. He felt his eyes filling with tears. He would die if he couldn't have her …

Bedaux had already suggested that they go away as soon as possible, so that Mr Eresby could forget. Bedaux meant abroad. Bedaux always imagined he had all the answers. Go where exactly, Bedaux? To the Continent, sir. Bedaux had suggested Carlsbad. Bedaux seemed to have a thing about old-world European spas of the statelier kind. Bedaux was particularly keen on Carlsbad, for some reason. But that was ridiculous. No one went to Carlsbad these days, did they?

He hated Bedaux. It was thanks to Bedaux that he had met Olga. It was all Bedaux's fault. Bedaux was a duplicitous bastard, well apart from being an anachronism and a bloody fake. Bedaux was his own invention. The gentleman's personal gentleman was an inane absurdity, an idealised nostalgic concept, nothing but a carefully cultivated phantasm. Charlie couldn't stand the look and sound of him, his carefully brushed hair, his blank crash-dummy face, his voice, which was of the silkily sinister variety and brought to mind a viper slithering through velvet. Bedaux had such an annoying way of saying 'sir' – he pronounced it 'sah'– another deliberate affectation.

Earlier on, at the house, after Olga's call which had caused Charlie to collapse on the sofa in the large gold-painted barrel-vaulted drawing room, Bedaux had stood gazing at him with a clinical unsympathetic eye, with more than a hint of ironic detachment. Charlie had had the sense of being coldly appraised. He might have been a specimen on a dissecting table. He had started to light a cigarette, to calm his nerves, only the match had jumped from between his shaking fingers and fallen among the sofa cushions. He had made no attempt to retrieve it. He remembered his thoughts. *An all-consuming conflagration would be a most welcome development. It would be marvellous if I went up in flames.* But then he had heard Bedaux clear his throat.

'Do not be alarmed, sir. I have been able to locate the fugitive ember. There will be no fiery consequences.'

That Bedaux should have chosen to act the stage butler at a moment like that! Perhaps he should sack him? Yes, why not? A bloody marvellous idea. Mummy wouldn't like it but Charlie really didn't care. If Mummy was so frightfully keen on Bedaux, she could offer him employment herself, couldn't she? Mummy could make Bedaux her butler or something. Mummy had been complaining about not having a butler. No, old Collingwood wouldn't allow it. Old Collingwood disapproved of Bedaux. He had warned Charlie against Bedaux. His stepfather was an interfering old fool, but he might be right this time …

A sound came from behind. It was Bedaux clearing his throat. Bedaux was reminding him of his presence, in case the young master decided he might need him after all.

Charlie blinked. He had seen the word 'nursery' in front of him. There was a sign on his left, saying 'SYLVIE & BRUNO NURSERY SCHOOL'. How funny. He seemed to know who Sylvie and Bruno were. Of course he knew. Lewis Carroll. Why, at one time he had known 'The Mad Gardener's Song' by heart! Absolute ages ago, but he believed he could still recite it!

Charlie stood gazing at the building. It was made of fine red brick. There was a picture window and framed in it he saw a woman. She was sitting at an important-looking desk and she was talking to someone. She was wearing a perfectly tailored suit amd exuded great authority and confidence. She looked stolid. Not a type he admired. Who was she? The head nanny – if there was such a thing? *Supernanny.* Charlie had watched a TV programme of that name, all about a super nanny who helped ineffectual parents cope with their difficult ultra-feral offspring.

For some reason Charlie couldn't tear his eyes from the picture window.

'A fact so dread,' he faintly said, 'extinguishes all hope.'

It was the Mad Gardener in *Sylvie and Bruno* who said that. Extinguish all hope, eh? Charlie laughed. He couldn't help himself. He hadn't meant to. He was feeling rather wobbly, actually. A touch of vertigo. More than a touch. Unwise to laugh. It was so terribly hot. Hot and stuffy.

Who was the super nanny talking to? There was someone in the room with her.

Suddenly a little boy appeared at the window. He stood there, looking at Charlie.

Charlie tried waving at the boy but his hand refused to obey him. He frowned. He knew that something was about to happen. Something momentous –

He shouldn't have laughed – it was wrong to laugh when he felt like weeping – his head felt bad – everything had started whirling around him – turning black – bright spots dancing before his eyes – all the hues of the rainbow – Olga loved dancing –

What was that? The sound of rushing water? Or was it footsteps? Someone – running?

I manage to catch Mr Eresby as he falls.

He feels as light as the proverbial feather. Despite my best efforts, he hasn't been eating properly.

I hold Mr Eresby in my arms and for a moment time stands still. I imagine we look like that famous picture, *Death of Nelson*. The heroic admiral, mortally wounded, uttering his last words, 'Kiss me Hardy.' Or did he really say, 'Kismet, Hardy' – as some claimed?

(Would I kiss Mr Eresby if he asked me to?)

'Ah, Bedaux. Good man. You caught me, didn't you? I knew you would. Always there for me, the way you promised Mummy … I think there was someone dancing, wasn't there? Rushing water. I am thirsty, actually …' Mr Eresby's hand creeps up to his forehead. His eyelids flutter. 'The sound of rushing water – yes – there it is again – can you hear it?'

I look round – I might need help – I might have to call an ambulance – I seem to have left my mobile behind and it doesn't look as if Mr Eresby's got his either – what's that building – a nursery?

'Look here, Bedaux, I did you an injustice. I thought of you as an anachronism. I apologise. I thought I'd sack you but of course I won't. I am not myself today. Would you do something for me?'

'Certainly, sir.'

'Do you promise?'

'I promise.'

'On your honour?'

'On my honour.'

'You sound as though you are humouring me. Do let's be serious, shall we? I want you to contact the Home Office.'

'The Home Office, sir?'

'That's what I said. The Home Office ... '

It is clear to me the strain on Mr Eresby's mind and the emotions have taken their toll. Mr Eresby appears to be losing his grip on reality. I believe he is delirious.

Who would have thought he would take Olga's rejection so badly?

For a split second I feel a stab of what I imagine is guilt. A glimmer of remorse daintily running along the steel of my conspiratorial dagger. It is a most unaccustomed sensation and I am surprised at myself. I wonder whether to tell him the truth, which of course, will be only *part* of the truth – namely, that his misery will soon be at an end ...

No, I can't. I mustn't. Not the truth.

It would mean revealing the plot. Or rather, the Plot.

'I want you to call the Home Office and tell them she is an illegal alien – that she must be punished – no, deported – tell them that she's got a false passport. That's a criminal offence. Actually, no. I've changed my mind. Don't tell them anything. I would probably want to go after her. I am weak, you see. I am emotionally immature. That's what old Collingwood says. I may be a little crazy too. I am in love with her. I'll go after her. Then – then the misery will continue –' Mr Eresby breaks off. 'I have changed my mind, you see.'

'Sir?'

'I might decide to follow her all the way to the Baltic, Bedaux ... That's where she comes from ... The Baltic ... She said she would take me there ... She promised to introduce me to her mother … It hurts so much, Bedaux – *here.*' Mr Eresby points to his chest. 'You can't imagine how much it hurts. I feel ill. I can't stand it any longer – the misery.'

'Shall I call an ambulance, sir?'

'Actually, I've got a better idea. I want her dead, Bedaux. Dead, yes. I mean it. I am not delirious or anything of the sort. *I want Olga dead.* Stop looking round and listen. I am not afraid of killing her, only if I did kill her, I would be the first to be suspected. Do you see? But if I were to have an alibi …' Mr Eresby licks his lips. 'If I were to go away … To Baden-Baden, as you suggested – or to good old anachronistic Carlsbad – but I'll go on my own – without you.'

'Without me, sir?'

'Yes. You will stay in London. I will give you money – a lot of money – any sum you wish to name –'

'Money?'

'Yes.' Mr Eresby grips my hand. 'You like money, don't you? I want you to kill her, Bedaux. That's the only way to stop the pain – stop the misery. Would you do it? Would you kill Olga for me?'

2

THE CHILDREN'S HOUR

'Are you Sylvie?' Eddy asked.

'I am afraid I am not.'

'Why are you afraid you are not?'

'Because 'Sylvie' is a lovely name and I wish it were mine but it isn't.'

'Are you Miss Bruno then?'

'No –'

'What is your name?'

'Stop asking questions, Eddy,' Antonia said.

'No, that's all right, Miss Darcy. We tend to encourage inquisitive minds here. I must say I find his lack of bashfulness refreshing. Most of the children I meet for the first time are too shy and too tongue-tied for my liking. Besides, Eddy does need to know my name since I am going to be his headmistress.'

'But you know Miss Frayle's name, Eddy. We told you. We told him.' Antonia gave an apologetic smile.

'He must have forgotten,' Miss Frayle said easily.

Eddy was Antonia's second grandchild. He was nearly five and it was going to be his first day 'at school'. A lot had been made of it at home, by both Eddy's mother and father – Antonia's son by her first husband. They had reassured Eddy he had nothing to worry about, certainly nothing to fear, that he would enjoy it, that it would be a truly memorable experience. They had frowned and shaken their heads when Hugh had said he had absolutely detested his first day at school. It had been hellish. Hugh had of course meant his prep school – or was it his public school?

'Miss Frayle,' Eddy said slowly and for some reason he sighed.

Must tell him it's ill-mannered to sigh, Antonia thought.

'Makes me want to sigh too!' Miss Frayle said with a loud laugh.

She doesn't look like a Miss Frayle at all, Antonia thought. Nothing *frail* about her, quite the reverse. Actually, she looks like a Miss Bruno. There was something reassuringly solid and dependable about the name of Bruno. Associations with 'brawny' and 'brunt' – as in the phrase 'to bear the brunt'. She must be a very patient woman too, Antonia decided.

Fenella Frayle might have read Antonia's thoughts for she gave her a nod and a conspiratorial smile then pulled a droll face while at the same time slightly hunching up her shoulders. She exuded a blend of reliability, competence and good humour. Antonia decided she rather liked her.

How old was she? Mid-thirties? Her hair was a glossy brown (*brun?*) and she had apple cheeks. She appeared to be in glowing health. She had a compact capable body and was clad in a smart dark blue suit, with a little gold-and-diamond brooch on the lapel. Her eyes were aquamarine blue, very bright, slightly exophthalmic, her chin well shaped and determined-looking. Her expression was unflaggingly cheerful.

Eddy will be in safe hands, Antonia thought.

'Is this your nursery school?' Eddy asked.

'It is mine, yes.' Something like a shadow crossed her face. Antonia saw her frown down at a sheet of paper.

'The house is called "Jevanny Lodge". It looks very old,' Eddy said. 'The name's written above the door – "Jevanny Lodge". I can read, you see. It looks spooky.'

'The house is very old, you are absolutely right, eighteenth century, a listed building, but it's completely renovated inside. It cost me a pretty penny to have it done up!' She laughed – a little ruefully, Antonia thought.

'Do you live here?'

'I do. My snuggery is upstairs.'

'What is "snuggery"?'

'My quarters.'

'Why do you call it "snuggery"?'

'Because it's terribly snug. I can put up my feet and have a cup of tea.'

'Do you like putting up your feet?'

'Eddy,' Antonia said. Really, the boy should be working for the Spanish Inquisition.

'Oh very much. I like it awfully. I am often tired, you know.'

'Can I see your snuggery?'

'I am afraid children are not allowed there. My quarters are out of bounds. As head mistresses go, I am fairly liberal but I do draw the line somewhere.' Miss Frayle laughed again. 'Anyhow. I am sure you will have a jolly good time with us.'

'Would I "adore" my time with you?'

'Goodness. You *are* clever, aren't you?'

'We read him your advertisement. That's how he learnt "adore",' Antonia explained.

'So that's my word, is it?'

'Yes, it's your word. Adore. *Adore.*' Eddy yawned.

'How funny! I'd completely forgotten!'

Must tell him it's rude to yawn, Antonia thought.

'I must say I am terribly impressed by you, Eddy.' Miss Frayle leant forward slightly. 'You said you could read and write, correct? Did your mummy and daddy teach you?'

'Granny taught me,' Eddy said. 'Granny is a writer.'

'I know.' Fenella Frayle gave a solemn nod. She smiled at Antonia. 'You must be very proud of your granny.'

'Her books are in all the bookshops,' Eddy said. 'In all the bookshops in the world.'

'No, not in all the bookshops,' Antonia said. 'Really, Eddy, I don't think you —'

'My granny writes about murders. She is very clever. She notices things no one else notices. In Granny's books people get killed.'

'I know. As a matter of fact I have read two of your granny's books. I enjoyed them very much indeed. I suppose you have read all her books?' Fenella Frayle said with a twinkle.

'I haven't. Granny writes about *murders*. I am not allowed to read about *murders*.'

'When you are a little older, you will,' Fenella Frayle said comfortably. 'Well, I must say I don't get to meet many grannies who write books.'

'Granny doesn't look like a granny, does she?'

'Not in the least.'

'That's what my grandfather says — he is not *really* my grandfather — he is my *step*-grandfather — he allows me to call him "Hugh" — he says he loves Granny in any and every state she happens to be in — especially when she is annoyed with him — he is very funny — he calls me a "fearful Jesuit"— because mummy is a Catholic, you see — Granny was married *twice* — Hugh married Granny after —'

'That's enough, Eddy.' Antonia's manner was brisk.

'You wrote little boys and girls would adore their time with you,' Eddy told Miss Frayle. 'You wrote that they'd love the "home corner". What is a home corner?'

As Fenella Frayle started explaining, Antonia's thoughts went back to the Sylvie & Bruno website. The Sylvie & Bruno Nursery School was renowned for its warm and friendly environment. Children were nurtured by well-qualified and caring teachers and enthusiastic assistants. They were taught how to develop coordination, concentration and independence. They were carefully instructed on how to interact positively with a wide range of other children and adults before they were ready to move on to the wider environment of pre-prep.

Jolly impressive, Hugh had conceded – though he was not sure he cared for the sound of 'pre-prep'.

At our nursery school your child is introduced to the fundamentals of early years education. To create a strong base for future learning, great importance is placed on literacy and numeracy. Children also begin French, music and PE. Sylvie & Bruno Nursery School is exceptionally well resourced. Sand and water play, the art and craft table, a computer corner and a construction area, all have an important part in the structure of our school …

'So you see, the home corner constantly changes from being a shop to a doctor's surgery, an estate agent's, a royal palace, even a jungle,' Miss Frayle was saying. 'Something tells me you will like our jungle.'

Eddy frowned. 'It's not with *real* animals, is it?'

'I am afraid not. Our children love dressing up as bears and zebras and wolves and foxes. We have the most wonderful dressing-up box –'

'No one dresses up as a *zebra*.' Eddy countered. 'That would be *silly*.'

'Eddy,' Antonia said admonishingly. Fenella Frayle's face had turned a little red.

He slid down his chair. 'Can I look out of the window?' Without waiting for permission, he strode up to the picture window and stood looking out.

'Eddy –'

'No, that's all right, Miss Darcy. Let him. Bored, poor thing. I don't blame him,' Fenella Frayle said. 'My fault, really. I do tend to go on, don't I?'

'No, no,' Antonia protested. 'Not at all.'

'Oh, look, Granny! A man fell – another man catched him!' Eddy pointed excitedly. 'I think he is dead!'

'Caught him,' Antonia said automatically.

'The man is dead!'

'I don't think that's terribly likely … I'll be very annoyed if –! Where? You're making things up, aren't you?'

'I am not, Granny – *look*!' Eddy pointed again. 'The man is dead!'

Fenella Frayle joined Eddy and Antonia by the picture window. 'He's right. I do believe someone's fainted in the street. I think they may need our help.'

3

THE KINDNESS OF STRANGERS

Jevanny Lodge was a tall, square, red-brick house, built in the reign of Queen Anne. A stone-pillared porch had been added in the purer classical style of 1790; the windows of the house were many, tall and narrow, with small panes and thick white woodwork. A pediment, pierced with a round window, crowned the front. There were wings to right and left, connected by curious glazed galleries, supported by colonnades.

'It looks like a fit. We'll take him upstairs, Miss Thornton,' Fenella Frayle told the teacher she had called, a freckled young woman whose physique suggested a gym mistress.

'He is not epileptic, is he?' Miss Thornton asked.

'I have no idea. I hope not.'

'Can I go with them?' Eddy asked.

'Certainly not.' Antonia kept a restraining arm across her grandson's chest.

'Why not?'

'It would be inappropriate.'

'What does that mean?' Eddy looked up at her.

'It means you would be in the way.'

'Will the man die?'

'He may, if you go on asking questions.'

She needed to keep an eye on Eddy. He was bored. A minute earlier he had taken advantage of the disturbance; as soon as Miss Frayle had left the room, he had walked up to her desk and started examining the papers that lay on it. Antonia had had to call him back.

Miss Frayle's office door had been left wide open. Antonia and Eddy stood beside it, looking at the little group in the hall, ranged round the base of the stairs.

'Are the children OK?' Fenella Frayle asked.

'Overexcited,' Patricia Thornton said. 'They know something's happened and they all want to be part of it. I left them in Frostbite's care. I mean Lilian Frobisher.'

'Good. Excellent. Poor fellow – can he walk or will we have to give him a piggyback?'

'I am fine, really.' Charles Eresby staggered between his manservant and Patricia Thornton. 'I can walk. I feel a little better. It's so hot.'

'You are not epileptic, are you?' Patricia Thornton asked.

'I am not.'

'You may be without knowing it.'

'I am not.'

'You haven't got a dicky heart, have you?' Fenella Frayle said.

'No. My heart is fine. It's broken but otherwise it's fine.'

'I'd hate it if you were to keel over and snuff it on the premises,' Fenella said cheerfully. 'We'd have to send the children home and the parents wouldn't like it. You gave poor Eddy a great fright, you know – that clever little boy over there –' She pointed towards the top of the stairs.

'He didn't give me a fright.' Eddy's eyes flashed indignantly.

'He thought you were dead!'

Eddy glanced up at Antonia and mouthed, 'I don't like her.'

The dark man in the alpaca coat cleared his throat. 'I am afraid Mr Eresby is not used to high temperatures.'

'Oh, you know each other? What a relief. Jolly good. Makes all the difference. I took you for a Good Samaritan. I thought you were a casual passer-by.'

'I am Mr Eresby's manservant. My name is Bedaux.'

Antonia gazed at them curiously. Master and servant promenading *en plein air*? A rare phenomenon these days, surely, even in this part of London? Antonia had imagined that only people like Prince Charles had valets. The master, as far as she could see, was a delicately built young man dressed in a somewhat crumpled white linen suit. His hair was very fair and floppy. He was probably quite good-looking in a young-Anthony-Andrews-as-Lord-Sebastian-Flyte kind of way, but was at the moment deathly pale, and somewhat slack-mouthed … What was it he said? It was something curious … *It's broken* … He'd meant his heart, which suggested his fainting fit might not be exclusively due to the heat …

Antonia's attention shifted to the servant who was a tall dark man with an impassive face, immaculately dressed. A gentleman's gentleman, eh? Clearly, they did exist … This one seemed to run to type … Was he really one of those chaps whose entire life, like that of the late Queen Mother, was based upon duty, obligation, discretion and restraint? Something monkish about him but the eyes were watchful and – what was it? – calculating? The eyes of a man who enjoys dice games for dangerous stakes … The eyes of a Machiavelli … I mustn't let my imagination run away with me, Antonia reminded herself.

Beside her Eddy chanted under his breath, something that sounded like, 'Aunt Clo-Clo must die, Aunt Clo-Clo must die', but she paid no attention.

'Are we ready? Let me go first – can Mr Eresby manage the stairs?' The irrepressible Miss Frayle led the way up. 'We normally have a resident nurse, but she phoned in sick this morning, now wasn't that a nuisance? Would you like us to call an ambulance?'

'It might be a good idea, to be on the safe side,' Bedaux said.

'No, thank you. No ambulance. No need. I'll be all right,' Charles Eresby countered. 'I just want to sit down quietly for a bit. I need to clear my head, that's all … I am frightfully sorry for being a nuisance.'

'Not a bit of it … Can happen to anyone, even to the best of us … I felt a bit faint myself this morning … Here we are. Journey's end.' Fenella pushed open a door. 'My cubbyhole … I call it my "snuggery" … How about a drop of brandy? Old-fashioned remedies are usually the best … You aren't a teetotaller, are you? It's a bit stuffy here … I'll open the window, shall I?'

'You are frightfully kind,' Charlie said. 'I already feel better.'

But the next moment he was seized with another giddy spell and once more he heard the sound of rushing water … The figures round him started moving in a nightmarish dance … He saw Bedaux and beefy Miss Thornton whirl round, they might have been waltzing … The super nanny in her blue suit and brooch started bobbing up and down like the piston of an old-fashioned steam engine …

Shutting his eyes, he allowed them to lead him to the sofa.

Our hostess is called Fenella Frayle and her sitting room is papered in sunny Georgian yellow – red chintz curtains hang from gilded pelmets at the windows – the large sofa is of a bright cobalt blue. Even on the dullest day, I imagine one would feel uplifted by the cheerful mix of colour and pattern, the sparkle of mirror and glint of glass. The overall effect is most envigorating.

Miss Frayle offers Mr Eresby a glass of sherry, which he accepts. It should have been brandy, but it turns out she has run out of brandy. Mr Eresby takes one tiny sip, then another. His eyes close. He coughs. Mr Eresby is not used to strong drink. He shouldn't be drinking, really. Miss Frayle raises her eyebrows at me and points to the sherry decanter. I politely decline. I remain standing, my hands behind my back. I preserve a sentry-like stillness. I am gratified to observe Mr Eresby's cheeks turn a little pink.

'Eresby, did you say?' Miss Frayle says. 'Unusual name. Any connection with Eresby's Biscuits? Hope you don't mind my asking? I believe they are defunct now, or are they?'

'My father. My late father. He sold the company. That was ages ago. I was two at the time.' Mr Eresby speaks haltingly. 'I have no recollection of any of it. The biscuits do exist but they are called something else now.'

'So you are the son of the man himself! How terribly exciting! My aunt used to love Eresby's biscuits.' Miss Frayle frowns slightly. I get the impression she doesn't like her aunt.

Miss Thornton has left the room, but another youngish woman enters, whom Miss Frayle addresses as 'Miss Cooper'. Miss Cooper appears to be Miss Frayle's secretary. Miss Frayle asks her to stay with us, she then apologises, says she will be back soon and leaves the room.

Miss Cooper is thin and bespectacled and she is wearing an attractively patterned silk dress. She sits down beside the desk. Her dress rustles.

'We are used to accidents here,' she says. 'You would never believe what happened last March. One evening it was very cold and we were sitting here, in this very room, reading by the fire. Suddenly we noticed a strange roaring coming from the chimney, then outside there were flames and sparks lighting up the sky like a beacon! Two fire engines and several gallons of water later, the danger was over, but Miss Frayle was sternly warned by the firemen that before we ever put a match to another fire, the chimney had to be relined.'

'Did you hear that, Bedaux? Relined and sternly warned,' Mr Eresby says. There are two bright spots on his cheeks. 'This is fascinating. We should have our chimneys relined and sternly warned as soon as possible, don't you think?'

I hope he is not getting drunk.

I suspect the main reason for Miss Cooper's presence is to ensure that we don't get up to any mischief. We are, after all, strangers. For all Miss Frayle knows, we may be a pair of confidence tricksters specialising in gaining entry into respectable households under false colours and relieving them of any valuable objects. Mr Eresby's fainting fit could have been no more than a charade, his deathly pallor the result of some artfully applied make-up.

Miss Cooper asks whether Mr Eresby would like to glance at *The Times*. He says he would like to die.

The next moment I remember something. 'I don't think I locked the front door, sir,' I tell Mr Eresby.

'A grave omission, Bedaux.' He doesn't sound particularly concerned. 'I suppose it was my fault, rushing out madly the way I did.'

'No, not at all, sir. Would you mind if I went back and checked if everything is in order?'

'By all means. Take a cab, if you like. Do you suppose the old homestead may have been burgled?'

'I consider that a most unlikely contingency, but it would be best to go and ascertain. It wouldn't take me long.' I glance at my watch. 'I could be back in half an hour ... Will you be all right, sir?'

'What a peculiar question. I will never be all right, Bedaux.' Mr Eresby takes another sip of sherry. 'Not as long as –' He breaks off. He leans his left elbow against one of the brocade cushions and once more shuts his eyes.

I give a bow and leave the room.

As I walk down the stairs, I hear the sound of a piano and children singing lustily: 'I'd rather be a colonel with an eagle on my shoulder than a private with a chicken on my knee –'

That is a First World War song, I believe. This is an unselfconsciously old-fashioned establishment and no mistake.

I am in luck. The moment I come out of the front door I spot a cab. I hail it and get in. 'Sloane Square,' I tell the driver.

What was it Mr Eresby was about to say to me but was prevented by Miss Cooper's presence? He would never be all right – not as long as – what? – *not as long as Olga Klimt lived*? I am certain that he intended to say something along those lines.

I lean back and dab at my forehead with my handkerchief. Did I say I was something of a student of English literature and that I sometimes indulge in making parallels between real-life people and personages in novels? It occurs to me that, odd as it may appear, the literary character Mr Eresby brings to mind most at the moment is the spinster schoolmistress in *Notes on a Scandal* – at one and the same time violently besotted and viciously vengeful.

Mr Eresby asked me to kill Olga Klimt for him but I don't think he really meant it. He would be devastated if I did kill her. I believe he is experiencing a temporary derangement, what is known as a 'psychotic episode'. This is not as uncommon as some may imagine. I read somewhere, I think it was in the *Telegraph*, that seventy-six per cent of the population of the British Isles have had at least one psychotic episode at some point in their lives.

As it happens, I have murder on my mind too, though, unlike Mr Eresby, I am perfectly serious and rational about it.

Murder, yes. I have been thinking of little else the last couple of days.

How ironic that Mr Eresby should want me to kill Olga Klimt. I smile, one of my rare smiles. If only Mr Eresby knew.

If only he knew.

4

THE ENIGMA OF THE EVIL VALET

'My wife,' said Lord Collingwood, 'likes to create illusions for herself, which I tend to encourage, but *only* if they are the kind of illusions that are likely to make her happy in the long run. Otherwise I take a firm line. I tell her not to be silly. Now, don't misunderstand me, Payne. I am awfully fond of my wife. Deirdre is a delightful woman, perfectly splendid, marvellous dress sense, but bonkers.'

'Surely not?'

'I meant that in the nicest possible way. No question of her being relegated to the attic or despatched to a *maison de santé*. Heavens, no. Nothing of the sort. But I must admit there are times when she does try my patience. One thing I find awfully hard to compromise with is rigid thought patterns. An Aconite addiction is another.'

'Lady Collingwood takes Aconite?'

'Indeed she does. She keeps saying it's only herbal Valium. She says it's completely harmless. She's quite unable to face facts.' Lord Collingwood lowered his cigar. 'Do allow me to ask you a question, Payne, if I may, but you must try to give me an honest answer. Does your wife wear high heels?'

'I believe she does at certain times, on special occasions.'

'My wife wears high heels at *all times* – even in the country! Says she feels uprooted and destitute without her high heels – says the backs of her legs start hurting if she takes them off for more than five minutes. That sounds like another addiction, don't you think? Then there's her conversation. Deirdre's conversation is marked by what – for want of a more precise phrase – I'd call "magnificent irrelevancy". And she seems to entertain some truly extraordinary ideas – I'm not boring you frightfully, am I?'

'No, not at all,' Major Payne assured him.

It was eleven-thirty in the morning and the two men were sitting in the smoking room at the Military Club in St James's.

'Deirdre's been pestering me to get a butler. Each time I say no, over my dead body! Butlers don't go with an urban setting. In the country yes, in Park Lane, no. I know people do have butlers in London but I am not one to go with the flow, Payne, as you may have gathered. I told her she would only get a butler over my dead body. She is also convinced that Charlie'll flood Sloane Square with his bath water should Bedaux let him out of his sight for one single moment, so she has instructed Bedaux to keep to Charlie's side at all times. Bedaux apparently follows Charlie like Mary's lamb. Charlie's my stepson,' Lord Collingwood explained with a scowl.

'Who's Bedaux?' Major Payne asked.

'Charlie's man. He's the sort of fellow that deserves to be flung over a precipice or, failing that, tarred and feathered. However, my wife won't accept any criticism of him. Bedaux is one of Deirdre's blind spots.' Lord Collingwood's face was very red now. 'He's been boasting about the regime he's managed to establish *chez* Charlie – that's the latest thing – every meal served at a precisely preordained moment, no dish on the menu ever repeated and every foodstuff of the highest quality!'

'Nothing wrong with that, is there?'

'No, but I doubt if any of it's true. The fellow's the worst slacker and scrounger who ever lived, Payne. Bedaux also told Deirdre he buttered and sliced Charlie's toast into convenient fingers every morning at breakfast. Deirdre's terribly impressed. Bedaux has her eating out of his hand. He's been overstepping the mark in the most outrageous manner, Payne. He is a malignant creature. Your wife writes crime, doesn't she?'

'She does, yes.' Payne blinked, somewhat startled by the change of subject. 'Very old-fashioned crime.'

'I understand her plots sometimes go wildly beyond the probable but not beyond the possible, that correct? Perhaps she may write a short story about someone like Bedaux one day? "The Enigma of the Nefarious Factotum" – something on those lines? Or she may be inspired to pen a novella about the facades most villains take such care to maintain?'

'Antonia does that quite a lot, actually. The characters in her books are rarely what they seem. Is Bedaux a villain?'

'Oh, without the slightest shadow of a doubt. Shall I tell you what's behind villainy, Payne? Bad blood, that's what. Bad blood has a lot to answer for. You'd never believe this,' Lord Collingwood went on, dropping his voice, 'but a couple of months ago I discovered that an early ancestor of mine had been one of the signatories to the death warrant of Charles I. Gave me quite a turn, I must admit. Couldn't sleep a wink for quite a while. Haven't had much peace since. Keep thinking about it. Still struggling to make sense of it.'

'A republican Collingwood, eh?'

'Just your saying it sends shivers down my spine. He was unquestionably mad. I find myself in a furnace of shame each time I think about it.' Lord Collingwood paused. He sat examining the burning end of his cigar. 'Sometimes you encounter a seemingly good family, perfect pedigree and so on, but what you don't realise, what you never get a glimpse of, is that behind the sunny facade a kink is being passed down the centuries, from father to son, from father to son, from father to son –'

'Or daughter?'

Collingwood shot Payne a startled glance. His eyes bulged a little. 'Or, as you say, daughter … Do you know anything about a Collingwood daughter?'

'No, nothing at all. Of course not.' Payne wondered why Lord Collingwood suddenly looked so agitated.

'Take the Hitler family, for example. Apparently there are three Hitler nephews who live in America. Under assumed names, naturally, so nobody knows who they are. Well, they are said to have made a pact never to marry and never to procreate, which strikes me as a jolly sound idea. They are clearly convinced that they carry a murderous mad-dictator gene … What do you think?'

'I don't know. Some have compared the bad heredity hypothesis to astrology –'

'The Hitler chaps did the right thing. Discontinue the line, that's the only way to deal with it. Crackpots cause havoc, Payne. Flawed thinking ruins lives. One must be radical in such matters. For the good of civilisation and so on. I am strongly in favour of the "final solution" where madness is concerned. I can't help holding awfully strong views on the subject. I wasn't brought up to compromise. In that respect I take after Mama. So you don't suppose murderers are born murderers, do you?'

'I am not sure.'

'*The Cain Anomaly.* How's that for a book title?'

'Sounds intriguing.'

'It does, doesn't it?' Lord Collingwood beamed. 'That's the title of the book I intend to write one day. All on the theme of bad blood. *The* Cain, don't you know. The very first killer who ever lived. You may have gathered that your wife is not the only one who scribbles. I do it myself. Now and then. Nothing serious so far. Nothing like your wife. How many books has she written to date?'

'Nine. She's just changed publishers.'

'Writing, I find, keeps the Black Dog at bay. Better than any pill! "A Soul-bartering Subaltern". That was a long poem I wrote once – it unspooled in a single movement, I remember. I had it published privately. Press owned by a cousin of mine.'

'Was it a hit?' Payne asked politely.

'All my friends liked it. But of course poetry doesn't sell, as I am sure you are well aware. Not that I need the money. Someone reviewed it in some publication or other, can't remember which one. A terribly clever review. My poem was described, if I correctly recall, as having stretched the capacities of free verse to the limits of their acceptability. That's damned clever, don't you think? I then wrote a Shavian skit about a lapsed atheist who loses his faith in godlessness.'

'Didn't Shaw actually use the concept in his play *Too Good to be True*?'

'Did he? I have no idea. I am sure he didn't. I think you are wrong.' Lord Collingood showed signs of annoyance. 'But I was telling you about Bedaux. Well, there are strong indications that Bedaux's devious and dubious, rather than devoted, if one may put it like that.'

'What's he done?'

'It's rather a tedious story. So boring, it's bound to send you to sleep. Sure you want to hear it? Very well. Don't say I didn't warn you.' Lord Collingwood leant back in his armchair. 'Charlie had a girlfriend. Girl called Joan Selwyn. Good family, on her *mother's* side – father a banker with JP Morgan – finishing school in Switzerland – all the rest of it. I used to – um – know her mother quite well at one time. Joanie is very spirited, though a little on the plain side and perhaps the tiniest bit bossy. She and Charlie are not together any more but it took her quite a bit to let go. She was awfully keen on Charlie. Head over heels in love. Would walk through broken glass for him! Heaven knows what she saw in him, but there you are. I mean, if I were a girl, Charlie's the last chap I'd set my cap at. The boy's a sap and a damned neurotic. In addition to being a confounded nuisance.'

'He is rich, I suppose? As far as I know the Eresby fortune –'

'Yes, yes. That's a circumstance not to be sneezed at, I know, but Joanie said she loved him for himself. For my part, I've found dealing with him to be as difficult as dealing with hunt saboteurs. As stubborn as Balaam's ass. Have you ever had to deal with hunt saboteurs, Payne?'

'No, not for some time.'

'Poor Mama's being driven out of her mind by hunt saboteurs. Those pheasant shoots at your aunt's place were quite something, weren't they? Shame she's had to sell Chalfont, but that's the way it is these days, I suppose … I'm thinking of selling myself though not before Mama kicks the bucket, perhaps. It would be unfair otherwise … Collingwood Castle's quite something but it costs a fortune to maintain … Shall we have some fresh coffee? This new chap's too slow – why is he so slow? I believe he's foreign. This place is going to the dogs, the country itself is going to the dogs, wouldn't you say?'

'The coffee's as good as ever,' Payne said brightly. Raising his hand, he managed to attract the waiter's attention.

'One wonders for how long! Where was I? Oh yes. Apparently things between Joan and Charlie started going wrong the moment Bedaux appeared on the scene. Joan found Bedaux's manner towards her cold and supercilious, bordering on the offensive. Bedaux made it glaringly obvious he resented her presence *chez* Charlie and considered her surplus to requirements. When she told Charlie about it, he said she'd imagined it.

'They were on the point of tying the knot, so they gave a party at Charlie's place, a kind of pre-engagement bash for some of their friends. Well, only hours before the party starts, Joan learns catering is to be provided by some firm she's never heard of before and not by the people she's recommended to Charlie. Charlie informs her it was Bedaux who did the hiring. Then the caterers arrive and they are revealed as three girlies, all of them foreign and pretty as pictures and wearing uniforms that don't look like uniforms at all. Poor Joan says nothing but, naturally, she is frightfully upset and cross —'

'There's our coffee,' Payne said. 'Jealous, was she?'

'Indeed she was. She told me all about it. She regards me as a kind of father figure. She said it wasn't just the way the girlies looked, it was also the way in which they acted — trying to catch Charlie's eye, leaning over him, letting their hands brush against his. Charlie has no head for drink. After knocking back half a glass of champagne he starts hitting on one of the girls — engages her in a conversation that goes on for some time. For quite some time. It's obvious he has taken a fancy to her. The girl's name is Olga Klimt.'

'Olga Klimt?'

'Olga Klimt. She was wearing a name tag — all three girls were. Charlie couldn't hide the fact he fancied her madly. Couldn't keep his eyes off her. Hands ditto. Joanie actually heard him asking Olga Klimt for her phone number. When later that night poor Joanie asked for an explanation, he denied being smitten, but from then on nothing was the same again. The long and the short of it is that he's ditched her since and has been seeing Olga Klimt instead.'

'What is she — Russian?'

'Of Baltic extraction. Latvian or Lithuanian or something. I haven't seen her but apparently she's something pretty special to look at. A beauty of luminous, shimmering fairness, with a figure to match, Joanie described her as. Charlie has severed all links with Joanie. And not a word of explanation! At first she couldn't believe it and she kept ringing him but he never answered his mobile phone. And d'you know what happened when she tried his landline?'

'It was Bedaux who answered?'

Lord Collingwood shot Major Payne a glance full of surprised admiration. Payne might have suddenly produced a rabbit from his coffee cup.

'What a clever chap you are! Yes! Each time she phoned it was Bedaux she got, and each time he said the same thing in his stuffiest voice, "Mr Eresby is out." The stage butler, you know. Well, Joan's jolly determined. She had a key to the house but when she went round, she discovered the lock had been changed. She rang the front-door bell but got no response. She said she stood outside the front door for ages. At one point she glanced up and she saw Bedaux standing at a first-floor window, gazing down at her. She said he had a little smile on his lips. Not a nice smile. Well, it confirmed what she'd suspected all along – that Bedaux was behind it. That it was Bedaux who was pulling the strings.'

'What happened next?'

'Well, she started to follow Charlie and Olga whenever she got the chance, once all the way to the Royal Albert Hall. "Stalked" them, I believe is the technical term? A confrontation or what-have-you took place at the Albert Hall, in the first interval of whatever it was they'd been watching. Joanie made a frightful scene. She said she couldn't help herself. She told Olga she'd kill her. Charlie threatened to call the police. Well, Joanie phoned me as soon as she got back home that evening, that's when I heard the whole sorry tale. She wasn't crying or anything. She sounded icily calm. She said she intended to kill Olga Klimt. Now, isn't that extraordinary?'

'People who publicly declare they are going to kill someone, rarely do it.' Payne raised his coffee cup to his lips.

'Joanie is an odd girl. She's unlike most people,' Lord Collingwood said thoughtfully. 'I got to know her quite well. She used to be my secretary, did I say? Bright as a button. Determined. She is convinced Bedaux and Olga Klimt are acting in cahoots and that they are out to get Charlie's money or some such thing. She holds Bedaux responsible for having engineered the whole thing – for corrupting Charlie, or rather for detecting his weakness for sluts and satisfying it.'

'She thinks it was Bedaux who pushed Olga into Charlie's arms?'

'She's convinced of it. She referred to Bedaux as "no more than a glorified pimp" and she regards Charlie as his innocent victim. Well, when we talked that night, she still believed she had a chance with Charlie. She begged me to have a word with him, which I did – against my better judgement. I managed to speak to him on the phone the following day.'

'What did you say?'

'I told Charlie I had received information from an impeccable source, to the effect that his man and the Lithuanian siren were in some kind of transgressional partnership. I said he might actually be in danger.'

'What did he say?'

'He sneered. He said that my impeccable informant had been talking through his hat. Bedaux had nothing to do with Olga. *Bedaux strongly disapproved of his affair with Olga.* Then he said he had every intention of marrying Olga and neither I nor his mother could do anything about it, so there.'

'He intends to marry her? Does Lady Collingwood know about it?'

'No, of course not. My mother is eighty-eight and her health is a delicate balance between cautious living and complex medication – oh, you mean Deirdre? Ha, ha. That's terribly funny. I did mention it to her, yes. Ha, ha. Deirdre wasn't at all perturbed.' Lord Collingwood took a sip of coffee. 'Far from it. She said Charlie was a big boy now and perfectly capable of making decisions for himself. She said she would rather set off for Valhalla in a flaming longship than interfere in the lives of her children.'

'I didn't know Deirdre had other children.'

'She hasn't got other children. Charlie's her only son. My wife's a delightful woman, Payne, perfectly splendid, but she does talk rot. Well, I got back to Joan and told her I'd drawn a blank. She then suggested I try to buy Olga off. Or scare her off. Make her leave England. Joanie seemed convinced that with Olga out of the way, the scales would fall from Charlie's eyes, the spell would be broken and he would return to her. Failing that she said she would have no other option but to kill Olga.'

'Did she sound serious?'

'I don't know. I tried to laugh it off. Told her not to be a chump. I think she was in a terrible mental state for quite a bit. Some women take being jilted badly. And she was jilted at the altar, as good as. Jilted women tend to brood and they go into black despair and turn bitter and eccentric and so on. Remember Miss Havisham?'

'But Joan got over it?'

'Yes, yes. It all happened some time ago. She has moved on since, found someone else. Some other young chap. I haven't yet met this Olga Klimt, yet I keep wondering about her.' Lord Collingwood cleared his throat. 'She's caught my imagination. Been meaning to go and take a look at her, actually. Curious to see what a young temptress looks like. Or would that be risky? Girls like Olga Klimt can get one into trouble, can't they?'

'They most certainly can.' Payne smiled. 'Do you know where she lives?'

'As a matter of fact, I do. Place in Fulham. Philomel Cottage, Ruby Road. Property used to belong to me, actually, but then Deirdre insisted I let Charlie have it. He bought it off me. I understand Olga's been set up there. It's in Fulham. I don't think I've ever encountered a luminous, shimmering kind of beauty, have you, Payne?'

'I am not sure. I may have done.'

This, Major Payne decided, was an imbroglio worthy of Antonia's pen.

5

TRUE LOVE

I walk across Sloane Square. The clear white stucco facade of Mr Eresby's house is as unbroken and unyielding as the heat. The front door has been left unlocked, as I imagined it would be. I go into the hall, which is spacious and painted white. I stand looking round. All the furniture is white. Perhaps I could persuade Mr Eresby to change the colour scheme? White rooms are invariably so chic in the eyes of those who don't have to clean them.

No sign of any disturbance. The small Vermeer is still on the wall. The Ming vase is on the console table.

I see my somewhat distorted reflection in the round convex mirror. On an impulse I stick out my tongue, open my eyes wide and twist my face into a demented grimace. I have no idea why I do it.

Who *is* the real Bedaux, you may wonder? Not a bad chef, a man of taste, an adroit flower arranger and of course, a first-class valet and all-purpose domestic, who can keep a large house spotless with the wave of a duster. Bedaux's exterior is cunningly conventional; what it hides are tremendous reserves of ruthlessness, of ice, of steel and of enterprise. You would scarcely believe me if I told you about the powers I exercise over some people …

I imagine I catch a sound from the direction of the drawing room. A tinkling kind of sound? I stand and listen. No, it's nothing.

I remind myself that I need to collect my mobile phone as well as Mr Eresby's phone but then I hear the tinkling again and I freeze. There *is* someone in the house. A burglar? The odious Joan Selwyn? No, unlikely to be her. It can't be the police, can it? I *have* been playing with fire …

I pick up a stick with a heavy bronze handle in the shape of a leopard's head and tiptoe to the drawing room. I hold the stick aloft.

The door is ajar –

I see Olga.

She is sitting on the sofa, drinking Tia Maria from a tall glass. The tinkling sound again. She has been in the kitchen and helped herself to ice.

The drawing room, in case you are interested, is not over-furnished; rather the effect I have aimed at is one of luxurious restraint.

'The front door is open. You leave the front door open! Why is the front door open?' Olga speaks in the silly peremptory voice she assumes with me when she believes Mr Eresby is within earshot. 'I sit here and I wait. I wait for light years. I try to phone Charlie, one, two, three times, but Charlie doesn't answer!'

'He doesn't have his mobile with him.'

'Where is Charlie?'

'He is not here. *Relax.*' I regard her with my head on one side. I am really glad to see her. I feel that very rare, very special kind of warmth rising in my chest. I lean over, hold her face between my hands and kiss her on the mouth. 'Why have you come?'

'You tell me to come, you don't remember? To come and tell Charlie it is all a game, a test!' She sounds sulkily impatient.

'I told you to come tomorrow, you silly goose.' I find it difficult to keep the affection out of my voice. 'But it's good you are here. The reconciliation may as well take place today. I have decided to truncate his ordeal.'

Anyone looking less like a goose I cannot imagine. Olga has short silvery-blonde hair, a wide sensuous mouth, high cheekbones and amber-coloured eyes – she is beautiful in a wild and rather animal kind of way. Strangely enough, she also brings to mind a dryad.

'Where is Charlie?'

'At the Sylvie & Bruno Nursery School. I left him in the capable hands of Miss Fenella Frayle.'

'What nursery? Who is this Miss Fenella? What is this foolishness? You joke, yes?'

I explain what has happened.

'He faints? Really? He is so upset when I tell him I don't want to see him that he faints? So he loves me?'

'He is mad about you.'

'He can't live without me.' She sighs luxuriantly.

'Operation Hard-to-Get has been an unqualified success, my darling. You can throw yourself into his arms without any reservation now.' I speak slowly, enunciating every word with care. 'You are now in a position to dictate your terms. He will be so relieved, he will probably insist on marrying you on the spot, or tomorrow at the latest.' I sit next to her on the sofa. Once more I kiss her lips, then I kiss her throat, then her lips again. Olga's lips are soft and pliant. 'Marriage or nothing, remember,' I murmur.

'He will be so happy when I tell him it is all a game, that I am only testing his feelings!'

'He will be ecstatic. In the circumstances, it would be unwise for us to prolong his ordeal. He said he couldn't bear the misery. He is in a bad way. We may have overestimated his stamina.'

'Poor Charlie.' Olga takes a sip of Tia Maria. 'You mean he is ill? Very ill?'

'I told you he fainted in the street right outside that nursery school. He had to be helped to Miss Frayle's sofa. His legs gave way. He is suffering pangs and agonies because you told him you didn't want to see him again.'

She shrugs. 'I only tell him what you tell me to tell him.'

'How elegantly you express yourself. Don't worry. You are a good child.' I pat her cheek. Although her passport says she is twenty, Olga is in actual fact only seventeen and three months. I found her birth certificate among the papers she brought with her from Lithuania.

'What else does Charlie say?'

'Well, he said his heart was broken and that he wanted to die. Oh yes, he also asked me to kill you.' I put my hands round her throat playfully.

'He wants you to kill me? Really? I like it. It is exciting, I think. But he is not serious, no?'

I look up at the ceiling. 'I don't know. He was extremely upset when he said it.'

'He loves me so much, he wants me to die ... It is poetic, I think ... It is pity I don't love him ... Charlie is nice and I like him but I do not *love* him. Love is special ... I love Mr Bedaux. Does Mr Bedaux love me?'

'You know he does.'

We kiss again. Would it surprise you to know that Olga is the first woman I have ever kissed?

She grips my hand. 'Tell me your first name. *Please.* What is your first name?'

'I haven't got a first name.'

'You joke, yes? What is your first name?'

'I will tell you some other time.'

I pull away. Well, business first. I look at the clock.

'Please, don't go,' she says. 'Stay with me.'

'We mustn't prolong Mr Eresby's agony. If we do, his brain may suffer some permanent damage.'

'It is your fault if he suffers damage! It is your idea, this stupid game! You say, make him suffer, make him cry, make his life hell, then, at right moment, at right psychological moment, go back to him, say it is all a game and ask him to marry you. This is what you say, isn't it?' She pronounces the 'p' in psychological.

'That's what I said, yes, but now it is time to end Mr Eresby's ordeal. We don't want the bridegroom to die of a broken heart, do we?'

'No. Charlie mustn't die before he marries me and before he makes a will.' She sits up. 'This is the plan. This is the plot. Our plot. He must leave all his money to me first. But I must become his wife first. And I must be good to him. *Then* he can die.'

'That is correct. Clever girl.' I rise. 'I must go now. I promise to bring him back to you as soon as I can. We'll take a cab. You wait here and when he comes in, you rush to him and embrace him. I will pretend not to mind. You kiss him with all the passion you can muster.'

'I know how to kiss.'

'You most certainly do.'

'Will he forgive me? Perhaps he doesn't forgive me? Perhaps he tells me, you play games with me, go away, you are a bad girl, I don't want to see you again?'

'He will forgive you. He is mad about you.'

She stretches out her hands towards me. 'Mr Bedaux, you make everything so simple, so easy! I love you so much. You know? I always like older men, *always*. You and I get married when Charlie dies, yes? And then we will be together for ever.'

'After a decent interval has passed, we'll get married, yes ... We'll go abroad ... To a place no one knows us ... Somewhere warm, near the sea ... Perhaps an island ... But remember, we must be very, very careful ...'

6

AN UNQUIET MIND

I spot Mr Eresby's mobile on the drawing-room table. I pick it up and check if there are any messages. No, nothing.

Just as I step out of the front door, a shaft of sunlight dazzles me and I am impelled to cover my eyes with my hand. Someone seems to have opened a car door. For a moment the blood rushes from my head and I have the completely irrational feeling that this is somehow a bad omen.

I feel like running back into the house and holding Olga in my arms, holding her as tight as I can. The impulse is powerful, but I manage to fight it down.

I decide not to hire a cab. I am going to walk. I need to collect my thoughts.

I glance round Sloane Square and note its solidity and grace, its charm and unostentatiously plutocratic decorum. The trees glow with cupreous tints. A woman is walking two Pekinese dogs on bejewelled leashes. They move at a stately pace. Although the day is warm, there is a mink stole draped round her shoulders. Her expressionless face is of the well-bred equine variety. Her pearl choker brings to mind a horse collar. The sight amuses me and I smile.

I head for Symons Street. I know I must hurry but I don't. I take my time. For some reason I do not feel like reaching my destination. I need to think and as I do, my mood changes. I stop smiling. I feel a cold hand clutching at my heart.

A vision slowly rises before my eyes.

I see Olga in Mr Eresby's arms – they are kissing passionately – it is their wedding night – they are in the double-poster bed in Mr Eresby's bedroom – they are making love –

I almost come to a halt. My heart is beating fast, too fast. Why, I believe I am jealous! Yes. The realisation frightens me. The truth is I hate the idea of sharing Olga with Mr Eresby. I try to be rational about it. I remind myself that one cannot make an omelette without breaking eggs, also that jealousy could be fatal since it is capable of destroying every careful plan Olga and I have made.

I make a conscious effort to steer my mind in a different direction. I think of the woman with the little boy at the Sylvie & Bruno Nursery School. Miss Frayle addressed the woman as 'Miss Darcy'. I have an idea I have seen that woman before. Like royalty, I rarely forget a face. I have seen her, yes. The exact place suddenly comes to me. Hatchards, in Piccadilly. It was three months ago. Yes. I had popped in to buy two books for Lady Collingwood. (*The Chalet School* and *Madame de …*)

A moment later I remember more. Her name is Antonia Darcy and she writes detective novels. When I last saw her, she was sitting at a small desk and signing copies of her latest book.

I have an uneasy feeling about her … I can't say why … I saw her looking down at me, from the top of the stairs … Well, so what? A cat can look at a king!

I used to read detective novels a great deal as a boy. I remember that I always tended to despise the police and side with the criminal. I identified with the criminal. I always thought it more fun. Didn't someone say that only as a criminal could one achieve ultimate freedom?

I believe Antonia Darcy writes traditional whodunits. I don't like whodunits. The artificiality and various contrivances of such stories irritate me. What I relish are crime stories in which you know who the culprit is from the very start and where the action is one long, unpredictable, frequently demented loop that keeps you on the edge of your seat and where all focus is on the villain.

I try to imagine how Antonia Darcy might see the situation I have engineered, how she would be likely to sketch it out in her plotting notebook, if of course she keeps one.

Two colluding lovers set out to dupe the heir to a vast fortune. The plan is to get the girl to marry the heir and subsequently kill him – but not before he has made a will leaving his money to her. The lovers will then marry and share the fortune. The male part of the conspiracy is the heir's valet who has managed to pull the wool over everybody's eyes by affecting animosity towards his master's girlfriend.

Something on those lines.

Perhaps Antonia Darcy will introduce a counterplot, or rather a complication, one that runs alongside the main murder plot … Mr Eresby asks his valet to kill Olga Klimt, not realising that the valet and Olga Klimt are intent on killing *him*.

I am smiling once more, remembering that this actually happened.

Poor innocent Mr Eresby!

How will he die? It will be a sudden kind of death, I think. There will be an accident, a freak accident, maybe. Mr Eresby will slip and smash the back of his head against the edge of the marble bath. Or he will fall in front of a speeding car. Or he may try to fix a faulty fuse by means of a stepladder and –

So many possibilities!

A vastness and variety of vistas.

(Count on a would-be murderer to have a fancy prose style.)

7

THE CONVERSATION

Phew, what a day! Fenella Frayle sat at her desk and thought back to the extraordinary conversation she had had with Charles Eresby.

After Antonia Darcy had departed and little Eddy Rushton had been introduced to his new class, Fenella went up to her snuggery to see how the uninvited guest was getting on. She found Charles Eresby – the 'biscuit heir', as she'd started thinking of him – crying into one of her sofa cushions, shaking his head and muttering to himself, or rather repeating the same phrase again and again.

'I want her dead, I want her dead, I want her dead.'

That's what it had sounded like.

Miss Cooper had apparently replenished his sherry glass twice, which was probably the reason for the strange mantra. Mr Eresby didn't seem to have a head for drink. Perhaps one day his name would appear in the *Guinness Book of Records* under the heading: first man to suffer delirium tremens induced by Croft's Original.

Fenella Frayle was good in a crisis. She had cultivated a mock-bully manner, which never became abrasive or overpowering. Like the man in the Kipling poem she was adept at keeping her head even when all about her were losing theirs.

She considered herself an expert at putting distressed souls at their ease — how many times had she had to provide comfort not only for a lachrymose child but for one of her staff as well?

She told Miss Cooper she could go, then she sat down in the armchair opposite the sofa. Charles Eresby slowly raised his head and looked at her and he started telling her his tragic story, some terrible rigmarole about a girl called Olga Klimt, whom he had loved more than anything in the world but whom he now hated.

He was in hell. That was why she had to die, Charles Eresby concluded. It was payback time. If he couldn't have her, no one else could.

'Do you know for sure if there is anyone else? Another man?' Fenella asked. She was a firm believer in the therapeutic effect of conversation.

'I have no idea. The little bitch didn't tell me. She used to have a boyfriend in Lithuania — maybe he's come to England? I am sure that's what's happened. She clearly thinks he is a better lover than I shall ever be. I'm sure they are together at this very moment!'

'You don't know that.' Fenella looked down at her neatly crossed ankles. 'You shouldn't jump to conclusions, you know.'

'If she thinks she can walk out on me, just like that, she is wrong. She can't. Well, as I said, it's payback time.'

'I do hope you won't do anything silly, Mr Eresby.'

'It won't be anything silly, I promise you. Oh no. Not *silly*.' He sniffed. 'If I can't have her, no one else can.'

'What's that supposed to mean exactly?'

'I am sure you can guess.'

'I can't. Please tell me.'

'I intend to take the ultimate drastic measure.'

'What's that?'

'*I will kill her.*'

Fenella felt the sudden urge to laugh. Really, she thought, the whole thing was too absurd for words. Of all the garbled, cliché-ridden tales of love, betrayal and revenge! The biscuit heir was clearly off his rocker. As for the Lithuanian girl, she sounded too trashy and trite for words. He wouldn't really try to kill her, would he?

'You can't go about killing people, Mr Eresby,' she said resolutely.

'Not people. Only one person. A girl called Olga Klimt. You see, I've already made up my mind.'

'They'll catch you.'

'They *won't*. I'll be really clever about it. All I need is an alibi.'

'They'll catch you.'

'They won't.'

'Alibis are tricky things, Mr Eresby. You won't be able to get away with it. Murderers almost invariably get caught these days.'

'Not always. Not if they are clever.'

'Nowadays the police have the most advanced technology –'

'Have you ever hated anyone? I mean, really hated?' Charles Eresby asked quietly.

'Sorry?' She blinked. 'Have I –?'

'Hated anyone?'

'Have I hated anyone? N-no. No! Of course not! I've never hated anyone!'

'You have.' He shook his forefinger at her. 'You have! I can see you have.'

'Nonsense. I haven't.'

'You have. You hesitated. You are a lousy liar. You are turning raspberry-red.'

'I am not.' Her hand went up to her cheek.

There was a pause.

'Who is it? It would help me enormously if you told me. Who is the person you hate? Please, tell me. Then I'll know I am not the only one. It would really help me.'

She tried to pull herself together. 'You are most certainly not the only one, Mr Eresby. All right. I agree. Everybody has hated somebody at some point in their life. A horrible boss or an obnoxious neighbour or a difficult husband or wife or –'

'Who is it you hate?'

'No one. No one.'

'It would really help me,' he said again.

'No one.'

'Please.'

'No one.'

'I should feel honoured if you confided in me.'

'The silly things you say!' Fenella laughed.

'Please.'

She threw up her hands. 'What a pest you are! Oh very well. I have an aunt who is difficult. I don't love her, though of course I wouldn't dream of killing her!'

'Who said anything about killing her?' He gave Fenella a look out of the corner of his eyes. 'So you hate your aunt?'

'All right, yes, I hate her. She is difficult.'

'How difficult?'

'Difficult enough. Very difficult. All right, extremely difficult.'

'Go on.'

'My aunt is unpredictable and can be unpleasant.' Fenella swallowed. 'She is volatile and, well, completely irrational. She enjoys saying terrible things, hurtful things, spiteful things. She is poison. Especially after she's had a drink. She enjoys intimidating me – humiliating me –'

'Go on.'

'Well, that's it. That's what she does. That's why I find her difficult. She wants to see me fail. As a matter of fact, she's been trying to sabotage my work,' Fenella suddenly blurted out.

'Oh? That sounds serious.'

'It is serious, yes … It's extremely serious … It's my life!'

He ran his fingers through his hair. 'I am interested in your aunt. I want to hear all about the old horror. You are in some way dependent on her, aren't you?'

'Well, yes. Aunt Clo-Clo started this place – this nursery school – she and I – we set it up together – we were business partners –'

'Aunt Clo-Clo? What kind of name is that?'

'That's what I used to call her when I was a child. "Aunt Clo-Clo". Her name is Clotilde.'

'What's her second name?'

'Why do you want to know? Lemarchant. Clotilde Lemarchant. She was the headmistress here before me – she is the one who owns this place officially – the Sylvie & Bruno Nursery School. Then she retired. Everything was OK for a bit – she was difficult but I could live with it – but then she decided to withdraw her financial support – I thought I could still manage but then she told me it was time for me to close down – *close down* – I couldn't believe my ears – she said she needed the building – Jevanny Lodge – for other purposes – she said she was planning to turn it into kennels!'

'She likes dogs?'

'She hates dogs. She detests dogs. She loves cats.' Fenella passed her hand across her face. 'It's sheer bloody-mindedness — she's doing it out of spite – she said I'd become too big for my boots – she said I needed to be taught a lesson – she told me to start getting rid of the "kiddies" –' Fenella's voice shook.

'Did you say she drank?'

'She drinks, yes – each time she rings, she sounds inebriated

— it's done something to her brain — she told me she'd always hated my mother, her late sister — my mother's been dead for years — she started referring to past injustices, most of them, I am sure, imaginary. I don't know what to do!'

'You sound at your wits' end,' Charlie said quietly.

'I am at my wits' end, yes — you are absolutely right — it's my life's work, you see — everything I care about is here — I can't just get rid of the children — we have some very exclusive parents — I have no life outside the school — I don't really know what to do!'

'Don't you?' He gave her another look out of the corner of his eyes. He looks like a corrupt cherub, she thought.

She took a deep breath. 'Aunt Clo-Clo told me to expect to hear from her solicitors very soon. Next week, in fact.'

It was at that point that Charles Eresby had come up with his idea. He had told her they were going to join forces. He had explained exactly what they were going to do and how it was going to work. Fenella Frayle had been unable to believe her ears — yet, what he said had a kind of mad logic about it — she believed it was the kind of thing that had been done before — in a book or in real life, she couldn't say at the moment, but somehow it made perfect sense —

No, it didn't. It was all impossible — fantastic — idiotic — completely insane, in fact.

Having outlined his plan, Charles Eresby had been violently sick all over her lovely cushions, after which he had passed out.

Fenella went on sitting at her desk, deep in thought. She jumped up when the door opened.

'Mr Bedaux,' her secretary announced.

'Who? Oh yes. Mr Eresby's manservant. Do show him in.'

A minute later Fenella was addressing the tall dark man with the carefully brushed hair who stood impassively before her. 'I am sorry, Mr Bedaux, but Mr Eresby was taken ill and we thought it prudent to call an ambulance. Mr Eresby passed out.'

'Most regrettable but I can't say I am surprised. Mr Eresby has rather a weak head for drink, I fear.'

She took this as criticism for she bristled a bit. 'It was only sherry. Anyhow. Mr Eresby was taken to —' She gave her visitor the name of the hospital. 'I wanted to phone you, but couldn't get a number. I looked under "Eresby".'

'We are ex-directory.'

'The paramedics didn't think it was anything very serious. They said Mr Eresby was dehydrated and his blood pressure seemed to be a little low. They are confident he will make a full recovery.'

Bedaux's face remained expressionless. 'That is most gratifying.'

'He will be properly examined by a doctor and may have to spend some time at the hospital.'

Bedaux gave a little bow. 'I must thank you but also apologise for all the trouble we have caused you.'

'No trouble at all! Happy to have been of assistance. Oh wait a mo —' she called out as he started retreating towards the door. She opened a drawer. 'Must give you something. This is Mr Eresby's wallet. I found it on the sofa upstairs. It is his wallet, isn't it?'

'This is his wallet, yes.'

'It must have slipped out of his pocket.' She handed the wallet to Bedaux and watched him put it into his pocket.

The next minute he was gone. Her secretary appeared at the door.

'A cup of tea, Fenella?'

'Yes, thank you, Isobel.'

'What a day, eh?'

'You can say that again. It's been a very … strange day … A dream-like feel about it … Is my poor snuggery fit for human habitation again?'

'I believe it is. Mrs Mason has cleaned up and we have kept all the windows open. Mrs Mason's removed the sofa cover and the cushions and taken them away to be washed.'

'Good show. Please, convey my thanks. I'll thank her personally when I see her.'

Fenella remained sitting at her desk. It felt like a dream, yes. Nightmare, rather. She remembered the way the biscuit heir had nodded and said, 'Don't you see? We are in the same boat. So how about it? I do yours, you do mine.'

No, none of it had happened. It couldn't have. People didn't go about exchanging – exchanging – she couldn't even bring herself to say the word!

Fenella shook her head.

The next moment she frowned. There was something she had to do, only what was it? She glanced round. Oh yes. Her scribblings! What she had written on a piece of paper earlier on, before Charles Eresby had been brought, before the arrival of Antonia Darcy and little Eddy Rushton. She had been feeling quite low, desperate, actually. It was a bloody stupid thing to have done – mad!

She had been willing her aunt to die …

Where was the blasted thing? Fenella Frayle's hand shook a little as she opened the top drawer of the desk and started rummaging inside. There it was! Thank God. How absurd to feel so relieved about it. 'Aunt Clo-Clo must die. Aunt Clo-Clo must die.'

Incriminating evidence, she murmured. It had been lying on her desk earlier on, then she'd pushed it into the drawer. She crumpled up the paper and thrust it into her pocket. She was going to burn it and she was going to flush the ashes down the lavatory. She was overreacting a bit. *Most* unlike her. How absurd to feel guilty!

By the time he had sobered up, she reflected, the biscuit heir would have forgotten all about his crazy scheme.

She started when Miss Cooper re-entered the room and placed a cup of tea on her desk.

'Little Viscount Esquilant has been caught telling lies again,' Miss Cooper said in a low voice.

'That boy will never learn,' Fenella said. 'What was it this time?'

'He told the other children his father was a housing agent.'

'His father is in the House of Lords. Wonder if we are dealing with a case of inverted snobbery. Make a note to mention it to the educational psychologist when she comes on Friday. Meanwhile, what's been done about it?'

'His lines have been doubled.'

'Jolly good. That'll teach him. It's very wrong to tell lies.' Fenella raised the teacup to her lips. 'We must discourage anything that smacks of the underhand.'

Her thoughts turned to Charles Eresby's wallet. She had examined its contents the moment she discovered it wedged between two sofa cushions. Apart from various credit cards, she had come across a photograph of a rather strikingly beautiful girl. The photo was inscribed 'From Olga to Charlie, with all my love'. Fenella had also found a piece of paper with Olga's name and an address in Fulham written on it.

Which meant she now knew not only what the perfidious Olga Klimt looked like, but also where she lived.

8

THE AFFAIR OF THE LUMINOUS BLONDE

'It's the most the remarkable coincidence. In detective stories, of course, remarkable coincidences are regarded as cheating – a lazy way of linking up important plot elements. Discerning readers feel their intelligence has been insulted and they tend to turn against the author. I do my best to avoid them in my books.' Antonia shook her head. 'I still can't quite believe that you and I, independently of each other and on the *very same day*, should have got involved with the same set of people!'

'Remarkable coincidences do happen,' Major Payne said.

'I meet Charles Eresby and his manservant at the Sylvie & Bruno Nursery School – while you – at the Military Club, of all places – sit drinking coffee with Charlie's stepfather and hear how, as a result of the manservant's machinations, Charles Eresby deserted his girlfriend and started an affair with Olga Klimt.'

'Small world, eh?'

'Staggeringly small.'

It was the evening of the same day and Antonia and Hugh Payne were at home in Hampstead.

'But perhaps today's extraordinary events prove we are meant to get involved in the Olga Klimt affair?'

THE KILLING OF OLGA KLIMT

'They prove no such thing,' Antonia said. 'Coincidences are precisely that, coincidences. Besides, there is no affair to speak of.'

'No, not yet, but there may be. Joan Selwyn has threatened to kill her. She is said to have got over it but what if she hasn't? What if she is still obsessed with Charlie? Perhaps she was merely trying to pull the wool over Collingwood's eyes? Aren't you tempted to weave one of your dauntingly devious plots round this particular group of characters?'

'I am not. Besides, they are not characters. They are people.'

'They are too good to be true. They should be in a book,' Major Payne said firmly. He produced his pipe. 'The neurotic young heir to a biscuit fortune, the manipulative manservant, the Aconite-addicted mama, the luminous blonde, jilted Joan Selwyn ... Then there's old Collingwood with his scribbling ambitions and peculiar preoccupation with bad blood ...' Payne reached out for his tobacco jar. 'I have a confession to make. I am haunted by that name. I can't get it out of my head.'

'What name?'

'Olga Klimt. It's the kind of name one might find among Freud's gruesome case histories, wouldn't you say? "The Case of Olga K." Freud's case histories are full of frustrated desires, devious thinking and savage urges, perhaps you've noticed?'

'I have noticed.'

'Same as in detective stories, actually –'

'Can't we talk about something else, Hugh? I don't feel like talking about detective stories. There's more to life than detective stories.' Antonia smiled. 'Eddy was very funny this morning. He kept asking Miss Frayle questions but then decided he didn't like her. He doesn't like to be teased. She is very nice, mind, in a reassuringly bluff, no-nonsense kind of way ... Are you looking for your matches?'

'How do you know I am looking for my matches?'

THE KILLING OF OLGA KLIMT

'What other reason could there be for patting your pockets, with your pipe clenched between your teeth, your features twisted into a ferocious grimace? You are clearly looking for your matches … They're by your elbow.'

'Thank you, darling.'

'See? We can talk about other things as well, like other people.'

'You know perfectly well we are not like other people. *The Mystery of the Luminous Blonde*. Sounds like the title of an Ellery Queen story, doesn't it? I know you don't care much for Ellery Queen. Um. How about *The Killing of Olga Klimt*? That's better, isn't it? Pleasantly alliterative. It's got a ring to it, what do you think? For some reason, I seem to think of Olga Klimt as no longer for this world. Odd, isn't it?'

'Very odd.'

'A lot of very beautiful women die young, I can't help noticing. Jean Harlow, Marilyn Monroe, Princess Diana. All blondes, as it happens. What is it about blondes that makes them so special?'

'Gentlemen prefer them … Diana wasn't a real blonde … You only have to look at those early photos.'

'Did you know Jean Harlow was actually decapitated? Sorry, darling. I seem to be in a peculiarly morbid mood tonight.'

'You are in a particularly annoying mood tonight. It wasn't Jean Harlow who was decapitated. It was Jayne Mansfield.'

'Of course it was. She was also a blonde! Another blonde! Who do you imagine is most likely to kill Olga Klimt?'

'No one is going to kill her. I find speculations like that tedious and distasteful.'

Payne looked surprised. 'Since when? It's the sort of thing we do all the time. You used to relish thinking up scenarios about people we met on planes and cruises and at hotels and so on.'

'I don't any longer. I have grown out of it,' said Antonia.

'No, you haven't. Do let's assume Joan hasn't got over Charlie. She told Collingwood that she intended to kill Olga, which makes it look a bit too obvious, but maybe proclaiming her murderous intentions to the world is only part of her cleverness? She says she's going to kill her, she does kill her, but no one believes it because it's too obvious?'

'This has been done before.'

'You are right, it has. In fact this particular plot-line has the crashing predictability of something produced by a Women's Institute writing circle.'

'It isn't as bad as that, actually. It all depends on the approach …'

'Let's consider the valet. Bedaux the blackguard. Though why should he want to kill Olga? You saw him. What's he like?'

'I don't know. I saw him only briefly. Inscrutable. The type that preserves the impassivity of a Madame Tussaud waxwork.'

'Collingwood's got his knife into him. Says the fellow's a scoundrel who deserves to be drawn and quartered, some such thing. Well, Bedaux may be regarding the future Mrs Eresby as a threat, couldn't he? Wives often take exception to their husbands' valets and have them sacked. Bedaux may also be a bit in love with his master, so there may be a green-eyed-monster element to his motive as well.'

'Bedaux may actually be in love with Olga,' Antonia said.

'Indeed he may. It was he who introduced her to Charlie, so he's known her for some time. Jealousy again! Charles Eresby himself should not be excluded from the list of suspects. OK, he is in love with Olga, but what if she has been double-crossing him? A femme fatale like Olga is bound to have an extensive circle of admirers … Incidentally, Vilnius is the capital of Lithuania, isn't it? Not Riga?'

'No, not Riga. It's Vilnius. They have the coldest winters out there. I wonder what it's like to skate out in the open,' Antonia said dreamily.

'Lady Collingwood may also have a motive. She may be strongly opposed to her son marrying a foreign adventuress. She doesn't seem to mind but that may be a front. Or we could have Joan Selwyn *and* Lady Collingwood locked in a murderous partnership. It would be a most unlikely pairing. I know you have a penchant for unlikely pairings. I don't think there have been many murders committed by female tandems. I mean in books … Have there?'

Antonia thought. 'No, not that many. There are the two women in Ruth Rendell's *A Judgement in Stone* … Genet's *The Maids* is also a possibility, though that's not exactly a detective story … What about Lord Collingwood? Could he have a motive?'

'He's been thinking of calling on Olga and he may kill her in the course of his visit.'

'I thought he was fascinated by her.'

'Oh he is. Very much so. He is dazzled by the very idea of her. That may be his undoing.' Payne nodded portentously. 'This is how it happens. He goes to the house in Fulham. All he wants is to take a look at Olga, to see how his mental image of her compares to the reality. He introduces himself as her boyfriend's stepfather and she lets him in. Collingwood finds her impossible to resist and makes a pass at her but is rebuffed. He attempts to ravish her – she fights back – he flies into a rage and hits her – she falls down, bangs her head on the fender and is instantly killed.'

'That would be a sordid case of manslaughter … Why do they call that kind of story "witty, civilised and amusing", I simply can't imagine. It is nothing of the sort,' Antonia said with an exasperated sigh.

9

TRUE LIES

'I used to be terribly fond of Rupert, perhaps I still am,' Lady
Collingwood said wistfully, 'but I have decided to face the
facts. Rupert imagines things which are not there. He has
constructed an image of me, for example, which he is only too
eager to present to the world – but that image, to put it bluntly,
is more or less counterfeit.'

Joan Selwyn frowned. 'Counterfeit?'

'Yes! Rupert takes pleasure in attributing to me opinions
which I have never given voice to – stances I have never
taken – attitudes I have never assumed. I usually learn about it
when some well-meaning soul reports it back to me. I have no
idea what exactly he hopes to achieve. It is not as though we
are going through divorce proceedings or anything like that.
I believe opinions are largely a matter of temperament, don't
you?'

'I suppose they are.' Joan hadn't the foggiest what Deirdre
meant.

Lady Collingwood raised her glass of gin fizz. She might
have been about to propose a toast but all she said was that
sooner or later *everything* came back to her. There was always
someone eager to spill the beans. 'Rupert discusses me with
you, doesn't he my dear?'

'He doesn't.' There were times Joan fervently wished she'd never got involved with the Collingwoods.

'Oh how I wish I could trust you! No, don't worry, I won't ask you to repeat what he said. I am sorry. I shouldn't be doing this. So terribly second rate, inquisitions like this.' Lady Collingwood waved a scornful hand. 'But I do know for a fact that you are his little confidante. He sees you quite often, doesn't he?'

'Not that often. I am no longer his secretary,' Joan reminded her.

The two women were sitting at a table at the Criterion. They were having aperitifs while waiting to be served lunch. It was Lady Collingwood who had issued the invitation.

'I believe you and he have some cosy little arrangement. You talk to him about Charlie and he talks to you about me. That's correct, isn't it? I don't suppose Rupert ever talks about me in a *sympathetic* way? No, you needn't answer. I am being a bore. I know it's silly of me, but I can't help feeling the tiniest bit jealous.'

'You needn't be. There is absolutely nothing between me and Lord Collingwood. And I don't talk to him about Charlie any more.'

'Rupert thinks the world of you, my dear. He keeps singing your praises. Says you were the best private secretary he ever had. He's been having dreadful problems with his current secretary. I believe he's thinking of sacking the poor wretch, perhaps he's sacked him already.'

'Lord Collingwood is extremely interested in heredity, isn't he?' Joan said.

'Well, yes. He is.' Lady Collingwood's hand went up to her forehead. 'I am sorry but I find sudden changes of subject a little disorientating. You are a very determined kind of person, aren't you, Joan? But you are right. Rupert is particularly exercised on the subject of "tainted blood". He has expressed some very radical – some may say dangerous – opinions on the subject, not dissimilar, in fact, to those entertained by the Nazi elite during the last war.'

Joan said that Lord Collingwood had struck her as a little preoccupied when they had last met.

'When was that? No, you needn't answer. You mustn't think I try to pounce on you each time Rupert's name gets a mention. I am not the least bit interested, I assure you. I don't know why we keep talking about Rupert. I do find his latest obsession a trifle puzzling. He says his family tree is "all wrong". What does he mean exactly? And he has started writing memos to himself. Or is that something people do? Doesn't that suggest some kind of split personality?'

'Not necessarily.'

'Last week Rupert ordered two pocketless suits. He says that's symbolic. Symbolic of what? He never explains what he means.' Lady Collingwood sighed. 'It seemed such a good prospect when I first married him, you know. Rupert was what we used to call a "good catch" – military-minded, Bellona's bridegroom, uncompromisingly Christian, descended from Scottish kings, his mother a former lady-in-waiting to the Countess of Athlone. There was also the sheer grandiose splendour of Collingwood Castle. I allowed myself to be won over. Not that I struggled much, mind!' She smiled. 'Have you ever been to Collingwood?'

'Once, as a little girl. With my mother.'

'Ah, your mother … *Of course* …' Lady Collingwood reached out for Joan's hand and held it in hers. 'You have been very brave, my dear. *Very brave.* I know what you have been through. I mean that whole unfortunate business of the phantom engagement.'

'If you mean Charlie and me, it wasn't a phantom engagement. It was a proper engagement, only Charlie left me soon after.'

'Unfortunately these things do happen. All break-ups are horrid. You took it rather badly, I understand?'

'I am OK now. So kind of you to ask me to lunch, Deirdre.'

'No, no, my dear, the pleasure is entirely mine! I always felt we should be friends. I must say this new colour is quite unusual. If you don't mind my saying so, it doesn't quite express your personality. It makes you look a bit frivolous, which you are not. I hardly recognised you. Did you do it because of Charlie? In the hope of getting him back? Did you attempt to bring about *un retour de flamme?*'

'No, it has nothing to do with Charlie. I have got over Charlie,' Joan said in a slightly louder voice.

'Are you sure, my dear? Rupert is not entirely convinced. He is a bit worried about you, you know.'

'He needn't be. I was upset and for a while I found it hard to cope but I managed to get over it. That's all there is to it. As a matter of fact I'm seeing someone else. So it is not as bad as you seem to imagine.'

'Sometimes, sadly, things are as bad as we imagine them. And sometimes they are worse.'

'His name is Billy Selkirk.'

'A young man? You are seeing a young man called Billy Selkirk? How marvellous. This calls for a celebration! But why did Rupert paint such a pessimistic picture of the situation then? He believes you are still pining for Charlie. Maybe because you don't smile enough? You should smile more, you know.'

'I am not pining for Charlie.'

'Oh well. Misunderstandings happen all the time. Only a couple of days ago one of my dearest and oldest friends thought that by "Foot Lady" I meant the racehorse of that name whereas what I had in mind was my chiropodist! As a result my friend lost an awful lot of money and now she refuses to speak to me … Did I say we moved Charlie to a private clinic?'

'You did say, yes. What was it exactly that made him so ill?'

'Charlie had sunstroke, poor lamb, or heatstroke, but now he is much better, I am glad to report. Really, the way the sun insists on shining! London is turning into a Luanda. It's Bedaux who keeps me informed about Charlie,' Lady Collingwood went on. 'Bedaux is my eyes and ears. I have no idea how we'd have coped without him. Rupert seems to disapprove of him, but then Rupert disapproves of most people. He even disapproves of himself! I don't think you have ever met Bedaux, have you?'

'I have.'

'Bedaux is one of the very few truly extraordinary people I know, my dear. Rupert says we mustn't fraternise with flunkeys, which is *such* an antediluvian point of view.' Lady Collingwood laughed. '*Us* and *them*, really! One might be excused for thinking *Jane Eyre* had never been written! Rupert should go back and live in the early twentieth century, say I. The Edwardian age would suit him perfectly!'

'Our oysters are coming.'

'*Did* we order oysters? I can't help having mixed feelings about oysters. No, no, my dear, you mustn't think I doubt your word! I am *famished*. You know of course that oysters are to be swallowed, *not* chewed? Little things like that do matter.'

'I do know.'

'When I rang Charlie last night, he said he was expecting a visitor this afternoon. I have an idea it might be the very same girl who caused the rift between you. Olga? He sounded enormously excited. Sorry, my dear. Tactless of me. Perhaps I shouldn't have mentioned it.'

At three o'clock in the afternoon I arrive at Dr Bishop's clinic. I find Olga in Mr Eresby's room. She is sitting beside Mr Eresby, on his bed. They are holding hands.

Mr Eresby's face is very pale and drawn, but it is clear that he has forgiven her completely. His cheeks and upper lip bear traces of Olga's bright-red lipstick.

I endeavour not to scowl or purse my lips.

They seem glad to see me, but their smiles strike me as somewhat strained and unnatural. There is a conspiratorial air about them.

Mr Eresby greets me amiably enough. Olga, on the other hand, avoids looking me in the eye. Her mascara is a little smudged. Has she been crying? Why has she been crying? Well, it was no doubt part of her act. Even though I remind myself she's had to play the repentant lover I am filled with misgivings.

'Another fine day, Bedaux! I wish they didn't keep me in conditions more suitable for tropical plants. In case you are wondering, I am feeling much better. Everything is, as they say, back to normal.' Mr Eresby's manner is exceedingly cheerful.

'Most gratifying, sir.'

'That nurse who ushered you in is the spitting image of Nanny Everett. Gave me quite a turn when I first clapped eyes on her. I don't suppose you remember Nanny Everett?'

'No, sir.'

'No, of course not. Before your time. *Long* before your time. I threw my Pierrot at her once. It – he? – hit her on the nose. Do toys have gender, Bedaux?'

'I imagine they do, sir.' I resent the silly whimsicality of Mr Eresby's conversation. It's the kind of silliness people employ when they want to hide something. I did say I could read Mr Eresby's mind, didn't I? I think Mr Eresby has decided he no longer requires my services. I think it is only a question of time before he gives me the sack. Am I being paranoid?

'You will be interested to hear that the coffee here is *nearly* as good as the coffee you make back home.' Mr Eresby turns towards Olga. 'Bedaux makes excellent coffee.'

'I don't like coffee. Coffee – what do you say? – puts stains on my teeth!' She tosses her head and pouts. She bends over the bowl of roses that stands on the bedside table and pretends to smell them.

She is as nervous as a cat.

'I believe the coffee has made me uncommonly talkative, Bedaux. At least, I *think* it's the coffee's fault, if "fault" indeed is the right word. Now I am talking like you!' Mr Eresby laughs, then he strokes Olga's fair hair. 'Can coffee have faults, Olga?'

'I don't know,' she says. 'Why do you ask such foolish questions?'

I clear my throat. 'I hope they put the flowers out at night, sir. It is not healthy to keep them beside your bed while you sleep. Most flowers exude a certain subtle poison.'

'Oh nonsense,' Mr Eresby says dismissively.

I watch Olga pick up a rose. She starts plucking off its petals. She starts speaking. 'A little, a lot, passionately, not at all. *Not at all.*'

I feel a cold hand around my heart.

'Everything quiet on the Sloane Square front, Bedaux?' Mr Eresby asks.

'Yes, sir.'

'We haven't been burgled yet, I trust?'

'No, sir.'

Olga says she wants to smoke.

'You know you can't, darling,' Mr Eresby says.

'Why can't I smoke?'

'Because it's not allowed here.' Mr Eresby strokes her hair again.

I don't like him touching her. I feel like ripping off his arm.

A minute or so later I leave Mr Eresby's room. As I walk down the corridor, I pass the nurses' room. The door is ajar. I catch a glimpse of the Nanny Everett nurse talking to another, younger nurse.

'*No*,' I hear the younger nurse gasp. 'Not *kill* him?'

I halt and listen.

'That's what she said. It was quite a confession. It was all part of some plan or other, she said, which she'd never intended to carry out. She threw herself across Mr Eresby's bed. Oh you should have seen her. She was in floods of tears. She didn't even wait for me to leave the room. She said she loved him, *only* him, that he was the only man she'd ever loved, not Mr Beddoes, whoever that may be. She said she hated Mr Beddoes but she was also scared of him.'

'She is Russian or something, isn't she?' the younger nurse says. 'She was probably play-acting.'

What the older nurse meant was 'Bedaux', of course, not 'Beddoes'.

I have been in a number of tight corners, but never for an instant have I lost my self-possession. Yet, I must admit this thoroughly unexpected revelation of Olga's treachery does give me a nasty shock.

She said she loved him, not Mr Beddoes.

This time it is I who is walking like a clockwork toy soldier.

As I leave the clinic, I wonder what my next move should be.

10

THE NIGHT OF THE HUNTER

Dusk had fallen and for the first time there was an autumnal nip in the air. Although it was some time before the clocks went back, the heat wave was over and one could already feel the insidious approach of winter.

The walk from the bus stop seemed endless. There was hardly any traffic and not a single person in sight. Something was wrong with the street lights, not one of them was on! It was also very quiet, oh so quiet! Olga thought it the deepest silence she had ever known since she had started living in London. It felt heavy and oppressive. One can't see a silence but she did; she imagined it as a great dark beast lying sprawled over the neighbourhood, over the street and the houses, deadening every sound beneath its soft fur …

There was a story that used to terrify her when she was a little girl, about the man who was coming to get you when you were upstairs in bed. Now the man was on the *first* step. Now he was on the second step. Now he was on the third, the fourth, the *fifth* step … and now the man was on the twelfth step, which was the last, crossing the landing and opening your door and creeping in – and now he was standing by your bed … *Got you!* It was her old ghoul of a grandmother who told her the story, each time making Olga laugh and scream.

What was the reason for that particular memory? Why had it come to her *now*? Well, it was dark – she was feeling a little sad and a little nervous and a little scared – and there was someone walking behind her.

Yes. She could hear footsteps. Left, right. Furtive, yet determined and purposeful. No. They were perfectly ordinary footsteps. Left, right. Just someone like her going home.

She wished it wasn't so dark!

Olga peered over her shoulder. She saw no one. But she thought she caught a movement.

The street was flanked with trees, so perhaps the person had dodged behind a tree? Her stalker wanted to remain unseen. Could it be Mr Bedaux? (Mr Bedaux had been very much on her mind.) Or perhaps it was Joan? Perhaps Joan intended to scare her. She had done it before, when she followed her and Charlie all the way to the Royal Albert Hall. Olga hadn't seen Joan for some time and Charlie said she'd given up her pursuit, but what if she hadn't? At one time Joan seemed to believe Olga could be persuaded to drop Charlie …

Who else could it be? Not any of her friends trying to give her a fright, she didn't think. Neither Inge nor Simona would play such silly games with her! They knew what it felt like to be on the receiving end of unwanted attentions. Besides, neither Simona nor Inge would have been able to keep it up. They'd have giggled by now! No, it wasn't them. The only games Inge and Simona played were the games their clients demanded of them.

Mr Bedaux had given them very careful instructions. *Do not frustrate the gentlemen with any pretence of maiden blushes.* Mr Bedaux spoke like that. Thank God *she* had never had any clients. She hated the idea of clients, of strange men who paid to have you in their houses. She had been extremely lucky. She was not a slut. She could have become one out of dire necessity, of course she could, but she had met Charlie and that had been her salvation. It was unfortunate that Mr Bedaux should have fallen for her too …

She had told Mr Bedaux she loved him, but that was a lie. Well, she'd had no choice but to lie. She had depended on Mr Bedaux, to start with. He had given her money, provided her with a place to live as well as with jobs, mainly in catering.

She should have gone to college, continued with her education, that's what her mother wanted for her more than anything else in the world. Olga's dream was to be an actress. Perhaps she could still go to drama school in London? Charlie said she could. Each time mother phoned, she told her she had to be a good girl. Mother worried about her all the time. 'You are in a foreign country, Olga, so be a good girl, don't do anything bad or they will send you back …'

Be a good girl … Funnily enough, that's what one of Inge's regular clients, a very rich old gentleman who lived in Bayswater, told her each time she went to his house. *Be a good girl and you will have nothing to regret …*

The old gentleman wished to be known as 'Mr X' and he never expected more than to be allowed to brush her hair, Inge said. He was really kind, a real old English gentleman with white hair, very neat, perfectly dressed, always wearing a silk cravat and a matching silk handkerchief in his breast pocket. Sometimes he would brush her hair for half an hour without stopping. He would put on a pair of surgical gloves first, which was a bit creepy, but Inge said she didn't mind. Mr X used an exquisite brush with an ivory handle that had belonged to his late mother, or so he told Inge …

Mr Bedaux still believed nothing had changed between them. He couldn't possibly know what Olga had done, what she'd said, could he? It wasn't as though he had been in the room when she made her confession to Charlie. Mr Bedaux had seen her holding Charlie's hand but he thought that she was still acting. Well, she was a good actress. She always spoke English in a silly way, mispronouncing words and phrases, the way she'd heard some of the other Lithuanian girls speak, but she did it on purpose. She made herself sound like a halfwit. She didn't want to show she was clever. She always felt it was safer that way ...

Back in Charlie's room at the clinic she had been aware of Mr Bedaux's eyes on her ... It had made her nervous ... He had kept looking at her, as though he suspected what she had done, as though he knew ...

What would he do if he knew?

There were the footsteps again – following her!

Olga stopped abruptly and turned round. This time she saw a figure, though not at all clearly. A long coat – a hat? A *woman*? It looked like a woman, yes. Was it Joan? The figure had stopped too. Olga stood looking into the darkness.

She wondered if it could be Mr Bedaux. Mr Bedaux had told her once that he liked to dress up in women's clothes sometimes. He liked to wear 'drag'. That was the English expression. He also told her he could *talk* like a woman too, if he chose. And he could also mince like a woman. That was very creepy, very scary.

Charlie had said, leave it to him, he'll deal with Bedaux, but Charlie wasn't well yet. Charlie didn't seem to take the murder plot seriously enough. He had laughed. 'So you and Bedaux have been plotting to kill me?' Charlie had then called Mr Bedaux a 'snake in the grass'.

Mr Bedaux was the age Olga's father would have been if he hadn't drunk himself to death. She'd pretended to enjoy Mr Bedaux's kisses, but she'd really hated being pawed by him. But she was a good actress, that's why Mr Bedaux had never suspected the truth. It was Charlie she liked and loved and that had nothing to do with his money and his big house, nothing at all ...

Once more Olga wondered what Mr Bedaux would do when he realised that she had lied to him. Sooner or later the truth would come out. Charlie had told her that it would be all right. He had told her not to worry. He'd get rid of Bedaux, he said. But she was worried, *very* worried. Mr Bedaux was creepy. She was scared of him. One never knew what went on inside Mr Bedaux's head. She didn't even know his first name!

Mr Bedaux would be very angry with her. He would be furious. He would want to hurt her. He might do something horrible. She hoped he wouldn't take it out on Inge and Simona. Poor Inge and poor Simona still very much depended on Mr Bedaux. Rich men, that's what Mr Bedaux specialised in. Rich clients.

She had been waiting for a chance to break away from him. Well, the moment she had seen Charlie in his hospital bed, looking so pale, so ill, all because of Mr Bedaux and her, she had made up her mind. Enough lies! She had realised how much Charlie loved her and how much she loved him. How much she wanted to be with him ...

The footsteps seemed to have stopped. Had her pursuer gone away?

Her house was at the end of a narrow cul-de-sac. Ruby Road. Lovely name. No one seemed to live in any of the neighbouring houses. Charlie had chosen a place where she wouldn't be disturbed by prying eyes ...

Olga stood in front of her little house. Charlie had bought it for her. Philomel Cottage. Lovely house with a lovely name. 'Philomel' meant nightingale, apparently.

She unlocked the front door and let herself into the hall. She switched on the light. She gave a great sigh of relief. Home is the one and only really good, warm, safe place, that's what her mother always said ...

She had heard a scratching sound ... The kitchen door was open ... There seemed to be someone in the kitchen ... She stood very still ... There it was again ... Scratching ...

The next moment she remembered – the kitten! Charlie had given her a kitten! It was very young and very, very silly. It was still without a name.

Olga gave a sigh of relief. She smiled.

She was still smiling as she started walking towards the kitchen ...

11

HEADS YOU LOSE

I don't know why I am doing this, I really don't, Fenella Frayle thought wearily. It's not as though I am going to do anything about it.

She was standing outside the house, but as soon as she saw the light come on in the hall, she moved into the shadow of the wall on the right.

Philomel Cottage. This was where Olga Klimt lived. No doubt about it now.

Fenella's hand went up to her hat and she pulled the brim down over her eyes. Then she swung round and walked briskly back to the main road and made for the Tube station.

She had spotted Olga come out of Doctor Bishop's clinic. Fenella had gone to the clinic with the intention of calling on Charles Eresby, to see how he was doing.

Olga Klimt looked *exactly* as in the photograph. The moment she had seen her, Fenella had changed her mind. She had turned her back on the clinic and started following Olga. She had acted on a wild impulse. Never before had she stalked anyone, let alone a perfect stranger.

This is so unlike me, Fenella thought.

The night before she had had another row with her aunt. It had been horrific. The situation had become quite impossible.

Aunt Clo-Clo had been vicious … She had really surpassed herself … *Such* nastiness … She had actually *enjoyed* seeing Fenella squirm and cower.

Her aunt had asked Fenella to come and see her at her house in South Kensington. Fenella should never have agreed but she'd had the idea she might be able to make her aunt change her mind … Some hope!

She had found her with a bottle of whisky beside her.

Don't say 'my school' in that proprietorial way, my girl — it was never your school. Actually I have a good reason to have you evicted, a very good reason. I have a moral reason. I have a duty to society. Moral, yes. Why do you look so surprised? You've put on weight, did you know that? You are as fat as a pig. Rather than curb your appetites, as would befit a moral person, you let them rule your life. I know what's going on under that roof, oh yes, I do. A bunch of deep-voiced dykes, that's what you all are — you shouldn't be left in charge of innocent little children — you should never be allowed anywhere near a child — man-mad harpies, that's what you are — that young man you lured in from the street — you didn't think I knew, did you?

Fenella had felt the blood rush from her face. It hadn't occurred to her to laugh at Aunt Clo-Clo's idiotic lack of logic — no woman could really be a dyke *and* man-mad. She had been possessed by fury. She had been standing beside the fireplace and had caught herself looking at the poker …

She remembered her thoughts. *How easy it would be to bash in her ugly old head, but if I did, I'd be caught in no time.* The battle over the Sylvie & Bruno Nursery School was ongoing and it seemed to be common knowledge among members of her staff. These things, alas, got around. That relations between her and her aunt were far from harmonious was also known. Isobel Cooper had actually spoken to Aunt Clo-Clo on the phone, several times. On one memorable occasion poor Isobel had been on the receiving end of Aunt Clo-Clo's drunken bile …

But how had Aunt Clo-Clo heard about Charles Eresby? That, surely, was what she meant by the 'young man lured in from the street'. She must have a spy somewhere among the staff … One of the teachers – which one, though? Martha Ransom? Martha had been unhappy with her extra duties and she had demanded a salary rise, which she hadn't got, so she had a grudge against Fenella … Or could it be Mrs Mason, the cleaner? Mrs Mason is not exactly the soul of integrity. Perhaps Aunt Clo-Clo had bribed Mrs Mason?

'I want the old bitch dead,' Fenella whispered.

What if Aunt Clo-Clo did die a violent death – and it was proven that Fenella couldn't have done it as she was hundreds of miles from the scene of the crime? What if the police found that she had a cast-iron alibi? She could go to France, or to Italy. Italy, yes. She loved Florence!

Had the biscuit heir been serious? They were in the same boat, he said. He wanted to be rid of trashy, mercenary Olga Klimt – she, on the other hand, wanted Aunt Clo-Clo dead …

His words came back to her.

'Do let's exchange murders. You do mine, I do yours, how about it?'

Fenella sat on the Tube, a copy of the *Evening Standard* on her lap.

What if she were to present Charles Eresby with the fait accompli? What if she told him she had killed Olga Klimt? Then he would have no choice but to go and kill Aunt Clo-Clo.

It was ridiculous, insane! She couldn't kill a perfect stranger, could she? That trashy blonde. But it wouldn't be difficult. She could follow Olga, exactly as she had done tonight, all the way to Philomel Cottage – and then what? Bash in her head? Stab her? Strangle her? Drive a hypodermic syringe filled with cyanide into her neck?

The girl doesn't know me, that's the beauty of it, Fenella thought. She's never seen me. I could easily engineer a meeting – engage her in conversation. Say that I am a friend of Charles Eresby. I don't think she'll be suspicious. I look eminently respectable, I exude common sense, I invite trust. I will tell her I have a message from her boyfriend – I will say it is urgent … *Your name is Olga Klimt, isn't it? I must talk to you.* I will suggest we have coffee at some café –

She would offer to buy the coffees – as she took them back to the table, she would slip a powder into the girl's cup – some slow-acting poison – the girl would collapse and die some time later, maybe in the street, or inside a shop – she was a foreigner – no one would care, really – the police would probably think Olga had committed suicide – that she'd poisoned herself – or that she was on drugs – foreign girls often killed themselves – they always had so many problems –

Madness – and yet – *how easy it would be.* Fenella Frayle felt excitement bubbling up inside her, thinking about it. I'll leave nothing to chance, she thought.

It would be easy for her to change her appearance – a Hermes scarf round her head, alter the colour of her eyes with contact lenses, put on her reading glasses, walk with a little limp, make herself look older – that was the image the CCTV cameras would capture.

Fenella nodded to herself. *No one would know it was her.*

12

DU CÔTÉ DE CHEZ COLLINGWOOD

Lord Collingwood lay strapped to an operating table. The walls around him were of a gleaming kind of white, which made him blink. The surgeon was bending over him, scalpel in hand, his face covered by a mask. The fellow was about to perform a trepanation – cut off the top of Lord Collingwood's head and remove whatever it was that needed to be removed – the thingummy that had been bothering him.

They didn't seem to have given Lord Collingwood any anaesthetic and yet he could smell the sticky reek of ether all around him. It put him in mind of old Coleridge. *Water, water, everywhere, nor any drop to drink.* Had they forgotten the anaesthetic or were they doing it on purpose? It was all highly irregular. It was going to hurt like hell, having the top of one's head sliced off –

In sudden panic Lord Collingwood tried to break free from the straps and failed. He might have been a pitiful rodent gripped in the coils of a great boa constrictor – the more he struggled, the tighter the pressure upon him grew …

As he screamed, the mask slipped from the surgeon's face and Lord Collingwood gasped in horror.

It wasn't a fellow – it was his wife – *it was Deirdre.*

At breakfast at their house in Park Lane he was silent. He couldn't get the dream out of his head. He had woken up and sat up in bed shaking like a leper in the wind. He found he had no appetite. He sat staring balefully at his boiled egg. The Black Dog, he couldn't get rid of the Black Dog.

'Are you seeing Joan today?' Deirdre asked from the other end of the table.

'Maybe I am.'

'You see her often, don't you?'

'What if I do?'

'Oh nothing. Nothing at all, Rupert. Simply curious.'

'Curiosity killed the cat.' Lord Collingwood smiled morosely.

It occurred to him that he occupied a hermetic, hierarchical kind of world where schedules and patterns of behaviour were constantly under some form of surveillance. It was a world filled with sinister potential. He remembered how his wife had pestered him to get a butler. He suspected Deirdre wanted a butler for the sole reason of bribing him to spy on him.

'Do you have to be so bad-tempered?' Deirdre helped herself to a piece of toast and started buttering it. 'It was an innocent enough question.'

'There is no such thing as an innocent enough question.'

'You aren't ill, are you?'

He was far from well, he said. He'd slept fitfully. He'd been tormented by bad dreams. At the moment he was feeling a vapourish kind of tightening around his brain. It was a most disagreeable sensation. He spoke slowly and patiently and rather loudly; he might have been addressing a foreigner or a refractory child.

'Why don't you go to the doctor?'

'No. Not today. He's already changed my pills twice.'

'Perhaps it's time you changed your doctor?'

'That would be damned disloyal. That's the sort of thing *you* would do.'

'You said your new pills left you emotionally cauterised.'

'I never said that.'

'You said your doctor was never pleased to see you.'

'I never said that.'

'How about some tea or coffee?'

Lord Collingwood stared back at his wife with an expression of profound dismay. 'The globe's monetary system is on the point of collapse, the whole of Western civilisation is under threat, the world's on the verge of a digital Armageddon, savages terrorise our embassies, and all my dear wife has to say is, how about some tea or coffee? What passes for conversation under this roof is no more than a list of utterances enfolding emptiness.'

Lady Collingwood remained unperturbed. She raised her coffee cup to her lips. 'Joan and I had lunch yesterday. At the Criterion. She thinks very highly of you, you know.'

Lord Collingwood said that that was the blandest, the most uncritically unctuous, the most appallingly sycophantic kind of remark he had heard in his entire life. When they had first got married, he went on, he had imagined her to be a different kind of woman – less conventional, less *county*, more hedonistic, brimming over with effervescent wit and theatricality. In short, the kind of woman who wouldn't think twice about wearing satin elbow-length gloves at breakfast.

'Would you like me to wear elbow-length gloves at breakfast?' Lady Collingwood asked.

'Must you take everything I say so literally?' He glanced at the clock. 'I am seeing little Joanie later today.'

'So you *are* seeing her.'

'Well, yes. I said so, didn't I?' He seemed surprised. 'I don't think she's quite given up on Charlie, you know. I may be entirely wrong, but I suspect she may be set on some unwise course of action.'

'She told me she was no longer interested in Charlie. She said she was seeing someone else. Someone called Billy Selkirk. Perhaps she was lying, I don't know.'

'It would be useful to find out if such a person exists,' Lord Collingwood said.

'You can't blame me for being suspicious about you and Joan. As middle age advances and one's youthful illusions recede, almost the only way of starting again, of being reborn, is to have an affair with a young woman. You said that once.'

'It sounds precisely the kind of thing I *would* say,' he nodded. 'Sometimes you do manage to hit the nail on the head, Deirdre.'

'Can you swear by your soul's salvation that you are not having an affair with Joan? You had an affair with her mother, you know.'

'You shouldn't listen to ill-natured gossip, Deirdre, you really shouldn't.' He shook his head. 'It seems to be the new religion, gossip. Afrikaners, Norfolk farmers and middle-class moralists are said to be the only ones who don't gossip, or so I read somewhere, but, sadly, they are *not* the sort of people one wants to see at one's dinner table, are they?'

'Do have some coffee, Rupert,' she urged him. 'It's excellent this morning. It's some exclusive brand. Kopi Luwak. Hideously expensive.'

'I think I shall have a cup of coffee, if only to please you. For some reason I have started feeling better, you know. It must be your conversation. I can feel the Black Dog lifting.' He reached out for the silver coffee pot. 'The affair with Joanie Selwyn's mother was a very long time ago,' he went on conversationally. 'You were probably not born at the time I had an affair with Joanie Selwyn's mother. That was a joke. Not meant to be taken literally.'

A minute or two later Lord Collingwood rose from his seat and strode up to his wife in a purposeful manner. For a moment or two he stood gazing down at her through narrowed eyes as though trying to distinguish something in her that was very distant. He then put his hands on her shoulders, stooped over and kissed her. It was a kiss of great tenderness. 'I am sorry, darling, but I've got to go.'

'But it's too early, surely?'

'No, it isn't. I've got an important job to do, several important jobs, actually. Promise me you will have a wonderful morning,' he whispered in her ear.

'I will miss you terribly.'

'I know you will. I will miss you too. But I have a boring tendency to stick to my principles.'

'I understand perfectly. And I admire you for it. *Noblesse oblige.*'

His expression changed. 'I was hoping you wouldn't say that.'

'I don't suppose you remember my very first visit to Collingwood, Rupert, do you?' Deirdre spoke with a faint touch of coquetry.

'Oh but I do remember. The weather was awful.'

'That was part of the magic. Your mother's dogs barked throughout the night. For some reason they didn't take to me. Then at breakfast your mother asked me whether my medical knowledge extended to the binding-up of wounds inflicted while playing billiard-fives. It sounded like some sort of a code. She seemed to be taking me for a spy or a nurse!' Deirdre laughed at the memory. She reached out for his hand. 'You won't get too tired, Rupert, will you?'

'I will try not to, darling. I can't promise.'

'I really worry about you sometimes, Rupert.'

'I am perfectly aware of it, darling. It means an awful lot to me. I don't know what I would do without you. I'd be lost, completely lost, darling. I have a giant and deranged ego. Sometimes I am quite unable to articulate the enormity of my thoughts.' He had started speaking with great urgency. 'I am troubled by perpetual and inextinguishable fears. I am tormented by nightmares. You don't really think I am losing my mind, darling, do you?'

'I don't. Of course I don't.' She gave his hand a reassuring squeeze.

'Promise you will always be here when I come back, you must promise.' He kissed her again.

'I am jealous, so terribly jealous.' Lady Collingwood moaned. Her hand flew up to her mouth. 'Every fibre, every neuron in my body militates against it but I can't help myself. It's a monstrous affliction. I am ashamed of it!'

'On no account must you feel any shame,' Lord Collingwood said. 'I don't mind you being shameless.'

'I have tried to like Joan, I really have, Rupert. But she and I are so different – poles apart – we do not breathe the same air. She always looks so – so superior. That very correct censorious stare!'

'I know exactly what you mean, darling … Lunch at the Criterion wasn't much of a success, I take it?'

'It was agony. She insisted on drinking only water. She *chewed* her oysters. I told her to swallow. She said she would but didn't. I know it sounds awfully petty but I think she wanted to show me that my opinions didn't cut any ice with her. She seemed keen on demonstrating her force of character.'

'I am no psychologist, Deirdre, but I think that may be the effect Charlie's rejection has had on her. She believes she should assert herself more. Incidentally I bumped into Payne at the club the other day and I told him all about Joan and Charlie and how Olga Klimt came between them. The whole sorry tale. Thought he might have some useful suggestions to make. Remember Payne?'

'Not Hugh Payne? Of course I remember Hugh Payne! Nellie Grylls' nephew. He's wonderful. He is terribly amusing,' Lady Collingwood gushed. 'Clever enough to wear his considerable intelligence lightly, I have heard it said. Reputed to be the second cleverest man in London but likes to play the buffoon. No idea who's the first. Similar in some ways to our beloved mayor, only ever so much more presentable.'

'Payne's wife writes. Murder mysteries. Don't know how good she is. Nowadays very few people are. We must get some of her books. Perhaps we could have the Paynes round to dinner some time?'

'I'd like that. Splendid idea.'

He patted her cheek. Then he straightened up, very much the cavalry officer he'd once been and examined his reflection in the mirror above the mantelpiece. He ran his forefinger inside his collar, straightened his tie, touched his little moustache, then smoothed his hair. His eyes, he noticed, were a little bloodshot. 'I really must go now.'

'I admire the rapidity of your intensely clever, quickly changing mind, Rupert ... You do love me, don't you?'

'I find you incomparable. Au revoir.'

'Au revoir.'

Deirdre Collingwood remained sitting at the table. She heard the front door open and close. As she considered the complex relationship she had with her husband, her smile slowly faded. She rang for fresh coffee, but then told the maid not to bother.

She rose decisively to her feet.

Five minutes later she was inside her husband's study, kneeling beside his desk, struggling with a bunch of keys.

13

THE PERFECT MURDER (1)

If I can't have her, no one else will.

I must admit I am extremely upset. Or this is what I believe being 'extremely upset' feels like. I remember that when I was a boy, I never cried.

Although at the moment I am quite unable to smile, the irony of my predicament has not escaped me. I feel very much the way Mr Eresby felt the day Olga told him she was breaking up with him. Mr Eresby, you may wish to remember, found his misery so acute, so unbearable, that he asked me to kill Olga Klimt for him.

I keep thinking about Olga Klimt's duplicity, about her lies, about the game she played with me. I then recall her kisses and tender caresses and, like Mr Eresby before me, I am filled with the desire for revenge.

I hold out my hands before me. I flex my fingers. I clench my hands into fists.

I want her dead. I want Olga Klimt dead.

The moment I think it, I feel better.

Beauty that is unfamiliar as it is perilous …

Making up his mind not to see Olga Klimt had been the right decision, of that he had no doubt, one should never take risks with girls like that, yet he felt quite unable to stop himself wondering whether his mental image of her matched the reality or not. He was of course going to see her when Charlie condescended to formally introduce her to his mother and to him, which was bound to happen at some point if there was going to be a wedding.

Lord Collingwood glanced at his watch. Risks, yes. Girls of that sort were known to make claims and cause trouble. He considered himself a man of the world but he was also a cautious man. He had after all a position to maintain. She might decide to complain that he had ravished her or some such ugly accusation, the papers were full of stories these days, or she might try blackmailing him. Better be safe than sorry and not visit Olga.

He was sitting at a table at Richoux's in Piccadilly, waiting for Joan Selwyn. He needed to concentrate. Producing a pad and a silver pen from his pocket, he wrote a little memo to himself. *Essential employ every bit of eloquence in case of sudden opposition.*

He had it all carefully mapped out in his head, the precise words he would use ...

It was so frightfully important!

(Later he was to give Payne a detailed account of his meeting with Joan Selwyn.)

Suddenly he saw her walking towards him. He held his breath. This, he reflected, was how Judith, of Holofornes decapitation notoriety, must have looked: an air of gravity, head high, chin resolute, lips pursed, eyes serious and steady. He felt his scalp prickle. He shivered. No, he wasn't being fanciful, dammit. There was something ruthless about Joan.

'Ah, my dear,' he said, rising and kissing her cheek. 'There you are.'

'I am sorry I am late,' Joan said.

'I'm so terribly glad to see you, my dear. I do apologise if I strike you as a bit on the low side but I slept badly. Besides, facing Deirdre across the breakfast table is always an unsettling experience.'

'She seems to be jealous of me!'

'She is jealous, yes. Went on and on about it. I almost wished we *were* having an affair! Ha ha! Flattering, in a way, shows one's wife does care, but such a damned bore! You should have seen her this morning as she sat gulping down cups of some superior black coffee. So magnificently groomed, so admirably garbed, so tantalisingly aloof! Some people I know find Deirdre extremely attractive.'

'Not Billy. Billy said Deirdre had all the allure of a cold hip bath. He's seen her somewhere, at some matinee, I think. She was pointed out to him.'

'Billy?' Lord Collingwood's left eyebrow went up. 'Is that your new beau? So he does exist! Hoorah!'

She pursed her lips slightly. 'Did you think he was a figment of my imagination?'

'I did wonder! You know I only want what's best for you! Such a relief! Jolly glad to know you are moving on, my dear.'

'What did you want to see me about, Rupert?'

He looked at her with mock solemnity. 'Well, Joanie, you promised to do something for me? You haven't forgotten, have you, my dear?'

'Oh *that*. Of course I haven't forgotten. I said I would help you, didn't I? You don't have to worry. You know I always do what I say. Who is this mysterious friend anyway?'

'He's an old fool,' Lord Collingwood said with a sigh. 'But he's done me several tremendous favours, so I feel under an obligation of sorts. I know the whole thing's rather awkward, but I didn't have the heart to say no, my dear.'

'Who *is* he?'

'He'd rather he remained anonymous, if you don't mind. I've been sworn to secrecy.'

Joan Selwyn tried to hide her exasperation. 'It's such an incredible story. Are you sure he wasn't making it up?'

'I don't see why he should want to send us on a wild goose chase, do you?'

'He may have some sinister motive.'

'No, no. I am convinced his request is entirely bona fide. He is an old fool. Ah there's the waiter, at long last! Service in London is no longer what it used to be. What would you like, my dear?'

'Just a cup of coffee. No, nothing to eat.'

'I'll have some scrambled eggs on toast. Feel ravenous. Hardly touched a thing this morning! Deirdre, on the other hand, kept stuffing herself with kedgeree. She generates *such* tension, you wouldn't believe it.' Lord Collingwood shook his head. 'She didn't want me to go out. If she could have her own way, she would keep me under lock and key!'

Fenella Frayle rose abruptly from her desk. Walking across her study, she locked her door. She then went up to a cupboard in the corner and producing a brand-new bottle of brandy, poured herself a glass. She took a resolute sip, then another.

She shut her eyes.

This is so unlike me, she thought as she raised the glass to her lips for the third time.

She could hear the children singing 'An Impossible Dream'.

To fight the unbeatable foe –

The unbeatable foe was of course Aunt Clo-Clo. Aunt Clo-Clo had been on the phone to Fenella about half an hour earlier – once again ranting and raving – it had been worse than usual, actually –

'I am giving you till Halloween to clear out. That's my final word. A letter from my solicitors is on the way.'

Fenella shut her eyes. She was certainly capable of killing Aunt Clo-Clo. Was she capable of killing Olga Klimt? No one could kill a perfect stranger, could they? Not unless they were mad. But she wasn't mad. She was the most sensible, the most rational person who ever walked the earth! But imagine – just *imagine* – for argument's sake – she did kill Olga Klimt – what guarantee was there that Charles Eresby would reciprocate?

Fenella took another sip of brandy. No guarantee at all. Chances were that the biscuit heir had forgotten all about his plan by now. But the killing of Olga Klimt might spur him on. It *might*.

I could blackmail him, Fenella thought. He wouldn't like it if I told the police we'd agreed to exchange murders. I could actually say that he'd *paid* me to kill his girlfriend. The heir to the Eresby biscuit millions wouldn't want the publicity, would he?

She laughed. It wouldn't work! All he'd need to do was deny the allegation. It would be her word against his. The whole thing was quite absurd!

She took another sip. He had sounded extremely serious and matter of fact. He had asked her where Aunt Clo-Clo lived, how old she was, what her habits were, whether she had an established routine. He had sounded as though he meant business …

'I do your murder, you do mine. We establish good, solid alibis for the murders that benefit us – we go away – thousands of miles away – the Amazonian Jungle – Acapulco – the police would never get us –'

Yes, he had sounded as though he meant business.

She kept her eyes firmly shut. It occurred to her that the present moment was perfect for the killing of Olga Klimt since Charles Eresby was at a private clinic, with doctors and nurses watching over him like hawks round the clock. She might never get another chance as good as this! He didn't have to go to as far as Acapulco. When Olga's body was found, *he would have the perfect alibi.*

14

THE PERFECT MURDER (2)

The murder took place later that same day.

Olga Klimt received the call on her landline at half past four in the afternoon. It was a stranger who spoke to her. It was a very pleasant kind of voice, cultivated, very English. The only odd thing was that she couldn't quite say if it was a man or a woman …

'Is that Olga? I am a friend of Charlie's. He asked me to call you. He needs to see you. It's rather urgent, in a way, but there is nothing to worry about. Could you go to the clinic at once?'

The caller rang off before she could ask any questions.

Olga panicked, she couldn't help herself. She immediately rang Charlie but his phone was permanently engaged. He couldn't be that ill then, she reflected, if he was on his phone? Unless someone else was using his phone?

Both the message and the way the person had spoken were very strange, now that she came to think about it. She wondered if it was Mr Bedaux who had phoned her. Mr Bedaux was a good mimic. What if Mr Bedaux was trying to get her outside Philomel Cottage for some reason?

No, nonsense. She couldn't stay in the house. She must go and see Charlie. It was getting dark but she had nothing to fear, really. All she needed to do was walk to the end of the cul-de-sac and then she would be out in the busy main road, where there were people, traffic, lights. She could run, run like the wind …

She put on her coat. Her hands were shaking slightly. She was scared of Mr Bedaux, of course she was. But he seemed to have disappeared! She hadn't seen him since that day at the clinic, actually, and Charlie had phoned her earlier on and said he had been unable to get in touch with Bedaux. Well, that was a good thing – wasn't it? Though, it was also very strange. At one time Mr Bedaux had been phoning her several times a day, asking her how she was, where she was, what she was doing, who she was with, what dress she was wearing …

There was something sinister about his silence. It suggested that Mr Bedaux somehow *knew* that she had confessed every-thing to Charlie. The thought caused Olga to shiver.

No, she *must* go! She picked up her bag and walked reso-lutely across the hall. She opened the front door and stood on the threshold. Not too cold. Looked like rain.

She glanced around. There was no one in sight. That green refuse bin. She imagined it had moved! No, she was being silly. She didn't really expect Mr Bedaux to jump out of it! She laughed nervously.

She turned and inserted the key in the lock …

There was something wrong with the key – it refused to turn or perhaps it was her – she was nervous – she'd heard a noise – plaintive wailing – the kitten was mewing in the hall, scratching the door –

Her hands were shaking really badly now. What was wrong with the key?

The knife had been carefully sharpened and it entered the girl's back without any resistance.

She didn't so much as utter a sound, only a kind of a gasp.

She pitched forward and fell.

There wasn't much blood but some of it seeped into her luminously blonde hair.

'What seems to be the problem now?' The Nanny Everett nurse stood at the end of the bed, regarding him with her faintly censorious expression.

'I can't get my girlfriend. She isn't answering her mobile.' Charles Eresby glanced at the clock on the wall. It was quarter to six.

'No need to get into a state,' the nurse said comfortably. 'Perhaps she is on the Tube. No network if you are on the Tube. You should know that.'

'Maybe she is on the Tube, yes.'

He didn't know why he felt so anxious.

He had had a call earlier on. Someone from his bank had phoned him and kept talking to him for a very long time. Now that he thought about it there had been something wrong about that call. The person's voice had sounded muffled – as though he didn't want to be recognised?

I mustn't get paranoid, Charlie thought. His heart was beating rapidly. It must be the coffee, he decided. He was drinking too much coffee. That was it.

'Would that be the young lady who paid you a visit the other day? The fair-haired young lady?'

'Yes, that's her.' He had no intention of discussing Olga with the Nanny Everett nurse.

'Were you expecting her?'

'No. Not really. Not tonight. She said she would come tomorrow morning. I – I just wanted to talk to her.' Charles Eresby looked down at his mobile phone and once more he pressed Olga's number.

He held the mobile to his ear. *Please, leave a message.*

'It will be the six o'clock news soon,' said the nurse. 'Would you like me to turn on the TV?'

'No, thank you.'

'Would you like a drink? A cup of tea?'

'No, nothing, thank you. I have a bit of a headache, actually.' Charles Eresby lay back on his bed and shut his eyes.

'You won't be able to go to sleep later on if you start snoozing now,' she warned him.

She clearly didn't see she was being a nuisance. If he had had a Pierrot, he would have thrown it at her!

Eventually he heard her leave the room. He knew she meant well but she could be annoying ... He mustn't be ungrateful ... They had been taking very good care of him here ... No, he didn't feel like going back to Sloane Square ... and to Bedaux ... There was no question of his keeping Bedaux ... If Bedaux tried to bother Olga in any way, he would call the police ... He hoped Olga's silence didn't have anything to do with Bedaux ... He had no need of a valet ... Ridiculous idea, when one came to think of it ... 'George V valet' ... That was private code for death, if Charlie remembered correctly, the invention of some controversial politician, now dead. No, not for death exactly, rather, for fear of dying while asleep and being found by a servant the following morning ... How morbid that was!

No more valets, Charlie thought.

'Sorry, sir, but there is a message for you.'

Charlie opened his eyes.

It was the young nurse with the silly snub-nosed face. She was standing by the door.

'What message?'

'Someone phoned – they left a number for you to call – they said it was very urgent.' Coming up to the bed, she handed him a slip of paper.

Charles Eresby stared down at the number. It was a mobile phone number he didn't recognise. For some reason, he didn't quite know why, he didn't like the look of it. 'Didn't the caller leave a name?'

'No, sir.'

'Man or woman?'

'Can't say, sir. I thought it was a gentleman at first but I am not sure. I think it was someone who knew you were here, with us, but they didn't know your mobile number.'

He nodded. 'That makes sense. Thank you, nurse.'

The door closed behind her.

He dialled the number.

His call was answered almost at once.

'Hallo?' Charlie said. 'Hallo? Who is that?'

There was a silence but he could hear someone's laboured breathing.

'Hallo? You left a message – It's Charles Eresby speaking –'

'Olga Klimt is dead,' a voice said. 'Exactly as you wanted it. Now it's your turn. You'll need to do your part of the deal.'

15

'PHILOMEL COTTAGE'

Sobs racked his body and tears streamed down his face.

He sat in the back of a cab. He was wearing his silk pyjamas, monogrammed dressing gown and slippers. He didn't really care if the driver saw his tears or not. He had rushed out of his room, unheeding of the alarmed noises Nanny Everett and the other nurse were making. He had expected some kind of opposition as he had run out of the main entrance, but no one had attempted to stop him.

Olga, Olga, Olga. He kept whispering her name.

His heart was beating violently. It's my fault, he thought. I did order her killing. He'd remembered. It had all come back to him. He had been in a befuddled state when he made his proposition. He had been drunk. That awful sweet sherry! Like drinking liquid Demerara sugar! He had wanted Olga dead. It had been his idea. But who would have thought that that fat lump would take it seriously? He couldn't even remember her name! He had sensed something in her, similar vibes, a similar aura, whatever it was. Perhaps would-be killers possessed some kind of radar?

Miss Frayle, that was her name. Yes. Miss Frayle had gone and killed Olga. She was mad, must be! *I never meant it*, he whispered. I never meant it. I was extremely upset – not myself! Please, Olga, forgive me!

It couldn't have been a prank call, could it? No. Something about the caller's voice had struck him as chillingly genuine. What was it? *Controlled panic.* Yes. Her voice had sounded harsh with suppressed hysteria ...

Someone less like a hired assassin he could not imagine – Miss Frayle had oozed stolid common sense – but now she seemed to expect him to do her murder! She wanted him to kill her aunt. He remembered the aunt's name because of its sheer absurdity – *Aunt Cluck-Cluck* – something like that.

He remembered his exact words. He had said he would kill the aunt – but Miss Frayle had to kill Olga first.

Oh Lord. Oh, Lord. He buried his face in his hands ...

His mobile phone rang. Automatically he put it to his ear.

It was Mummy. He didn't want to speak to Mummy. He sobbed.

'Charlie? What's the matter, darling?' Deirdre Collingwood asked.

'Olga – Olga is dead.' At once he regretted saying it. No one should know Olga was dead! He turned off the phone.

It rang almost at once. His mother clearly wanted to know details. I am not answering, he thought.

'My fault, my fault, *my fault,*' he whispered. He hadn't been himself. It was a misunderstanding. A terrible misunderstanding. People uttered the most appalling idiocies when they were drunk and upset. The fat nanny had deprived him of the one person he loved more than anything else in the world!

He tried to get a grip on himself. He blew his nose and dabbed at his eyes with his handkerchief.

No – she couldn't have killed Olga – impossible – Olga was not dead – Olga couldn't be dead – things like that did not happen – strangers didn't exchange murders – she could not be dead ...

But she was.

The body lay across the threshold, half in, half out of the open front door. He had asked the taxi to stop at the end of the cul-de-sac and had got out and run the short distance to the house ... Philomel Cottage ... It was he who had bought it for her ... He remembered how Olga had clapped her hands in delight when he explained that it meant nightingale ...

Tears streamed down his face. He knelt beside the body – reached out and touched her hair – there was a dark patch on her back – it felt sticky –

Blood.

She must have been stabbed, though there was no sign of a knife. At least he couldn't see a knife. Had Miss Frayle taken the knife with her?

He thought of going into the house and turning on the hall light, but decided against it. There was a full moon, bathing the ghastly scene in its silvery light and with every second he saw more – the dark stain on Olga's back became darker – she was wearing a light-coloured coat –

He heard a scratching noise followed by faint mewing – something soft brushed against him – the kitten – the poor little kitten – it was he who had given it to her. He picked it up. The kitten licked his fingers. He put it inside his breast pocket. They had meant to give it a name but had never got around to it ...

His nostrils caught the whiff of a perfume – Olga's perfume?

No, it wasn't. He was familiar with Olga's perfume.

He had the uncanny feeling of being watched and turned abruptly.

He saw a silhouette – a man standing very still, very straight, only a couple of paces away, looking not at him, but at Olga's body.

Charlie rose. The man's figure was familiar – *too* familiar. 'Bedaux?'

I keep my hands inside my pockets as Mr Eresby tells me that Olga is dead. I remain silent. I believe Mr Eresby is wearing one of his five dressing gowns: the dark blue one with the dove-grey lapels.

In my right hand I clutch at the length of rope I brought with me. I clutch at it as though my life depends on it. It occurs to me that I won't need it now.

I am motionless, speechless, breathless. I am aware of my lips moving, articulating her name. *Olga. Olga.* I can't tear my eyes from her body. I can't see it very well from where I stand but I feel no desire to go anywhere near it.

This, I tell myself, is the end.

Suddenly the choking sensation in my throat lifts. Now I feel nothing.

Nothing at all.

'She has been killed – I found her – she – she's been stabbed!' Mr Eresby stammers.

Without a single word I turn round and walk back towards the main road.

Charlie made no attempt to stop him. The last thing he felt like doing at this very moment was talk to Bedaux. Somehow he didn't believe Bedaux would call the police. From what Olga had told him, Bedaux had too many skeletons in his cupboard to want to have to anything to do with the police.

The kitten in his pocket mewed again …

Some instinct of self-preservation then began to assert itself and Charlie emerged from his stupor. He rose.

The police. He must call the police. That was what any law-abiding citizen would do in the circumstances. He knew he would immediately become their prime suspect. Olga had been his girlfriend. He was the rich boyfriend. It was his house. They wouldn't bother to look for anyone else –

But he had an alibi! He had been in bed at the clinic when he got the phone call. The murder had been committed by then – that could be proven quite easily – he would have to do a lot of explaining, though – he would have to tell them about the woman from the Sylvie & Bruno Nursery School and their conversation – how they'd exchanged murders – then the ball would be back in his court – oh God – what was he to do?

The nursery nut – that bloody Miss Frayle! He couldn't very well tell the police it was her without implicating himself – would they believe him that he'd never meant her to kill Olga?

He sniffed the air – that perfume again! Where had he smelled it before?

There was something wrong, though he couldn't say what it was. Well – *everything* was wrong! Things couldn't be more wrong.

He couldn't possibly go on standing there any longer, with the front door to Philomel Cottage gaping open and Olga's bloodied corpse lying across the threshold ...

The next moment his mobile rang again.

He stood staring down at the name displayed on the illuminated monitor in shocked disbelief.

Olga? Olga was ringing him ...

No, it couldn't be her. *Olga?*

Shivers ran down his spine and his hair stood on end, but then realisation dawned on him and his irrational horror turned to outrage.

It was Olga's killer calling him. Miss Frayle had taken Olga's mobile. It was Miss Frayle who was ringing him from Olga's mobile phone.

And of course that was Miss Frayle's perfume that hung round the body.

16

CALL ON THE DEAD

Major Payne lowered the book. 'Nobody's ever drunk, they are "inebriated". Nobody hurries, they "hasten". And flowers are invariably "bedecked". It is all unbearably sycophantically courteous. It might have been written by a courtier.'

'Wasn't Shawcross a courtier?'

'I don't think so. He's a journalist.'

'I bet her gowns and hats and boas are described in vivid detail?' Antonia smiled.

'Yes, they are. In vivid vacuous detail ...' Payne opened the hefty tome at random. 'Listen to this. "Cream chiffon moiré with appliqué bars of silver lame ... Ivory georgette, heavily beaded ... Japonica-pink velvet ..." It's strictly for readers that are secretly drawn to sartorial orgies ... This seems less a biography of a person than a swatch of high-end dress fabric!'

'No satirical edges?'

'None whatsoever. All deadly serious, solemn, bland and adulatory.'

'She lived to be a hundred and one. How could anyone write about her without a satirical edge?'

'That's what I keep asking myself.'

'Doesn't one get to know what she was like? I mean – really like?'

'Well, no. I don't think so. I was particularly curious to find out what it was that made Hitler call her the "most dangerous woman in Europe", also more details of her treatment of Diana, but there is nothing about any of that. What one gets instead is the highly dramatic account of how, on one memorable occasion, she almost walks into a diplomatic reception wearing the *légion d'honneur* on the wrong shoulder.'

'Wow,' Antonia said.

'The key word, please note, is "almost". There are lots of opportunities for high comedy, but they have been missed.'

'It's such a big book.'

'Yes! More than a thousand pages.'

'I suppose we could employ it as a rather unusual doorstop?' Antonia suggested.

'Not a bad idea!'

The phone rang and Payne picked it up.

It was a woman's voice that he didn't recognise.

'Hallo – is that Hugh Payne?'

'Speaking.'

'Oh hallo, Hugh. It's Deirdre Collingwood speaking. Hope you remember me? We met at a party at the Peruvian embassy some time ago, last February, I think.'

'Of course I remember you. Those grisly canapés!'

'They were rather awful, weren't they?'

'What a remarkable coincidence.' Payne grimaced at Antonia. 'My wife and I were just talking about diplomatic receptions.'

'It was Rupert who gave me your number,' Lady Collingwood explained. 'I do hope you don't mind terribly. I am at my wits' end. Rupert was against my calling you. He said I couldn't possibly bother you about it, that it wasn't the done thing, that I should call the police –'

'What's happened?' Payne asked.

'Charlie isn't answering his phone. I don't know where he is. He answered his phone just once. The first time. That's when he told me about Olga. I have no idea where he is or who he is with. He was in a car – I could tell by the noise. I don't want to call the police, not yet. I am afraid Charlie would be furious if I did. Rupert is not much help. He is in one of his moods. He's gone to his study now. Rupert's study is – well, inviolable. I simply don't know what to do. Could Charlie have been kidnapped, do you think?'

'What makes you think so?'

'I am perfectly aware that this is a terrible imposition, Hugh, but I was wondering whether I could ask you for help. Rupert said you knew all about this girl Olga Klimt. I understand he told you the whole story.'

'He told me about Olga, yes.' Payne cast another glance at Antonia. 'What happened exactly?'

'To be perfectly honest,' Lady Collingwood said, 'I couldn't care less whether Olga is dead or alive. It's an awful thing to say, but I am mainly concerned about Charlie's safety and state of mind. He should never have got involved with that girl, never, but you know what young men are. I called Charlie about half an hour ago. He was in a dreadful state. He was sobbing. I have no idea where he is at this very moment. All he said was that Olga was dead.'

'Is that all he said?'

'Yes. Olga is dead.'

Payne asked her a couple more questions. He reached out for the pad and pen they kept on the telephone table and made some notes. Eventually he rang off. He looked at his watch. 'That was Deirdre, Lady Collingwood.'

'So I gathered.' Antonia rose slowly from the sofa. 'Something's happened to Olga Klimt, hasn't it?'

'Olga Klimt is dead. Deirdre doesn't know any details. She has no idea how accurate the information is. She phoned her son earlier tonight. All he said was, "Olga's dead". Then he rang off. She hasn't been able to contact him since.'

'What does she expect you to do?'

'She wants me to track him down.'

'She should have called the police.'

'She doesn't want to call the police because she is afraid it may infuriate Charlie.'

'What has Lord Collingwood got to say about it?'

'He appears to be incommunicado. He has shut himself in his study.' Payne looked down at the pad. 'Deirdre rang the clinic where Charlie's been staying – place in Bayswater – but was told that, following a phone call, Charlie left – he was seen running out of the building – then the porter saw him get into a cab. He was wearing his dressing gown and slippers. He appeared to be crying.'

'We could assume that the phone call he received was something to do with Olga. Someone told him that Olga was dead,' Antonia went on thoughtfully. 'It was either the person who stumbled across her body or else the killer announcing their deed to Charlie.'

'Why should the killer want to declare their deed?'

'I don't know … Oh.'

'What's the matter?'

'No, nothing.'

But there was something. Something impossibly silly and irrelevant. She had remembered Eddy chanting, Aunt Clo-Clo must die. Aunt Clo-Clo must die. It had happened that day at the Sylvie & Bruno Nursery School. When she had asked Eddy who Aunt Clo-Clo was, he said he didn't know, but he had seen it written on a sheet of paper on Miss Frayle's desk. The sentence had been written at least ten times, he had counted them! He had sworn he wasn't lying.

Well, Antonia did remember him going up to the desk after Miss Frayle had left to attend to the man who had fainted and been brought into her nursery school. That man was Charles Eresby.

As it happened, it wasn't Aunt Clo-Clo who was dead but Olga Klimt. Could there be a connection? Did Fenella Frayle have an aunt called Clo-Clo? Did she wish her dead? Antonia then remembered that Fenella Frayle had struck her as preoccupied when she and Eddy were first ushered into her office that morning ... No, nonsense ... Miss Frayle couldn't have anything to do with Olga Klimt's death!

Payne was talking, 'Charlie may be anywhere at the moment, but we might as well start by visiting Olga's little house in Fulham. It is called Philomel Cottage. Collingwood told me the address. It's in Ruby Road ... We've got the satnav, so we'll get there in no time ... Perhaps that's where the body was found ... Though it may be somewhere else ... What do you say?'

'Do we need to get involved in this?'

'We most certainly do. I have been thinking of little else since Collingwood told me the Olga Klimt story. Things have now come to a head ...' He started patting his pockets. 'Car keys?'

Antonia sighed. 'I've got them.'

'*Allons-y!* Cometh the hour, cometh the man. *And* the woman.'

'She should call the police ... There are better things we could do with our lives, Hugh.'

'I am sure there are, my love, though not perhaps at this particular moment in time. We expected Olga Klimt to be killed and she was killed. How could we not get involved?'

In the car Antonia said, 'She may have died a natural death. Sorry to be a wet blanket, but we shouldn't immediately assume that she's been killed. Or she may have died in an accident. Or she may have committed suicide.'

Payne looked at her.

17

THE UNNATURAL ORDER OF THINGS

Fenella Frayle was on her knees, in a prayer-like position, heaving over the lavatory bowl.

She gasped for breath …

Eventually she rose shakily to her feet. She went up to the sink and splashed cold water over her face. She then brushed her teeth frantically and gargled with two different mouthwashes. She avoided glancing at her face in the mirror. She knew she looked dreadful – all blotched and mottled, her eyes puffy, wild and staring.

She had gone to Fulham in her car and driven back about half an hour ago.

She staggered into her unbearably cheerful sitting room, and collapsed on her freshly cleaned sofa. Her teeth were chattering. She thought of pouring herself some brandy but she couldn't trust herself to get up. She suddenly felt drained of all her strength … She needed to rest … She hadn't slept a wink the night before …

But the moment she shut her eyes, the flashbacks started … She saw herself bending over the body and making sure the girl was dead … She kept seeing the blood … She had touched the blood … The sickness returned … In normal circumstances, she was not squeamish about blood … She was used to seeing to nosebleeds and grazed knees in the nursery … But this time the circumstances were far from normal …

She felt panic rising inside her. *Macbeth has murdered sleep and therefore Macbeth will sleep no more …*

Now that she had made the phone call, there was no going back … It had been an impulsive action … One of those moments of madness … The words she had spoken on the phone kept coming back to her. 'Olga Klimt is dead. Exactly as you wanted it. Now it's your turn. You'll need to do your part of the deal –'

She couldn't quite believe she had said that. It felt like someone else now!

She tried to predict Charles Eresby's likeliest line of action. Would he do his part of the deal? She should have waited for him to say something. She shouldn't have just rung off. Well, she had been terrified. She had lost her nerve … Would he call her back? He hadn't so far … What did she want him to say? 'Thank you ever so much, Miss Frayle, and please don't worry, this will be our secret. I'll deal with your aunt in the next three days, so you'd better go away and make sure you have a sound alibi …' And even if she got some such reassurance from him, if he did eliminate her aunt, what then? Could she resume her life and carry on as though nothing untoward had ever happened?

But what if she had misjudged the situation completely? He had been very drunk when he asked her to kill his girlfriend … What if he never really meant her to do it? What if he had already called the police and reported her?

It looked like a garden and it seemed to lie on the outskirts of a wild forest. Pushing open a gate, he sauntered along a lane of sighing cypress trees. He noted with pleasure that there wasn't a single weed in sight. The air was fresh and bracing. Everything looked extremely neat and orderly. It was the kind of place where a gentleman could stretch his legs without having his eyes or nose offended!

Then he saw the tombstones and realised that this was no garden but a cemetery …

Now and then a date, an epitaph, a name on a marble slab or a weeping angel arrested his attention. Suddenly he saw a woman walking between the graves. She looked very much like Deirdre, though he was sure it was not her. She was wearing an elegant evening dress, elbow-length gloves and a stole. She stood pointing to a tombstone. When he got closer he saw a grave that was only half dug. There was a spade abandoned on the ground.

'Feel free to look round,' the woman told him with a smile. She struck him as being simultaneously over-willing and over-elusive, he couldn't quite put his finger on it, but found it a titillating combination.

He took off his black homburg. 'They seem to do you pretty well here.'

'No one knows better than I that you are a very important person. I am perfectly aware that you hold a position of unquestioned social eminence.'

'I am the last of the Collingwoods now,' he said. 'My mother is a Collingwood by marriage only.'

'Slips of the tongue can be dangerous,' she warned him.

He thought carefully how best to formulate his answer. 'We lead lives that are methodically regulated, but we have acquired a great number of little idiosyncrasies. Some brains hum incessantly, but I, for one, tend to drink coffee through a straw —'

Lord Collingwood woke up with a start. He was sitting in the swivel chair at his desk. His study was a large rectangular room lit by a Venetian glass chandelier converted to electricity. Two of the walls were lined with books. There was a luxurious carpet under his feet and two sash windows overlooking the back garden.

He discovered with some surprise that he was wearing his dinner jacket, though of course, following his contretemps with Deirdre, he'd refused to sit down and break bread with her.

On the desk in front of him there lay his morocco-bound gardening book, in which he religiously recorded his gardening experiences. He glanced at the last entry. *The finest of all camellias is the* Magnolia campbellii *by the tennis court. If February is mild, it is bound to yield a thousand crimson blooms.*

He looked up. Only nine-thirty? Not that late after all! For some reason he felt exhausted.

The sheet with the Collingwood family tree lay beside the gardening book. He frowned. It was no longer a sheet. It had been cut to ribbons.

He should perhaps join his mother at Collingwood Castle for a day or two? Scotland agreed with him. He could indulge in a spot of shooting. He and his mother could play billiards after dinner. There was no question of Deirdre joining him. London was Deirdre's natural habitat.

He wondered how Deirdre had spent the day. He had caught her looking down at her hands as though – as though what? – as though she hated them? Perhaps she suspected she was getting liver spots?

Deirdre – sleek, smiling and enigmatic in her long golden dress. She brought to mind a Byzantine Madonna. They had been about to have dinner, but then she decided she needed to phone Charlie. On previous occasions these calls went on for hours, though not this time – ten seconds, if that – she had put the phone down and looked at him. *Charlie said Olga was dead.*

Then they had had a row. Deirdre had provoked him. She said he was hopeless in a crisis. She seemed to expect him to hire a cab and go round London looking for Charlie as she had no idea where he had phoned her from. Charlie seemed to have left his clinic and gone off God knew where. She really was the most annoying woman in the universe. He had lost his temper. He told her that by marrying her he had swallowed a form of slow poison, which had been corroding his life.

And that wasn't all. He was sure Deirdre had been rummaging in his desk – some papers were not the way he had left them. When he challenged her, she denied it. She seemed to imagine he was an eyeless sap …

Lord Collingwood wondered if she had seen Ada's letter. And what about the draft of his new will? Had she read it? Did she now know that he was leaving everything to Joan?

He rubbed his temples. He didn't feel too well.

Olga Klimt couldn't be dead. Of course not. Charlie was mistaken.

'Nonsense,' Lord Collingwood said aloud. 'An utter impossibility.'

Whose was the name on the tombstone to which that woman had been pointing? He had an idea it might be his. He had meant to take a closer look. A half-dug grave waiting for him?

He couldn't remember if had taken his 'balancing' pill. Maybe he had. 'Balancing' wasn't its brand name of course. That was what he called it. Would one get over-balanced if one took an overdose? His doctor had told him to 'complete the course'. His doctor had changed his pills twice already, so it was high time his dreams began to make more sense!

As they approached Fulham, Antonia said, 'I may be making a complete fool of myself, but I do believe the solution to the Olga Klimt mystery lies at the Sylvie & Bruno Nursery School.'

'I've got a good one,' Payne said. 'Olga is actually an Oleg. A transvestite rent boy, a clever female impersonator, who has been shared by Charlie and Lord Collingwood. Collingwood is the killer – Oleg has been blackmailing him – no, it doesn't fit in with any of the facts.'

'What ghouls we are,' Antonia said. 'We don't even know for certain if Olga is dead!'

18

TO WAKE THE DEAD

'Olga? Is that you, Olga – really you?'

'Of course it is me, you silly boy! Why are you talking in this funny way?'

'Is that really you?'

'Stop saying that! Yes! Of course it's me!'

'I – I thought you were dead.' His voice shook. He pressed his mobile to his ear.

'I am not dead. I am at the clinic.'

'The clinic?'

'Yes! The clinic! Your clinic! I came to see you!'

'You are at the clinic?' Charlie's relief was so great, so over-powering, he was not surprised that tears were rolling down his face once more.

'What's the matter?'

'I am so happy you are not dead. What – what are you doing at the clinic?'

'I am having a cup of tea. The nurses are very nice, especially the older one.'

'Nanny Everett! She's always asking people if they want a cup of tea! I can't tell you how happy I am. But – but what are you doing at the clinic?'

'You asked someone to tell me to come to the clinic. Some friend of yours.'

'I didn't. What are you talking about?'

'Somebody phoned me, and said, go to the clinic at once – Charlie is not well. So you are at my house now, did you say? At Philomel Cottage, yes?'

'Yes.' He swallowed. 'Why didn't you answer your phone?'

'I was on the Tube!'

'That's what Nanny Everett said … Who the hell is that then?'

'Sorry?'

'There is a dead body here, outside the house!'

'What dead body?'

'No idea who it is. It's a girl. A blonde. I thought it was you. Someone rang me and said you were dead.'

'Did you say a girl?'

'Oh lord. I haven't seen her face yet. Can you come at once, Olga? I'll need your help. Please come at once.'

He pulled the body into the hall, shut the front door and turned on the light. He knew he shouldn't have touched it, but he was thinking that perhaps the body should be made to disappear. Calling the police would be asking for trouble.

He believed he knew now who the dead girl was. It had come to him in a flash. It was one of Olga's friends. Inge. Or Simona. Olga had given them replicas of the front-door key, she had told him. He'd said nothing but he didn't like it. He had no illusions as to what these girls did. It was Bedaux who provided them with 'jobs' and he knew what those jobs were. And officially Bedaux was still in his employ!

The trail would inevitably lead to me, Charlie thought.

The two girls were Olga's age, give or take a year. He had seen them. Like her they were blondes and quite pretty – though not a patch on her in the sheer-loveliness department!

He knew now what had happened. The nursery nut had made a fatal mistake – *she had stabbed the wrong girl.*

He bent over the body and slowly turned it over.

At Philomel Cottage all the lights were on.

Major Payne rang the front-door bell. As no one answered, he rang it again. Eventually the door opened and a girl stood on the threshold.

She was slim and was dressed in jeans, t-shirt and trainers. Her hair was very fair and it shimmered in the lamplight. Since she was lit from behind her face remained in shadow. Her shoulders, he noticed, were extremely tense.

'Yes?'

'So sorry to disturb you, but we are looking for Mr Charles Eresby,' Payne delivered with old-fashioned formality. 'He lives here, doesn't he?'

'Who are you?'

'I am Hugh Payne and this is my wife Antonia. We are his mother's friends. You see, Lady Collingwood wanted us to make sure Charlie is OK –'

'I don't understand.' The girl made a gesture that was exaggeratedly foreign.

'Charlie's mother was on the phone to Charlie but they were cut off,' Payne said slowly. 'Charlie only managed to tell his mother that a friend of his, the girl who lives in this house, actually, is dead. A girl called Olga Klimt?'

The girl took up a defiant pose, her arms akimbo. 'I am Olga Klimt and I am not dead!'

Payne's eyebrows went up a little, 'You are Olga Klimt?'

'Yes, I am! I am Olga Klimt! You want to see my papers? I am sorry but I am very busy. Please to go away –' It looked as though she was about to shut the door.

'Is Charlie here?' Payne was looking over her shoulder, into the hall. He believed he had caught a movement. 'Hallo, is that you, Charlie?' Payne called out.

'Charlie is not here – I can't talk – I am sorry – I don't understand – I am very busy.'

The door slammed.

'Curiouser and curiouser,' Antonia said.

'Watch,' Payne whispered and he gave Antonia a little wink. He then spoke in a histrionically loud voice, 'We have no option but to call the police, my love, don't you think?'

'Yes, we must call the police. We have no option,' Antonia agreed, equally loudly.

'Have you got your mobile? I don't seem to have brought mine,' Payne said, playing for time. '999, shall we?'

They thought they could hear agitated voices, then the front door opened once more and a young man wearing a dressing gown over pyjamas appeared.

'I'm so terribly sorry. I am Charles Eresby.' He sounded a little breathless, 'I was upstairs. I am afraid Olga didn't understand you. She doesn't speak English very well. Did you say you were friends of Mummy's?'

'Yes. My name is Hugh Payne and this is my wife Antonia.'

'I am so sorry. Do come in, do come in,' Charlie said and he opened the door wide. His floppy fair hair fell into his eyes.

His heartiness was a bit on the faux side, Payne thought.

19

THE HOUSE OF FEAR

The hall floor was made of expensive terracotta tiles, which gleamed in the electric light. Wet? Yes, the floor seemed to have been recently washed.

Odd time to wash the floor, Antonia thought. Could there have been something spilt on it?

Charlie seemed eager for them not to linger in the hall. He piloted them into the sitting room.

They stood beside the sofa but Charlie did not ask them to sit down. It was transparently obvious that he was anxious for them to go away as soon as possible. The girl – Olga – if she was really Olga – stood beside the door.

'Your mother is in quite a state about you,' Payne said.

'I am so terribly sorry,' Charlie said. 'It's so frightfully embarrassing that you should have come all this way on my account!'

'That's perfectly all right.'

'Poor Mummy. I'll get in touch with her as soon as I can. Most remiss of me. There's been the most diabolical muddle –' He faltered. He didn't seem to know what he should say next.

They hadn't had time to prepare their story, Antonia decided.

'You told your mother that Olga was dead. That was before you went off the radar.' Payne smiled.

'I lost the signal, for some reason. Happens all the time in some parts of London. I haven't had a chance to call her back.'

'So Olga is not dead?' Payne glanced in the direction of the girl. 'This is excellent news. Your mother thought you said Olga was dead.'

What was it Collingwood had said? *A luminous, shimmering kind of beauty*. Well, yes – the girl matched that description all right – no doubt about it – it was Olga.

Charlie ran the tip of his tongue over his lips. 'There was a fearful misunderstanding. You see, Olga was taken ill … Um … I panicked when she called me … Idiotic of me, I know, but I have been feeling rather run-down lately. So I – I overreacted a bit.' He gave a charming self-deprecating smile. 'She called me and said she thought she was dying – it was something she'd eaten – she'd been violently sick – she passed out, then came to – it made her feel very ill.'

'She seems to have made a remarkably quick recovery.'

'Well, yes. She has. Thank God for that! Sometimes Olga tends to dramatise, but I took it seriously, you see. I worked myself up into a state. I love her very much, you see. I love her to distraction. We are planning to get married.'

'Congratulations,' said Payne.

'It's all terribly embarrassing, but that's all there is to it, really. I'll explain everything to Mummy. Awfully decent of you to take so much trouble. I am deeply grateful –' Charlie now spoke a trifle impatiently. He started moving sideways towards the door. He was clearly desperate to see the back of them.

'I am terribly glad there's been no calamity.' Payne smiled amiably. He steered Antonia towards the door. He saw Charles Eresby relax.

'Have you come a long way?' Charlie asked as they walked back into the hall.

'Hampstead.'

'How intrepid of you.'

'We didn't mind one little bit,' Antonia said.

'Mummy is lucky to have such obliging friends.'

'It was a very pleasant drive. Not much traffic at this time of night.' said Payne. 'We do enjoy driving through London, don't we, my love?' He stood looking round. 'This is a cosy little place you've got here. Had it long?'

'A couple of months. It used to belong to old Collingwood. My stepfather, you know,' Charlie explained. 'I bought it from him. Had it done up and so on. Took some time, but it was worth it.'

'I daresay it is wonderfully secluded.' Payne wondered if Lord Collingwood had used Philomel Cottage as a clandestine love nest himself.

'You must come again some time. I mean, for a proper visit.'

'We'd love to. Thank you very much.'

'For drinks – or tea – or why not dinner?'

Payne inclined his head slightly. 'You are most kind. Dinner would be splendid. Incidentally, what did you do with the body?'

They heard Olga gasp.

There was a pause, then Charlie spoke. 'What the hell are you talking about? What body?' He had turned a livid shade of pale.

'I believe there was blood, wasn't there?' Payne said quietly.

'It was the body of a girl in her twenties. She looked like Olga – from the back at least.' Antonia enjoyed the process of reconstructing a crime. 'She is about the same height – has the same fair hair –'

Charlie put his hands into his dressing-gown pockets, clearly to stop them from shaking. Olga's hand had gone up to her mouth.

'There was blood,' Payne repeated. 'That's why it was imperative that you should wash the floor.'

'We have met before, actually.' Antonia addressed Charlie in conversational tones. She had decided to stop being embarrassed about her hunch and put it to the test instead.

'I don't think we have met. I am afraid you are mistaken,' Charlie said coldly.

'You clearly don't remember, but that is hardly surprising since you were quite ill that day. You fainted in the street and were taken into a place called the Sylvie & Bruno Nursery School?'

He stood staring at her. 'I am sure you are mistaken,' he said again but with less conviction.

'I am not mistaken. I happened to be there. We watched you as you climbed the stairs – I was with my grandson – it was his first day at school – we'd gone to meet the headmistress. You, on the other hand, were accompanied by your manservant – what was his name now? – Bedaux?'

Olga gave a little cry.

'You said you were perfectly capable of going up the stairs; or words to that effect. You *must* remember,' Antonia went on. 'Miss Frayle had you taken to her private quarters on the first floor.'

'Miss Frayle?'

'Yes. Fenella Frayle – the nursery school's owner-cum-headmistress. You remember her, don't you? She took you to her snuggery.'

Suddenly he swayed, as though his feet had turned to clay. He leant his back against the wall.

It looked as though he was about to be sick. So that was the effect Fenella Frayle's name had on him. Antonia now saw with absolute clarity exactly what had happened, or more precisely, what must have happened and why. The idea had occurred to her earlier on. A very ingenious premise, the crime writer in

THE KILLING OF OLGA KLIMT

her reflected, though of course it had already been used; it had served as the basis for a book and a film …

'Fenella Frayle wanted her aunt dead,' she said slowly. 'Aunt Clo-Clo? You, on the other hand, were unhappy about Olga. Extremely unhappy. If I remember correctly, you described yourself as heartbroken, or something similar, I'm not sure of your exact words. You and Olga had had a tiff – more than a tiff – a serious argument? That was the reason for your terrible state that day, wasn't it? It wasn't only the heat. You wanted her – dead?' She could see from his haunted expression that she was on the right track.

'I think you are mad,' Charlie said. His voice was hoarse.

'I don't think somehow that the idea came from her, did it? But Miss Frayle is a good listener. She's got the kind of personality that most people find reassuring. Very important for someone working with young children.' Antonia paused. It occurred to her that Fenella Frayle was not going to work with children for much longer. They must get Eddy out as soon as they could. Poor Eddy. Well, he had never quite taken to Miss Frayle. 'Perhaps Miss Frayle meant to help you by encouraging you to tell her your story? There's a lot to be said for getting a grievance off your chest.'

He remained silent. Olga had snuggled up against him. She continued holding her hand over her mouth. Standing side by side they looked very young.

'I do believe it was your idea. You detected her fatal weakness somehow. Perhaps she told you about the difficulties she was having with her aunt to show you that you were not the only one with seemingly insoluble problems? It is always reassuring to know you are not the only one with what looks like an insurmountable mountain in your life. Maybe that was her intention, to reassure you? Anyhow, you managed to tease it out of her. Her Aunt Clo-Clo dilemma. I have an idea you might have sensed the misery and despair that lurked behind the sturdy exterior?'

'What the hell are you?' Charles Eresby muttered. 'A witch? Or some bloody writer? You talk like a book!'

'The long and the short of it is that you and Miss Frayle exchanged confidences. She told you about her aunt whom she wanted dead. You, on the other hand, told her you wanted Olga dead. As I said, you and Olga had had an argument – it was serious – it seemed terminal – it ended in a break-up?'

'It was not serious!' Olga cried. She looked close to tears. 'I was only pretending! I didn't want to do it! I didn't intend to do it!'

'Shut up, Olga,' Charlie said.

'Well, you clearly managed to make Mr Eresby believe it was all over between you,' Antonia said.

'Mr Bedaux made me do it!'

Curiouser and curiouser, Antonia thought again. So the monkish Machiavel was involved too!

'That's enough, Olga! Not another word.'

'You told Miss Frayle you wanted Olga dead – in return you were going to kill her aunt. Isn't that what happened? *You exchanged murders.*'

'You need to have your head examined,' Charlie said.

'He never meant it!' Olga cried. Tears had started pouring down her face. 'Charlie, you must tell them you never meant it – I don't want her to go on – I don't like it – you are not a murderer – she frightens me – Charlie loves me! – He loves me – always! He was very ill – it was my fault – he didn't really want me killed – he told me all about it – that Miss Frayle is mad!'

'I said, not another word, Olga.' Charlie suddenly sounded very tired.

'But don't you see? *Don't you see?* They can send you to jail for something you didn't do! Let them go and get that woman

– that Miss Frayle! You must tell the truth, Charlie, please! It – it was crazy to hide the body – we were crazy – please, Charlie. Tell them – I am frightened!'

'Ah the body. I am glad you mentioned it.' Payne cleared his throat. 'I suggest you lead us to it and the sooner the better. It's the best course of action in the circumstances, I assure you. It would be utter idiocy to try to hide it, you know. What were you planning to do? Bury it in the back garden?'

Charlie suddenly covered his eyes with both his hands.

Olga went up to Antonia and clutched at her arm. 'Please. I know you will help us. You believe us, don't you? You have a kind face. I trust you. I'll show you the body.'

20

WHOSE BODY?

Deirdre Collingwood had read Le Maistre's delightful little book, *Voyage Autour de Ma Chambre*, at her finishing school and now she resolved to imitate the French author, and find occupation and amusement enough to take her mind off her worries over Charlie and Rupert and her other discoveries and all that had been happening. She intended doing this by making a mental inventory of every article of furniture she could see around her in her drawing room and by following it up with the associations, which a sofa, a chair, a chaise-longue, an occasional table or a lamp might have for her.

Only it didn't quite work. She was in an anxious, unsettled state of mind and she found it hard to concentrate.

She had had dinner all by herself and she was now sipping black coffee out of one of her tiny fragile-looking Meissen cups extravagantly fashioned like seashells. She was also smoking a purple gold-tipped Sobranie. It was one of her very rare cigarettes. The cup was so tiny, the sip didn't amount to more than a tongue-dip. Deirdre tried to amuse herself by pretending she was a cat but that didn't cheer her up much either.

She was sitting on the exceedingly uncomfortable Empire sofa upholstered in maroon and silver, which had once been at Collingwood. The sofa was uncompromisingly hard. She might have been sitting on a wooden bench – or on two planks put together. Well, sometimes Deirdre wanted to be uncomfortable. It helped her to concentrate. The Buhl desk in the corner, on the other hand, was an object of exquisite beauty. It sported some unusual red tortoiseshell decorations on its lid.

Thank God for Hugh Payne! Hugh Payne had been able to locate Charlie. Charlie had since called her and reassured her that all was well. There had been a mistake, a misunderstanding, which was a relief. She wondered whether to ring Bedaux. She craved a chat with Bedaux. Bedaux *understood* her. There was a special kind of rapport between them, one of those mysterious bonds that were impossible to explain in a rational manner.

She took another tiny sip of coffee. 'Meow,' she said. Perhaps one day Bedaux would help her get rid of Rupert?

She had a headache. She should bathe her temples with eau de cologne. And then – an Aconite? Yes. It would be bliss. She was unhappy, oh so terribly unhappy!

As she heard the clock strike ten, her thoughts strayed back to the morning and the discovery she had made.

She had gone up to Rupert's study and rifled Rupert's desk. She wasn't sure what she had hoped to find but she had been convinced that there would be *something*. She had always wondered if the theft of the Reynolds and the Vlaminck from Collingwood the year before hadn't been staged by Rupert and his mother, so that they could claim the insurance, which they had done … Or perhaps there would be love letters …

Well, she found a letter, not exactly a love letter, and it was linked to the draft of a brand new will. The two were together, inside a slim black folder.

The letter was from Ada de Ravigny, with whom, some twenty-five years ago, Rupert had had an affair. Well, that didn't come as a particular surprise. Rupert had never denied the affair. It was an exceedingly short letter, no more than a few lines. The date at the top indicated it had been written a couple of months ago, back in May. Ada informed Rupert that she was dying – and she wanted to tell Rupert something which he needed to know –

Simona snapped her fingers in Mr X's face and laughed when he blinked, but then she became serious again.

'I want to see where my friend is, Grandpa, I am very worried, can't you see I am worried? Are you so insensitive? Can't you wait a little? Are you a child?'

'I want us to start. Please.'

'Are you a child? No, you are not. Of course you are not.' She spoke with contempt. 'You are an old man. You are a very old man.'

'I am not that old.'

'You are *very* old. You are seventy-two and two months. I saw your passport. That's very old. In my country that is very old. So you need to be patient.'

'At my time of life being patient is a luxury I can ill afford. I endeavour to live every moment as though it were my last.' Mr X stood in his perfectly tailored suit, his silk handkerchief peeping out of his breast pocket, looking piteously at her, the ivory brush held aloft in his hand.

'Don't quote the Bible to me! I don't like the Bible. Religion is the opium of the people, that is what my grandparents were taught at school and I believe that. Shush. I don't want to know. I am not interested. I don't want you to speak. I've got a headache.' Simona took out her mobile. 'I am worried about my friend.'

'Is that Inga?'

'*Inge*,' Simona corrected him contemptuously. '*Inge*. Is it so difficult to remember a name? You are an educated man.

You had the best education money can buy. You told me so yourself. Your parents spent thousands and thousands on your education.'

'I have problems with my memory,' Mr X said.

'It's because you are old, that's why. Of course you have problems with your memory. Your brain is melting. I don't want you to speak now. No, don't say a word.' She held the mobile phone to her ear. 'Come on, where *are* you?' Simona muttered.

'Why do you have to talk to your friend now?' Mr X asked.

'Because I want to.' It wasn't like Inge to vanish like that without getting in touch for – what was it? Five hours? Six?

Simona hoped nothing had happened to Inge. In a job like theirs one met all kinds of problems, all kinds of men. Simona remembered something Inge had told her. Inge had been visited by a woman some time ago. A young woman, Inge said. English. Very polite, very well dressed. The woman had asked her questions about the job they did. What they called 'escort'. Not about the catering. The woman had assured Inge that her name wouldn't appear anywhere. It was some kind of anonymous survey. The woman had paid Inge to talk and Inge had talked. Inge was a fool. Mr Bedaux wouldn't like it if he knew …

Where was Inge?

The idea that the dead girl might not actually be Olga occurred to Fenella Frayle at about ten-fifteen in the evening and it pushed the nightmare into a completely new dimension. *She had never had the chance to look at the girl's face.* It was the conjunction of the blonde hair and the open front door that had made her believe the girl was Olga …

She had got up and picked up the brandy. She was now on her second glass. She didn't feel calmer, exactly, rather she felt resigned.

If the dead girl wasn't Olga, Fenella reasoned, that meant she hadn't really carried out her part of the deal, so she couldn't possibly expect Charles Eresby to go and kill Aunt Clo-Clo in return, could she?

But who was the girl if not Olga? What other blonde would have been standing outside Olga's house?

Billy Selkirk was not at all sure he wanted to marry Joan Selwyn. He doubted whether he loved Joan Selwyn, though he was certainly fond of her. Well, to love was to invent. Love filled the imagination before taking possession of the heart. Would love ever take possession of his heart, where Joan was concerned?

As it happened, it was Mortimer whom Billy loved passionately and unconditionally. His life, he had decided, had no meaning unless lived alongside Mortimer.

Well, discretion would be the name of the game. After he and Joan were married, he and Mortimer could carry on seeing each other in a seemingly casual manner, though with clockwork regularity. There wouldn't be any slackening. After all, they had been together since Haileybury. Billy firmly believed Joan could be made to slip into the equation somehow. (He was a bit vague on that point.) He thought that things could be made to work somehow. He was an optimist – though he wished Mortimer wasn't so hideously jealous and possessive. Mortimer would never admit to it, but he was. Sometimes Mortimer was a little bit too temperamental for his own good, though you wouldn't think it looking at him. He had said he would kill Joan. He said he would slit her throat. He didn't mean it of course. At least Billy didn't think so.

Billy smiled at the memory of one of Mortimer's rare outbursts. Mortimer had gesticulated and shouted. He had made himself sound like a Corsican or something, though anyone looking less like a Corsican Billy could not imagine. For one thing, Mortimer was awfully keen on laws and rules and such-like, which Billy believed to be completely alien to the Corsican nature. (Mortimer's latest invention was a punishment called the Cupboard and Its Perfumed Depths, at the thought of which Billy gave a little shudder.) Then there was the fact that Mortimer was fair-haired while the whole world knew that all Corsicans were dark.

Billy glanced at his watch. He was sitting at a table at Porters in Covent Garden, waiting for Joan to turn up and secretly hoping she wouldn't. She was often critical and disapproving, a little *too* severe for his liking.

She was already ten minutes late, which wasn't like her at all. She hadn't phoned him, so he didn't know where she was or what had happened. He hadn't tried to call her either, though he had rung Mortimer and explained the situation. Mortimer had laughed and said that was what one should expect when one went out with *girls*. 'We are going to Gstaad for Christmas, Selkirk!' – this, despite the fact Billy had made it absolutely clear to him that he and Joan would be doing something completely different at Christmas ...

It suddenly came to Billy that the reason Joan couldn't phone him was because she had left her mobile at his flat the day before. He remembered now. He had been meaning to let her know but hadn't had a chance yet. Some people had a second mobile, but Joan didn't seem to. Not even her worst enemies could have accused Joan of extravagance or profligacy.

For some reason Billy had the uneasy feeling that Joan's lateness might have something to do with Mortimer. The last time he had seen Mortimer, which was six and a half hours ago, Mortimer's fair hair had been at its sleekest, his face alight with mischief. Mortimer had teased him that it would be silly

137

for a Selkirk to marry a Selwyn – Wilt thou, Selkirk, take this Selwyn – it sounded, well, *wrong*.

Mortimer didn't like Joan. He was always terribly polite to her, he jumped to his feet the moment she entered the room and so on, but once or twice Billy had caught him gazing at her in a speculative kind of way. As though – what? He wasn't sure, but it had made him uneasy.

Gstaad for Christmas, eh? He was certain it was the kind of place he would enjoy. Skiing and drinking punch in front of cosy fires and so on. He looked at his watch. Could Joan still be with Lord Collingwood? She had told him she was going to see Lord Collingwood, but that was in the morning, wasn't it? Joan and Lord Collingwood seemed to be on extremely friendly terms, of which Billy approved. He thought that Lord Collingwood might be a useful contact for him to have one day. Mortimer, who knew Lord Collingwood, said Lord Collingwood was as mad as a hatter – or was it Lady Collingwood who was as mad as a hatter? Billy remembered Joan telling him some rigmarole about some mysterious friend of Lord Collingwood's – now, what was that about?

Billy reached out for the bottle of wine and poured himself a second glass. It was getting terribly late. Something told him Joan wouldn't be coming. He felt himself relaxing. His spirits soared. She cometh not! He held up his glass and drank a toast to it, then he took out his mobile and gave Mortimer a ring.

Olga led the way across the hall to what looked like the door to a broom cupboard, which she opened and then moved to the left without looking at what lay inside.

Payne said sharply, 'Is there a light?'

Again without looking, Olga reached out and flicked a switch.

Our fingerprints are everywhere now, Antonia thought in mild panic. This is all most irregular. What would the police say?

The body had been placed on a piece of tarpaulin, face up. It was the body of a young woman with blond hair. The eyes were open and they stared back at them.

Not a natural blonde. The hair's roots were dark, Antonia observed.

'Who is she?' Major Payne asked. He turned round and glanced across the hall. Charlie remained silent. He hadn't joined them; he was leaning against the wall, his head bowed.

It was Olga who told them. 'This is Charlie's *ex*-girlfriend. Her name is Joan Selwyn.'

21

THE ANATOMY OF MURDER

It was quarter of an hour later and they were back in the sitting room.

'Well, that's – that's been done. Filial obligation fulfilled. Mummy sends her love.' Charlie put away his mobile. He sounded dazed but appeared more composed. He had told his mother that there had been a mistake and that he and Olga were both all right.

He hadn't mentioned the murder. He hadn't referred to Joan at all. Major Payne had advised him against it. It wouldn't have been a good idea for Deirdre Collingwood to hear about Joan's death *before* they had informed the police of it.

Payne leant back in his chair and brought the tips of his fingers together. 'Now then, be kind enough to give us the sequence of events that led to your finding the body, but try to make it snappy.' He glanced at his watch. 'We haven't got much time. We'll need to call the police, you know.'

'Must we call the police?' Charlie said.

'I am afraid we must. And it would look really bad if we delayed too long, so get on with it, there's a good chap.'

'Very well. I was in bed at Dr Bishop's clinic in Bayswater. A nurse came and told me there had been a call for me. She gave me a mobile number I didn't know. She couldn't say if it was a man or woman. The caller hadn't given a name, but had asked me to call back as soon as I could. Which I did.'

'Didn't you recognise Fenella Frayle's voice?'

'No. No. For a couple of moments I had no idea what she meant by 'your part of the deal'. I'd forgotten all about it, you see. That's why it came as such a shock when she told me that Olga was dead.'

'But then you remembered?'

'Yes.' Charlie swallowed. 'I remembered all right. I can't explain how it made me feel. I – I was overcome by guilt. I realised it had all been my fault. "Olga Klimt is dead. Exactly as you wanted it. Now it's your turn. You'll need to do your part of the deal." Those were the exact words. It all came back to me and it – it hit me very hard. I wanted to die. I thought of killing myself. I honestly did. I couldn't imagine life without Olga. I thought of killing myself,' he repeated. 'Thank God Olga called.'

'It's like in *Romeo and Juliet*,' Olga whispered. Her eyes filled with tears. She had been holding the kitten but now she put it down on the floor – they had had to keep the kitten from licking the blood in the hall, she explained. 'Romeo thinks Juliet is dead and he kills himself. Then she wakes up and sees him and she too dies!'

'Did you read *Romeo and Juliet* in Lithuanian?' Payne turned to her. He was intrigued.

'Yes. We did it at school.'

'Did you find it difficult?'

'No, not difficult. It was very sad but it was beautiful!'

'She is a clever girl,' Charlie said. He stroked Olga's hair. '"She doth teach the torches to burn bright." Doesn't she?'

'She most certainly does.' Payne smiled.

Olga and Charlie were sitting on the sofa side by side. They were holding hands. They looked like frightened children.

Well, they were in a terrible mess. Poor things, Antonia thought. Who was it that said that being young was the one great adventure of our lives?

'I wasn't myself when I suggested to that woman that we exchange murders,' Charlie said. 'I know it was highly irresponsible of me, but I was in a frightful state. Besides I'd been drinking Miss Frayle's sherry. I shouldn't have touched it but she said it would be good for me. I am not used to drinking. I can't believe I said what I said. People do say terrible things when they are drunk and when they are upset with someone, don't they?'

'They certainly do.' Payne nodded. 'So what happened after you got Miss Frayle's call? You leapt out of bed and –'

'I ran. I was dressed the way you see me now, in my dressing gown and slippers. I didn't care what people might think. I got into a cab –'

'What time was it?'

'About six, I think. When we got to Fulham, I asked the driver to stop at the end of the cul-de-sac. There was no one around. There never is. I ran to the house. It was getting dark but it wasn't too dark. I saw the front door was open. Then – then I saw the body lying face down; half in, half out of the hall. I saw the blood on her back. A dark stain. I saw the blonde hair and I had no doubt it was Olga. I – I just stood there. I wanted to die. Then – then Bedaux suddenly appeared –'

'Your man? Really? How terribly interesting,' said Payne. 'Are you sure he didn't come out of the house?'

'No. He came from the direction of the main road.'

'Did he say anything?'

'No. Nothing. He didn't say a word. He just stood and stared at the body. He had his hands in his pockets. I think he was holding something in his pocket but I may be wrong. I told him Olga was dead, that she had been stabbed. He said nothing. He just turned and walked off.'

'I think Mr Bedaux wanted to kill me,' said Olga. 'He hated me — because I lied to him. He scares me!'

'Stop calling him "Mr Bedaux",' Charlie said.

'Why should he have wanted to kill you?' Antonia asked.

'It is difficult to explain. He is a very strange man.' Olga hesitated. 'Well, he is in love with me.'

'Is he? Really?' So, Antonia thought, I was right! Master and servant in love with the same girl. She saw Olga tighten her grip on Charlie's hand.

'I pretended to be in love with him, that was my mistake,' Olga said with a sigh.

'I don't think Bedaux will ever want to come back,' said Charlie. 'Which is just as well. I was planning to get rid of him. He thinks that you are dead, so he is unlikely to bother you again … A minute after Bedaux walked away, my mobile rang. It was Olga. At first I thought it was Fenella Frayle calling from Olga's phone but then I heard Olga's voice. I couldn't believe it at first. I can't explain how I felt! The relief! Oh my God, the relief!'

'You told her to come here?'

'Yes. While I waited I pulled the body into the hall and turned on the light – that's when – that's when I saw it was Joan. That was another shock. She was the last person I expected to see!'

'Why the last person? Why were you so surprised? Wasn't Joan Selwyn obsessed with you? Hadn't she been stalking you? Your stepfather told me the whole story, you see.'

'Well, it's true. She did stalk us once. And she kept ringing me. But then she stopped. I hadn't seen her for quite a while. I didn't treat her well and I am sorry, but then I couldn't help falling in love with Olga –' Charlie broke off. 'I can't believe she is over there! I can't believe she's been killed.' He glanced in the direction of the hall. Payne had thought it unwise to move the body yet again and they had left it lying inside the broom cupboard.

'Have you any idea why Joan should have wanted to come here?' Antonia asked.

'No. No idea at all.'

'Perhaps she wanted to kill me?' Olga suggested. 'When we were at the Albert Hall, she said she would kill me, didn't she, Charlie?'

'She did, yes, but that was some time ago. I can't believe she still wanted to do it. I'd have thought it highly unlikely.' Charlie stroked Olga's hair.

'Some girls don't forget such things,' Olga pointed out.

'You said the front door was open and the key was in the lock,' Payne said. 'You mean on the outside?'

'Yes. I took it out.' Charlie nodded. 'Oh my God, my fingerprints are everywhere now, aren't they? All round the place!'

'I am afraid so. You will have some explaining to do when the police come.' Payne glanced at his watch. 'But don't worry. We'll all have some explaining to do. My fingerprints are also all round the place, so are my wife's. So it seems Joan was killed as she was letting herself into the house,' Payne stroked his chin with his forefinger. 'Now then, how did Joan get hold of the key?'

'She might have stolen it from old Collingwood. She used to be his secretary,' Charlie explained. 'This used to be his property. I am sure he still has a couple of front-door keys. The locks haven't been changed since his time.'

Payne turned to Olga. 'If my calculations are correct, you arrived at the clinic only moments after Charlie left?'

Olga agreed that she must have done. The nurses had told her that Charlie had suddenly left, they had no idea where he'd gone. 'They were very worried. They were wondering what to do. They asked me to sit and wait. They thought that if I stayed there, Charlie would come back. They thought Charlie was looking for me. They made me a cup of tea. Then I phoned Charlie.'

'Thank God you did!'

'Charlie was so happy! Oh he was so happy! He couldn't believe it was me at first! He said he was here, at Philomel Cottage. He told me to come.' Olga's smile faded. 'The body was in the hall – it was horrible – the blood! There was blood on the floor. She had been stabbed in the back. There was blood on her coat. It was horrible.'

'No knife?'

'No knife. The nursery nut must have taken it with her,' Charlie said. 'She must have got rid of it by now. Dropped it in the river or into the Serpentine or something.'

Olga said, 'Charlie wanted to hide the body. I told him it was stupid. How do you hide a dead body?'

'How indeed. It would have been an incredibly daft thing to do.' Payne nodded. 'You are absolutely right.'

'He wanted to bury it in the back garden,' Olga said.

'I couldn't think of anything else.' Charlie looked sheepish.

'The police would have been able to trace Joan's movements to this place soon enough,' Payne said. 'Her disappearance would have been noticed – by tomorrow lunchtime at the latest. There are CCTV cameras everywhere. What does she do? I mean, did – did she have a job?'

'She used to be old Collingwood's secretary, as I said.' Charlie frowned. 'Then she went to work for some Tory MP, I think. No idea which one. If she ever told me, I've forgotten.'

'Where did she live?'

'She shared a flat with two other girls. In Kensington or was it in Chelsea? She doesn't get on with her father. Didn't. Her mother is in a hospice in Wiltshire. She's terminally ill. Cancer, I think. It's all terribly sad, I see that now.' Charlie bowed his head.

'D'you have any idea why she dyed her hair blond?' Antonia asked suddenly.

Charlie blinked. 'No. No idea at all. The last time I saw her, her hair was brown. Joan's hair was light brown. That was her natural colour.'

'She didn't do it in the hope of making herself look like Olga? With the intention of winning you back?' Major Payne suggested. 'Girls do odd things in the name of love.'

Charlie frowned. 'That would never have worked … I thought she had got over me … I keep telling you … Actually, I heard she's started seeing someone else … Came as a relief … '

'It's horrible – we are sitting and talking about her while she is lying in the cupboard, dead!' Olga cried.

'Well, it's time we called the police.' Payne produced his mobile phone.

'No, wait.' Olga rose abruptly. She went up to where Antonia sat and took her hands. 'It will be all right, won't it? I am very frightened. The police won't think it was me that killed Joan, will they? I mean they may think I have a reason to want her dead – because of Charlie? They won't think she came here to see me and that we quarrelled and then I got angry and stabbed her, will they?'

'I can't say what the police will think, but you don't stab people in the back when you are quarrelling with them. Don't worry.' Antonia tried to be reassuring. 'We also seem to be forgetting that there is already someone who has confessed to the murder. Fenella Frayle did, didn't she? All Charlie will have to do is tell his story. Wait a minute,' she told Payne. 'Don't ring yet.'

'Will they believe me though? That's what worries me,' Charlie said. 'I mean, it will be my word against hers, won't it? OK, there is the call she made to the clinic and they will probably be able to trace it to Miss Frayle's mobile phone, if she used her mobile phone, that is, though she may not have. In the end it will be only my word that she told me she had killed Olga. I don't think they'll believe me. The whole thing is too fantastic! Do you see? It's too idiotic for words.'

'I do see,' Antonia said. 'It *is* fantastic.'

'All Miss Frayle will need to do is deny it. Somehow,' Charlie went on gloomily, 'I don't see her admitting to the police she killed a perfect stranger to oblige me – do you? She is a highly respectable figure. She invites immediate trust. She doesn't look like a nut at all. She sounds frightfully composed and rational. You wouldn't say she looked like a nut, would you?'

'No, I wouldn't.' Antonia gave a little smile. 'Though my grandson seemed to have some reservations about her. I wonder if that means he'll grow up to be a fine judge of character.'

'Unless they traced the knife to her in some way, there would be absolutely no proof that it was a case of mistaken identity, that she killed Joan thinking it was Olga!'

There was a pause. Antonia came to a decision. She slowly got to her feet. 'I think we should go and see Miss Frayle, Hugh. She lives at a place called Jevanny Lodge. She lives above her school.'

'She calls it her "snuggery",' Charlie said.

'Actually it would be best if I went alone. You stay here and wait for the police.'

'Are you sure?' Payne asked.

'Yes. I'll go in the car, if you don't mind. I think it would be better if I saw her before the police did. She knows me. It would be well, kinder. She'll be more inclined to open the door to me at this time of night. I am after all little Eddy Rushton's grandmother. Besides she's read two of my novels.'

Charlie stared at her. 'Good God. Do you write *detective* stories?' Suddenly he grinned. 'Well, *that* explains it!'

Payne cocked an eyebrow. 'You think you have a chance of getting her to confess?'

'I don't know. I will try my best.' Antonia shrugged. 'Wait about ten minutes before you call the police, will you? I want to talk to her without being interrupted.'

'Very well, my love. Do be careful,' Payne said.

22

JOURNEY INTO DARKNESS

Antonia drove in the direction of the Sylvie & Bruno Nursery School as fast as she could. 'Hell for leather,' she murmured. (Did anyone ever use the expression nowadays?)

She found herself trying to imagine the experts in violent death arriving at Philomel Cottage. She hated police procedurals, so she was vague about it. There would be a team consisting of a detective inspector, a police sergeant, a police surgeon, a photographer or two, a print man, whom she envisaged as having small delicate hands, several plain-clothes men who would no doubt subject every room in the house to a methodical search. They would be carrying with them their peculiar paraphernalia and specific skills.

She could see them very clearly now, hard-faced, bleary-eyed men and, possibly, a woman or two, standing around, looking as though they would rather be somewhere else …

Antonia had forced herself to read a couple of police procedurals and found them tedious, but she understood they had a following. Well, *chacun à son goût* …

She imagined Hugh sitting patiently on the sofa, smoking his pipe, his legs crossed, giving every appearance of being unperturbed, waiting for his turn to be interviewed.

'Major Payne? You say you have nothing to do with any of this? Then what the hell are you doing here?'

No, they wouldn't say 'hell'; they would be politer. But they wouldn't allow Hugh to smoke his pipe inside the house, would they? They might even confiscate it if he refused to put it out! Poor Hugh. Would the inspector take Charlie's story of the exchanged murders seriously? Actually she had no idea. Poor Charlie.

The scene of the crime would be taped off. Every scrap of paper, threads of fabric, shreds of wood, pieces of plastic, hairs from the kitten, bits from Olga's make-up, the detritus of everyday living would be rescued and examined to see whether it could add to the picture of how Joan Selwyn had died and at whose hands …

In her detective novels Antonia (writing as 'Antonia Darcy') never attempted to mystify her readers with the mechanical, the technical, the ballistic, nor, for that matter, with the forensic. Some thought it a weakness, but Antonia didn't care. She hated doing research – she feared she wouldn't get it right because she found the process so boring. Procedural verisimilitude simply had no place in her kind of plot.

Antonia was famous – some said notorious – for allotting the police only a tangential part in her novels. Actually, in one or two of her books the police did not appear at all. The investigation was invariably conducted by a pair of gifted amateurs. Gifted amateurs might be an anachronism, but hers were carefully camouflaged by mobile phones, references to Google, Twitter and Facebook and lashings of self-deprecating wit. (Were Charlie and Olga on Facebook? They were the right age for it.)

Antonia pulled her thoughts back to the murder at Philomel Cottage. There were some questions that needed to be answered. Who was the person that had phoned Olga and told her to go to Doctor Bishop's clinic? Why had that phone call been made in the first place?

Joan Selwyn must have arrived at Philomel Cottage soon after Olga left. What had Joan Selwyn been hoping to achieve? She had had a front-door key in her pocket and she seemed to have been stabbed in the back as she was about to enter the house. Miss Frayle must have followed her ... Well, yes ... Miss Frayle was the killer ... Miss Frayle had believed Joan to be Olga, so she killed her ...

Antonia wondered whether they were not dealing with two murderers, both intent on the same target. How did that work out? Enter First Murderer, former girlfriend Joan Selwyn. Joan had only pretended to be over Charlie whereas in point of fact she was still hankering after him. The fact that she had dyed her hair blonde could be interpreted as pointing in that direction. Unrequited passion, as Hugh had put it once, was the devil.

Antonia tried to envisage the scene. Joan has acquired a key and she is in the process of unlocking the front door with it, her intention being to hide somewhere inside the house and wait for Olga. But just then the Second Murderer arrives. Fenella Frayle is carrying a knife in her pocket. It's getting dark and she sees a blonde girl standing in the doorway with her back to her. She is convinced that it is Olga and she goes up to her and stabs her in the back – which introduces the joint elements of dark irony and poetic justice into the proceedings.

But Joan had no weapon of any kind on her. They had checked her pockets. No gun, no knife, no blunt instrument. Could she have intended to strangle Olga? Or had she hoped to use something from inside the house? The poker? There had been no gloves on her hands or in her pockets either. Had she planned to do it with her bare hands then? It was possible, people did do illogical things, especially if they were in the grip of a powerful emotion, but Antonia was not convinced ...

There it was. Jevanny Lodge. The Sylvie & Bruno Nursery School. That was where it had all started. There were enough street lights, so the place did not look as sinister as it might have done. Only one window on the first floor was lit. Miss Frayle's snuggery? So she was in.

Antonia pushed open the little gate and walked up to the front door. Suddenly she shivered, though the evening was not particularly cold. Someone walking on my grave, Antonia thought. She remembered Hugh had urged her to be careful …

She rang the front-door bell.

23

CHARLIE'S ANGEL

As there was no answer, she rang the bell again. She stood and waited. Nothing. She glanced up at the lit window. No shadowy silhouettes. No movement. The curtains were drawn across the window.

Antonia reached out for the knocker. She heard the 'bang-bang-bang' reverberate inside the house. Then she did it again. Someone was passing in the street and, with the corner of her eye, she saw them pause. Possessed by a spirit of recklessness, Antonia drew back a little, away from the door, and called out, 'Miss Frayle? Miss Frayle? Are you there? Are you all right?'

Miss Frayle wouldn't want a rumpus, Antonia reflected. Not at a moment like this.

'Miss Frayle! Will you open up, please?' Antonia called out in a louder voice. She then picked up a pebble and threw it at the window. She heard a tinkling sound as it hit the pane.

Nothing. A thought crossed her mind. *Fenella Frayle might have killed herself.* Some murderers committed suicide. Fenella Frayle was not a hardened criminal; rather she was someone who had had a moment of madness …

'Miss Frayle?' Antonia shouted again. 'I am going to call an ambulance!'

She felt extremely self-conscious since she hated raising her voice, but she realised she was doing this for her own personal safety as well. Fenella Frayle was less likely to attempt killing her if there had been a rumpus outside her front door. Passers-by might remember the woman bawling outside the Sylvie & Bruno Nursery School shortly after ten in the evening ...

The next moment she saw a light come on in the coloured-glass panel of the front door.

Antonia could hardly recognise the woman who stood in the doorway.

'Miss Frayle?'

'It is very late. The nursery is closed.' Fenella Frayle made a peculiar gesture with her hand, at once pitifully defensive and peremptory. 'Please, come tomorrow. Some time after nine o'clock would be best. We are closed now.' She was slurring. Antonia smelled brandy. Oh dear.

'It is me, Antonia Darcy. Eddy Rushton's grandmother.'

'I am sorry but the nursery is closed. All the children have been taken home. I am sure they are all safely in bed. I don't think I can do anything for you now.'

'I would like to talk to you,' Antonia persisted. 'It's important.'

'I am afraid that would be impossible. This is a most inconvenient time.'

'It's very important. I must talk to you.'

'What is it about?'

'May I come in?'

'No. What is it about?' It looked as though Miss Frayle was about to shut the door. She had a dazed and disoriented air about her.

'It is about Olga Klimt. It's about the killing of Olga Klimt,' Antonia said boldly. Sometimes, though not always, shock tactics worked.

'I don't know anyone called Olga. I am not familiar with anyone of that name. Please go away.'

Antonia cast a glance at her watch. 'The police will be here very soon. I may be able to help you.'

'The police? Are the police … coming?'

'Yes!'

There was a pause.

'How can you help me? No one can help me.' Fenella Frayle suddenly sounded breathless. She stood peering at Antonia. 'You are Miss Darcy. You write detective novels. You write about murders.'

'That is correct. But that has nothing to do with why I am here,' Antonia said quickly.

'Detective-story writers are not at all nice-minded. They always think the worst of everyone they meet, don't they? They are ghouls. You are here for "copy", aren't you?'

'No, that's not the reason I came. I want to help you.' Antonia knew that if she had been asked exactly how she proposed to do that, she wouldn't have been able to provide a satisfactory answer.

'I think it is too late for help. But come in. You might as well come in,' Fenella Frayle said.

She led the way into her snuggery and slumped heavily on the sofa, making it creak. She didn't ask Antonia to sit down and Antonia didn't. It was better to remain standing, actually, in case Miss Frayle suddenly lunged at her and tried to stab her. (Perhaps there was a knife hidden behind one of the sofa cushions? *Sharp Blades and Soft Fabrics*. That could be an interesting title for a novel.)

Fenella Frayle's stoutish body was encased in a black, baggy trouser suit. Her hair had been pulled back into a tight bun. She

THE KILLING OF OLGA KLIMT

looked like some grotesque version of a Charlie's Angel. Her face, once so pleasantly firm and apple-cheeked, was mottled and puffy and it sagged a little – the left cheek more than the right one. From a certain angle her face gave the impression of being lopsided – she might have had a facelift that had gone badly wrong. Her eyelids were actually quite swollen, they might have been injected with some mysterious serum. The whole effect was very disconcerting.

Antonia glanced at the brandy bottle and empty glass on the coffee table in front of the sofa. There was no time to waste.

'The body at Philomel Cottage is not that of Olga Klimt. You made a mistake. You killed the wrong girl.'

Miss Frayle frowned. 'You were here when he came, weren't you? I mean the biscuit heir. I should never have allowed him to be brought in. Never. Then none of this would have happened. But that was the humane thing to do. One is frequently punished for one's kindness, have you noticed? I was good to him and how did he repay me?' She tapped her forehead. 'By playing with my mind. He was very clever about it. *Very clever*. I wouldn't have thought it of a pretty boy like him, but there you are. Pretty boys are usually silly. But he was clever.'

Antonia nodded. 'Yes. You were in a vulnerable state and he took advantage of it. We know it was Charles Eresby who came up with the idea of exchanging murders.'

'That is correct. I am glad you believe me. I wouldn't have dreamt of asking him to kill my aunt. I am famous for my self-control, you know. For my rationality.' She gave a mirthless guffaw. 'But he said he would kill my aunt for me. He promised. Spoilt rich boy! *I do yours, you do mine*.' Fenella frowned. 'Are you telling me he's made a confession?'

'He did make a confession, yes, sort of. His line is that he wasn't himself at the time. He was upset, besides he'd drunk too much of your sherry.'

'So my sherry is to blame, is it?'

'He said he never thought you would act on the suggestion. He never meant you to.'

'He never meant me to? But he asked me to kill Olga Klimt! He was most specific. He said it would be foolproof. No one would think of linking us when it was all over and so on. It's been used before, hasn't it? The strangers-on-a-train scenario.'

'It has been used, yes.'

'He said he wanted Olga dead. I don't understand. What do the police make of it?'

'The police haven't questioned him yet, but they will, soon. In fact, I believe they may be questioning him at this very moment.' Antonia glanced at her watch.

'You don't look the kind of person who would volunteer to do jobs for the police,' Fenella said slowly. 'I can't believe it was they who sent you here. They wouldn't do anything like that, would they?'

'No. I am here entirely on my own initiative.'

'And you believe you know exactly what I did?'

'You phoned Charles Eresby and told him that you'd killed Olga. Then you reminded him that he should do his part of the deal. You expected him to kill your aunt. Aunt Clo-Clo.'

'Aunt Clo-Clo.' Fenella echoed. 'You know about Aunt Clo-Clo? You seem to know too much.' She reached for the brandy bottle, seemed to change her mind and didn't pick it up. 'But you can't possibly know what I have had to put up with.'

'I can imagine – if what you wrote was anything to go by,' Antonia said in apologetic tones. 'You wrote that Aunt Clo-Clo should die – you wrote it several times.'

'How – how do you know that? You can't possibly know that.' Fenella shook her head. 'Well, I was pushed to the limit. I didn't know what I was doing, really. My aunt's a monster. I am facing ruin. You see, they are going to take this place from me. My life's work. I haven't been sleeping well. I catch myself doing odd things, like the scribbling you mention.'

'A doctor might have been able to help you.'

'You think I need help? You are right, I damned well need help. My nerves are all to hell. Look at me, just look at me! Normally I never dress like this – never. Look at the way I've done my hair!' She sniffed. 'But I was pushed to the limit. I had a phone call from Aunt Clo-Clo earlier today. She said some truly appalling things to me. More appalling than usual. So I thought to myself, enough is enough. Aunt Clo-Clo is a noxious weed in need of uprooting. Let's go and do it. Let's get cracking!'

'What did you do?'

'Well, I got up, put on this suit – I have never worn it before though I have had it for ages. I got into my car and I drove to Fulham. I knew the address. Philomel Cottage. I found it in Charles Eresby's wallet.'

'You brought a knife with you, didn't you?'

'A knife?' Fenella looked puzzled. 'No, I didn't. You won't succeed in catching me out, so don't you try it! I took no weapon with me; that was the idiotic thing. I'd convinced myself I meant business, but I didn't have a weapon with me! This should show you how adept I am in the art of murder. This should show you!' Suddenly she threw back her head and laughed.

'Did you perhaps pick up the knife on the way – perhaps you bought it? Or maybe you found it somewhere?' Antonia said after a pause. She knew this sounded feeble, but extraordinary things did happen.

'No, I did nothing of the sort.' Fenella shook her head. 'I didn't have a knife when I arrived at Philomel Cottage, I keep telling you. You clearly don't believe me but that's God's truth. I hadn't the foggiest what I was going to do exactly. I admit I had fantasised about killing Olga, wondered how I might do it, but deep down I knew I couldn't do it.'

'But you went to Fulham? You went to Olga's house?'

'I went to Fulham, yes. I drove to Fulham. I went to Olga's house. Strange, isn't it? Or would you call it mad? I don't expect you to understand. Or perhaps you *do* understand? You write about people like me.' She shook her forefinger at Antonia. 'I read one of your books. You like odd people.'

'I don't like them. Not really. I find them interesting.'

'Olga's house is in a cul-de-sac. No neighbours on either side. *Perfect for murder.* I thought that, yes – I thought it as I started walking towards the house – even though I had no weapon on me! Even though I knew very well that even if I had a weapon I could *not* kill Olga – strange, isn't it? Isn't it?'

'Go on.'

'Then I stopped. I saw the body lying there, half in half out of the door. I got closer. I saw the blood on her back. She was wearing some light-coloured coat. I saw the dark patch on the back. I bent over her. I touched her neck. She was warm but there was no pulse. I have had first-aid training, so I knew she was dead. *Olga was dead.* It never occurred to me that the body might not be Olga. You said it wasn't Olga, didn't you? I was shocked to find her dead but I was also delighted – you see why, don't you?'

'Go on,' Antonia said again.

'This, I thought, was an answer to my prayers! *Olga Klimt was dead.* She had been killed. Someone else had gone and killed her. That was all that mattered. Oh the relief! It was exactly as Charles Eresby wanted it. I knew I couldn't do it and now I didn't have to do it! It had already been done. Someone else had done it for me – I didn't care who or why. That was the only thing I could think of as I ran back to my car. It has been done for me. And I knew what I should do next. *I should claim it.* That's what I told myself.'

'Claim it?' Antonia echoed.

'Yes, claim it,' Fenella said firmly. 'Well, I drove away – then I stopped the car – no idea where I was – in some small street. I took out my phone and I rang the clinic where I knew Charles Eresby was. I asked the nurse to tell him to ring me, I gave my number, and when he did phone, I told him I had done my part of the deal.' Fenella took a deep breath and blew out her cheeks. 'I told him Olga Klimt was dead. I then reminded him that now it was his turn.'

Antonia stood looking at her in a fascinated manner. Why, she believed Fenella Frayle was telling the truth! In fact she was convinced of it. But that meant –

'I don't know what possessed me, I really don't. I should never have made that phone call. It was utterly idiotic of me. Utterly! I knew I had made a mistake as soon as I rang off. I was terrified – but it was too late. I was beset by doubts. I saw the madness of it. How could I think Charles Eresby would go and kill Aunt Clo-Clo for me? But, as I said, it was too late. The fat was in the fire. I knew I was in for it. I had confessed to a murder I never committed. Well, there you are, Miss Darcy. I don't think you believe me, do you?'

'As a matter of fact I do,' Antonia said.

'You do?' Fenella looked startled. She made an effort to sit up. 'Well, that's something! Would the police believe me though?'

'I am sure they will listen to your story very carefully.'

'So that wasn't Olga Klimt … Well, I never saw her face. The fact that she had fair hair seemed to be enough for me … Such a stupid mistake … I was rushing … I was terribly nervous about the whole thing … I am hopeless, hopeless! Who is she then?'

'Charles Eresby's former girlfriend. Her name is Joan Selwyn.'

'His former girlfriend? Would she have been Olga's "love rival", by any chance?'

'They were love rivals, yes,' Antonia admitted.

'She died at Olga's house,' Fenella said thoughtfully. 'It was most probably Olga then who killed her, wouldn't you say? The obvious solution, as you probably call it ... I mean, it stands to reason ... Doesn't it?'

24

UNDER SUSPICION

'Odd that she should have said that. The police also seem to think that it was poor Olga who killed Joan Selwyn,' said Major Payne after listening to Antonia's story. 'But perhaps it was her? I know she has turned out to be extremely sweet-natured, nice and likeable, in addition to her luminosity – and she clearly loves Charlie very much – but the police are notoriously down-to-earth and unsentimental. Their hearts refused to be warmed by the sight of young love.'

'No, it isn't Olga.' Antonia shook her head. 'How could she have killed Joan Selwyn? Why should Olga Klimt have wanted to kill Joan Selwyn? She had no motive. It was the other way round!'

'I know, I know – but there you are.'

'Did the police actually voice that suspicion?'

'Well, yes. I happened to overhear an indiscreet remark the sergeant made to one of the plain-clothes chaps. It was not meant for my ears. And then of course there was the sight of Olga emerging from her interview with the inspector in floods of tears. She seemed distraught. She looked really scared. Charlie did his best to comfort her, but I could see he was rattled too.'

'So they didn't take his story of the exchanged murders seriously?'

'I don't think they did, no. They didn't seem to regard Charlie as someone whom they could entirely trust. There was a time when toffs could do no wrong, now it's the other way round, have you noticed? I saw the way they looked at his monogrammed dressing gown.'

'How did they look at it?'

'With an air of amused contempt. It didn't help that at one point he lost his temper and accused them of serving a corrupt undemocratic system, of lacking emotional intelligence and – what was it? – oh yes, of using bully-boy tactics. That wasn't wise at all.'

'So Miss Frayle is out of it? After everything! Lucky Miss Frayle.'

'Lucky Miss Frayle indeed. I believe they intend to pay her only what is known as a "routine visit". She is most certainly not in danger of any immediate incarceration. She may have been our prime suspect, but she isn't theirs.'

'They don't think the murder of Joan Selwyn was a case of mistaken identity?'

'I may be wrong, my love, but I had the distinct feeling they thought the idea a little on the fanciful side.'

'We didn't think it at all fanciful!'

'We are not exactly paragons of pragmatic, down-to-earth thinking, are we? As far as the police are concerned, a young woman called Joan Selwyn has been stabbed to death on the doorstep of a house occupied by a foreign girl, one Olga Klimt, who is the mistress of the young wastrel whose former girlfriend until not so very long ago the victim was – or had been – and that is all there is to it.'

'How unimaginative! How crass!' Antonia fumed. 'Do they suspect Charlie as well?'

'I don't know, but as I pointed out, they didn't take to him at all … They will soon find out he couldn't have done it since at the time of the murder he was at an exclusive private clinic in Bayswater. Still, they think it damned suspicious that he should have monkeyed about with the body. At the moment I think they are concentrating on Olga. I believe that Olga is their main suspect.'

'Poor, poor Olga,' Antonia said. 'My heart goes out to her. What about you? Did they treat you as a nuisance?'

'I should say they did! Pretty much.' Payne scrunched up his face. 'They simply couldn't understand what I was doing at Philomel Cottage, given that I was neither a relative nor a friend of Mr Eresby's or Miss Klimt's. I was not a doctor, neither was I a solicitor or a priest. It was the inspector who pointed out these rather obvious facts to me. So what was I doing at the house?'

'You could have said you were a social worker.'

'Do I *look* like a social worker?'

'You didn't tell them you were playing at detectives, did you?'

'No, of course not. But I think the inspector guessed. There was a satirical glint in his eye, though that might have been occasioned by the sight of my pipe.'

'Did they allow you to smoke it?'

'I was already smoking it when they arrived. They asked me to put it out. It was all rather grim.' Payne pursed his lips. 'There was Olga crying her eyes out and Charlie staring down at his slippers, his face a picture of guilt. I am sorry to have to say this, my love, but I didn't care for any of the representatives of the law. Not one little bit. I know we are supposed to be on the same side, but there are certain things one simply has to draw the line at.'

'Such as? Banning your pipe?'

'Not only that. The sergeant actually called me 'Hugh' at one point.'

'Did he really?'

'Yes! That particular outrage took place soon after I had given them my full name and military title. "Ex-service" used to count for a bit more once upon a time, but there he was, this ungainly youth, addressing me as "Hugh". I couldn't believe my ears and I actually glanced over my shoulder since I thought at first there was another Hugh in the room, his closest friend, perhaps or maybe his best man? I managed to restrain myself with tremendous difficulty.'

'They took a statement from each one of you?'

'They most certainly did. As well as fingerprints. Everything happened exactly as it says in books. They also looked us up on their computer system, to see if we had any convictions, cautions, fines, outstanding debts or whatever. They discovered that Charlie had perpetrated eleven driving offences, which resulted in his being deprived of his driving licence. Olga Klimt, on the other hand, had no black marks against her name. When asked what she did, she said she was in "party catering". Rather neat, that, don't you think? And her Lithuanian passport was in perfect order, thank God.'

'Did they look for the murder weapon?'

'They conducted an incredibly thorough search for it. I can't fault them on that count. They appeared to be looking for a knife with a thin blade of the stiletto variety, but they failed to find any object matching that description anywhere inside the house or in the garden. They will no doubt continue their search tomorrow morning. They were really cross with Charlie for moving the body, did I say? I mean, really cross.'

'They didn't arrest either of them, did they?'

'No. I heard the inspector warn them that they should be available for further questioning.' Payne reached out for his glass of Scotch and put his feet up on the coffee table. 'Let's take a glance at the crucial times in the affair, shall we?'

'It is half-past-midnight, Hugh.'

'It won't take a moment. I have written it all down. Take a dekko, my love. I've done some jottings. I want you to take a dekko. You are after all the expert.'

'I am nothing of the sort. I hate timetables.' Antonia sighed. 'I am exhausted. I suggest we go to bed.'

'No, not yet. Let's do it while it's all fresh. Take a dekko.' Payne pointed with the stem of his pipe. 'Olga gets a phone call at quarter-past-five, asking her to go to Dr Bishop's clinic. The caller says it is very urgent. Olga leaves the house five minutes later, at twenty-past-five. She runs to the Tube station. Miss Frayle says she arrived at Philomel Cottage at about a quarter-to-six, that's when she found the body. The body was still warm. We assume that Miss Frayle was telling the truth, don't we?'

'I believe she was telling the truth, yes.'

'That means that Joan Selwyn must have been stabbed just a short while earlier, say, between twenty-five-minutes-past five and twenty-to-six, give or take a minute? Does that strike you as plausible?'

'It does. Exceedingly plausible.' Antonia yawned.

'You don't think it's plausible?'

'I do, but I happen to be mortally tired. Sorry, but I feel a little sick. I have been driving around in the dark. I want to go to bed.' Antonia rose.

'Who do you think did the stabbing?'

'I haven't an earthly notion.'

'Really?'

'Really.'

'Where are you going?'

'To bed, Hugh. To bed. I suggest we continue our discussion tomorrow morning, if we must.'

'What d'you mean, if we must? Of course we must!'

25

THE RULE OF TWO

Sieg Mortimer was talking to Billy Selkirk. 'Shocking state of affairs, I know, old man, but do try to get some brekkers into your system. There's Wilkin & Sons Tiptree Little Scarlet Strawberry Conserve. I got that specially for you. I hope you don't think me callous or unfeeling. Remember what we agreed?'

'We agree about so many things.'

'That's true. We walk in complete agreement. But I meant specifically about death and the soul. Death is the absolute end and there is nothing we can possibly do about it. It doesn't help to brood. We don't believe in a soul, do we?'

'No.'

'In the same way as we find the idea of collective unconscious too vague to be of any great importance?'

'Yes.'

'In the same way as we don't revere any twenty-first-century sensitivities, such as shame, guilt and the desire for meaningful relationships?'

'No.'

After a pause Billy said he couldn't understand why the police hadn't contacted him yet. It made him nervous, wondering. He had let *The Times* fall on the floor and it now lay beside his chair. He was staring at the butter dish.

'Surely, it is a cause for wild rejoicing, that the police haven't contacted you yet,' Mortimer said. 'Perhaps they never will.'

'Oh, I am sure they will.'

'Jeepers-creepers, you sound as though you want them to, Selkirk. Remember what we agreed about irrational impulses? To recognise and acknowledge and – remember the rest?'

'I am afraid I don't. Sorry, Mortimer, but I feel a bit – odd.'

'A bit odd? You mean a bit 'off'? That's only natural in the circs.' Mortimer nodded. 'You were actually about to marry the victim. Sorry to appear callous but I can't pretend I liked her. And duly suppress, Selkirk. To recognise, acknowledge and duly suppress.'

'Yes. Sorry, Mortimer.'

Mortimer moved away from the breakfast table. He stood by the window, hands in pockets, his back very straight, looking out. He and Billy looked rather similar in a blonde, blue-eyed, crew-cut *Herrenvolk* kind of way. They wore identical black dressing gowns with pale silver-blue lapels that matched the colour of their eyes. They might have been brothers, or even twins. Anyone entering the room at that moment would have thought them exceedingly good-looking and distinguished and somewhat sinister.

'But maybe I should contact them and make them aware of my existence?'

'Why should you want to do that? Are you going to offer to identify the body?'

'No, no. I hope they don't ask me to do that. I'd hate it! I am sure that's already been done. She's got a father, I think. But the fact remains that I was her fiancé.'

'Well, no longer. All I can say, Selkirk, is I am awfully glad you are no longer Miss Selwyn's fiancé. There, I've said it. It wouldn't have worked anyhow. You would have hated being married. It would have made you sick.'

'It wouldn't have made me sick.'

'It *would* have made you sick.'

'I suppose her father has already identified the body. Or one of those girls.' Billy spoke abstractedly. 'I mean one of her flatmates. She shared a flat. I didn't care for any of them. I thought they were trying to poison Joan's mind against me. I am sure I am imagining things.'

'You are not. They were trying to poison her mind against you. They are truly awful, so they managed to do it very well but maybe not well enough.'

'What do you mean? How – how do you know?'

'I put them up to it.'

'I don't believe you! You didn't!'

'I am afraid I did. I couldn't think of anything else. But Miss Selwyn was determined to get you, so whatever they said fell on deaf ears.'

'You are fibbing!'

'I told them things about you, Selkirk. Some true, some not so true. I actually paid one of them, Minerva, I think, to bring a particular fact about you to Joan's attention … I gave her – um – I can't remember how much … You don't believe me?'

'They are all bitches, but Minerva is the worst!'

'I thought you liked girls,' Mortimer said.

'I do like girls. I don't happen to like those particular girls.'

'You don't like girls. You are in denial.'

'I am not in denial.'

'A large part of you still craves conventionality, Selkirk. That accounts for the marriage idea. You have an obstinate way of clinging to a thoroughly illusory notion of yourself. There is a vast crevasse between what you are and what you want to be. You don't feel *bien dans ta peau*. Well, Minerva said she'd have done it even if I hadn't paid her. She doesn't like you for some unknown reason, or else she was lusting after Joan, I don't know which.'

'I don't believe you paid her.'

'I did pay her. We talked about trust only the other day, didn't we, Selkirk?' Mortimer spoke in a quiet voice. 'Perhaps we need to have another session? Don't you remember what we agreed?'

'No, I don't,' Billy said defiantly.

'I am sure you do. "Now these are the laws of the jungle" – Go on, please. I want to hear you recite the rest.'

'I don't feel like it.'

'I said, go on, Selkirk. I know you are upset but I want you to make an effort. Remember what happened the last time you refused to comply? Remember the clothes cupboard and its perfumed depths?'

'Oh very well. "And many and mighty are they,"' Billy said sullenly. 'Sorry, Mortimer, but I keep getting distracted. I suppose I am still in a state of shock. I've still got Joan's mobile.'

'"But the head and the hoof and the haunch and the hump is –?" What's the last word? Tell me.'

'You know perfectly well what the bloody word is.'

'I do yes, but I want you to say it. It's important. Say the word, please.'

'Say it yourself.'

'Say it, Selkirk. Say it. It rhymes with "they" and "dismay". Oh, and with "Bombay". Come on, say it. What is it?'

'Obey.'

'Obey. Yes. Well done. You are a gem without price, Selkirk. I believe you need a diversion. Not a distraction. A *diversion*.'

Billy said he needed to be left alone for a bit, if Mortimer didn't mind.

'Oh, but I do mind. No, not alone. That would be wrong. The time for enjoyment is always too short and fleeting. As you know I strive to make pleasure something very charming which has no consequences. As it happens, I've got two tickets for a show tonight. I won't tell you which one. It will be a surprise.

You may think it in poor taste, given the circumstances, but that's a risk I am perfectly willing to take.' Mortimer hummed a tune under his breath. He was holding a mobile phone. He had started pressing its buttons.

Billy frowned. 'That's not your mobile, is it?'

'No. It's Joan's mobile. It's a Blackberry, to be precise. I think she left it behind the last time she was here. When was it? The day before yesterday?'

'Last night I meant to tell her I'd got it. She'd probably have come back with me and collected it. She has only one mobile, she said. Only – only she didn't turn up.' Billy swallowed.

'It never crossed your mind you'd never see her again, did it, Selkirk?'

'No, of course not. What are you doing with her mobile?'

'I am playing Wingless Officers. It's a game. Want to have a go? It's thrilling.'

'I don't think you should be handling her phone, Mortimer. The police will most certainly want to see it. You may get into trouble.'

'The worst I could ever be accused of is thoughtlessness.'

There was a pause, and then Billy asked, 'What did you do yesterday afternoon? After I left?'

'I believe I sat dreaming of Gstaad.'

'The whole afternoon?'

'No, of course not. Don't be silly. At some point I went out.'

'Where did you go?'

'I can't remember. Are we playing Twenty Questions now? I think I went for a walk in Kensington Gardens. It was such a languorous, odorous kind of afternoon. I couldn't get down to doing anything else.'

'I told you I wouldn't be able to go to Gstaad with you because Joan had already made other plans.'

'Too late now, Selkirk. It's already done.'

'What's done?'

'The booking. I've already made a booking. We are going to Gstaad for Christmas. Caroline will be there. Also James Middleton and his set. I mean Princess Caroline of Monaco, of course. You said you wanted to meet James, didn't you? I'll introduce you. He may not come from the finest landed blood-stock, but he is highly intelligent, waspish, worldly, sophisticated, emotionally complex and extraordinarily good company. And that cake business of his is such a hoot. So refreshingly uncon-ventional. Besides,' Mortimer went on, 'you can't go anywhere with Joan as Joan is dead. Your mouth is open, Selkirk. Do shut it, please. You look like a goldfish.'

'When did you make the booking?'

'Why are you gazing at me with such peculiar intensity, Selkirk? You do look quite absurd.' Mortimer laughed. 'Remember what we agreed? If you really insist on knowing, I made the booking yesterday afternoon. Some time after you left. Satisfied?'

'Yesterday afternoon? But you couldn't have known then that – that –' Billy broke off.

26

DANGEROUS KNOWLEDGE

'It's only the shortest of news items – page four – no details – the police are clearly keeping their cards close to their chest at this early stage of the investigation.' Major Payne pushed *The Times* to one side. It was the following morning and they were having breakfast. 'I've no doubt our brains are much more advanced than theirs, wouldn't you agree?'

'No, I wouldn't. "Pride cometh before destruction and haughty spirit before a fall,"' Antonia quoted. She took a sip of coffee. 'Have you fed Dupin?' Dupin was the cat.

'Of course I haven't. I've been busy thinking about the case. Wait, I gave him a piece of fried bacon.'

'You shouldn't have! Hugh! Not *bacon*. Not *fried*.'

'It won't kill him. He seemed to like it, rather.'

'That's exactly it! He'll get used to it and won't eat any of the tinned Felix we've got him.'

'You fear he may forget he is a cat?' Payne poured himself some more coffee. 'The really important question at the moment is – would we be able to get to the truth before they do? Are we capable of outwitting them? It is imperative that we do, you know.'

'Who is "they"? Oh you mean the police. You make it sound as though this time it's personal somehow.'

'Well, in a way, it is.' Payne gave a rueful smile. 'Unprincipled use of first names is not something an officer and a gentleman of the old school should forget or forgive that easily.'

'Don't be an ass, Hugh.'

'I am perfectly serious. This is war. It is imperative that we prove our superiority.'

Antonia buttered a piece of toast. 'What was Joan Selwyn's reason for wanting to go into Philomel Cottage? I keep thinking about it. She was killed after she'd unlocked the front door and was about to enter the house. That does look suspicious, doesn't it?'

'Perhaps she was intent on giving Olga a fright. Perhaps she was still keen on Charlie?'

'We need to establish the exact nature of her feelings towards Olga Klimt since we have had some very mixed messages on the subject. Charlie believes she'd got over him and that she was seeing someone else. Lord Collingwood, on the other hand, is not convinced she'd got over Charlie … That correct?'

'Yes.' Payne helped himself to a boiled egg and cracked it with his teaspoon.

'How reliable a source is Lord Collingwood?'

'Not particularly reliable. He is something of a windbag. He is a dangerous reactionary. Some of his ideas have a whiff of the crackpot about them. He wrote a long poem once called "A Soul-bartering Subaltern".'

'But he was close to Joan Selwyn and he is of course married to Charlie's mother … He may know things … Will he talk to you, do you think?'

'I am sure he will. He thinks very highly of me. I served in the same regiment as his late brother. He told me things about his wife I didn't really want to know. Deirdre Collingwood is an Aconite addict, apparently. I will ring him after breakfast, if you like.'

'Yes, do.'

It was half-past-ten now. The September morning was sunny and so garishly gorgeous, it could be cut into pieces and rearranged as a jigsaw, Lady Collingwood thought.

She was sitting in her bed, propped up on pillows, a breakfast tray across her knees and a book beside her. She had her phone in her hand. She was speaking to her son while gazing out of the window, at the fiery red of the rowans and beeches in the garden and ardently wishing she could float away – float away in poetic appreciation …

'Oh my poor darling, how perfectly horrid. And you knew all along? You actually stumbled over the body … But why didn't you tell me last night? I see. No, I haven't seen the paper yet. Rupert's got it. He's bound to see it, no matter how tiny it is, he reads the paper from cover to cover … We are not on speaking terms, I am afraid … We had a scene last night … I am forlornly banished to my room, my choice … No, no … Helps me to have some semblance of normality … Yes … Yes … Well, melodrama is better than melanoma, as a very dear friend of mine once put it …'

Lady Collingwood took a sip of coffee.

'How about lunch, Charlie? I could book a table at Harry's Bar? No? Oh never mind. Some other time. I quite understand, darling. No, don't worry. How is she? Such a marvellous name, I always thought … Is she? Poor thing. Olga speaks English, I trust? Everybody seems to nowadays … Poor Joan, yes. So much unfulfilled promise. I imagine Rupert will be distraught as he loved her dearly. She had a very special place in his heart, you see. More special than I ever thought possible … You'd never guess what I found … I would rather not talk about it now … I am not supposed to know … Sorry for speaking in riddles, darling but if Rupert realises that I know it may provide him with ammunition for further attacks … Shall we say I came across some rather

revealing papers? I'll tell you all about it when I see you …
Yes … Bye, darling.'

Deirdre put the phone down. She glanced at the book she had
been reading. It was one of Antonia Darcy's. She'd got it from the
library the day before. She leant back and shut her eyes. Well, that
was that. Joan Selwyn was dead and Rupert was in the process of
discovering that he had wasted time, paper and ink writing that
new will …

She heard the opening and closing of a door. Rather, the
slamming. She heard something that sounded like a sob followed by 'Oh God!' Clearly Rupert knew. It had been in the
paper. She glanced at the little blue enamel clock on her bedside table: quarter-to-eleven.

Rupert had left his room. She wondered if he was wearing
a black tie.

Lord Collingwood was more than willing to see Major Payne.
As a matter of fact he'd been about to give him a tinkle, he
said. Payne was just the fellow to whom Lord Collingwood
wished to speak. He said the matter required urgent attention.
Could they meet at the Military Club later in the morning, at
eleven-thirty, say?

'Look here, Payne. This is a wretched business. Absolutely
wretched.'

Lord Collingwood was immaculately dressed in a grey suit
and a double-breasted waistcoat in port-wine red. He wore a
black tie and in his buttonhole he sported a black orchid – from
his conservatory, the 'new crop', he explained.

Major Payne said that the murder of a young woman was
always particularly appalling.

'The blasted paper said "Fulham" but gave no details. It's an outrage. Few things annoy me more than ellipsis. Do they expect readers to fill in the blanks for themselves? Sorry, Payne, but I believe that chap's trying to eavesdrop on us. It's the same chap we had last time, I think. The slow chap – remember? Damned impertinence, don't you think?'

'I think he wants to know if we want to order something.'

'Of course we want to order something. We want coffee, don't we? What else could we possibly want at this time of day? *Artichauts aux fines herbes*? Sauerkraut?'

'A pot of coffee, please,' Major Payne said to the waiter.

'I wouldn't say "please" if I were you, Payne. These chaps tend to take advantage of one's good nature. You risk setting a dangerous precedent, you know.' Lord Collingwood glanced round. 'This place is going to the dogs. I have a good mind to resign. It's been a foul morning, absolutely ghastly. Talk about the heavy and weary weight of an unintelligible world! I opened the *Telegraph* and got the shock of my life. Little Joanie Selwyn!' His hand went up to his eyes. 'Can't believe I'll never see her again! Brutally butchered! Don't suppose you know any details?'

'As a matter of fact I do,' Payne said and he gave a summary of how he and Antonia had got involved in the Olga Klimt affair.

'I see. So it was Deirdre who started the ball rolling and then one thing led to another, eh? And she was killed at Philomel Cottage! Good grief! Did you say your wife went with you? You seem to make a good team. I have heard some remarkable stories about your exploits. That Sphinx Island business last year! Took my breath away. Wish I had a wife like yours. And she writes! What a lucky fellow you are. Deirdre only manages to set my teeth on edge. She generates such tension. I have now decided to stop talking to Deirdre altogether.' Lord Collingwood mimed zipping his lips. 'Ah, here comes our coffee. Jolly good. The best coffee in London, at least that's how it used to be.'

'Still is, I believe,' Payne said.

'Thank you, my good man,' Lord Collingwood said to the waiter.

'I'd like to ask you a question or two if I may, Collingwood … Or do you want to go first?'

'No, no, you first. Be my guest.' Lord Collingwood dropped a sugar lump in his coffee and stirred it with the silver spoon. 'Fire away. It's probably about Joanie, isn't it?'

'Yes. When did you see her last?'

'Yesterday morning. I'd arranged to meet her at a place in Piccadilly. Richoux's, some such name. Pleasant enough place but not enough leg room. I had scrambled eggs on toast.'

'What did you talk about?'

'Nothing of any particular interest. Fool of a friend of mine wanted me to do something for him. Not exactly a *friend*, rather a chap who'd done me a favour and expected me to do likewise. I decided Joanie could be of assistance. She was terribly efficient, you know. Don't think she was wild about the idea but said she'd do it.' Lord Collingwood sighed. 'Then I told her that having it out with the Lithuanian houri couldn't possibly be expected to lead to anything constructive. She told me not to worry. She said that was old hat. I was behind the times. She confirmed that she'd got over Charlie, which was a relief. There was a new man in her life now, name of Selkirk, and she was looking forward to starting a new life.'

'D'you think she was telling the truth?'

'Yes. I am sure she meant it.' Collingwood nodded. 'I congratulated her on her good sense. But then something very odd happened. As a matter of fact that's one of the things I wanted to see you about.'

'What happened?'

'Her mobile phone rang and she answered it. I saw her expression change. She said, "Speaking. Who is this? You mean today? At Philomel Cottage? Some time after five?" Those were her exact words. It was a very brief exchange. Before I knew it, it was over. Strange, isn't it, Payne? I knew you'd be interested!'

'I most certainly am,' Payne said slowly. 'Someone asked Joan to go to Philomel Cottage?'

'Yes! She was told that she would learn something to her advantage. That's all she was told and then the caller rang off. I must admit I didn't like the sound of it at all and it seems I was right to feel uneasy! Dammit, Payne, Philomel Cottage was where Joanie was killed, wasn't it, that's what you said?'

'Yes. It's also the place where Olga Klimt lives.'

'Precisely, Payne. *Precisely*. Where Olga Klimt lives!'

'But she didn't think it was Olga?'

'She said she didn't recognise the voice. She couldn't even tell if the voice was male or female. It might have been female. I said it would be madness to go. I told her it looked like a trap to me.'

'You thought it was a trap?'

'My exact words.' Lord Collingwood nodded. 'And it seems I was right! She said, how very peculiar, I wonder who that was. Or words to that effect. I asked her to promise me she wouldn't go. Well, she did promise and then we talked about other things but I was uneasy. I didn't like the way she looked. Pensive. Distracted. Soon after that we said goodbye ... But I remained uneasy. I was worried ...'

'You feared she was going to go?'

'Yes. It was the way her eyelids had fluttered. And she'd avoided looking at me directly. The more I thought about it, the more anxious I became. I didn't know what to do. I had the idea of going to Philomel Cottage, of following her to her assignation, so to speak, to see what it was all about. I thought I'd have a stab at unveiling the mystery of the strange phone call, as your wife might put it. I suspected Olga Klimt might be behind it – or that villain, Bedaux – who else is there? In fact I thought the two were acting in cahoots. I have a special reason for suspecting Bedaux. I'll tell you about it in a second. I feared for Joan's safety but I was also – well, curious.'

'Did you go?'

'No, I didn't. And that's something I will regret to the end of my days.' Lord Collingwood shook his head. 'An incident took place early in the afternoon and that put me in a bad mood. Altercation with a cab driver. Most impertinent fellow. I am no good in enclosed spaces. I lost my temper. I'd forgotten to take my balancing pill, you see – it's some damned pills I've got to take. Got cross with the driver. He said something that annoyed me, you see. I am afraid I flew into a rage. I banged on the glass partition with my umbrella and it seems I cracked it. Anyhow, won't bore you with it. The long and the short of it is that I spent most of the afternoon in Green Park, sitting in a deckchair, trying to read this new book on orchids I bought at Hatchards. It was a jolly warm afternoon.'

Payne agreed. 'Apparently the last days of the heatwave.'

'I sat there and tried to read but I couldn't concentrate. I kept thinking about that phone call. I became convinced Bedaux was behind it, that it was he who'd lured Joan to Philomel Cottage! Well, it was too late for me to do anything about it, apart from phoning Joanie and making sure she was all right.'

'Did you phone her?'

'I did. I phoned her after I got back home. It was some time after six, I think. There was no reply. I tried some time later but again there was no reply.' Lord Collingwood put down his coffee cup. 'The truth is I am overcome with guilt, Payne. You do see why, don't you? If only I'd gone to Philomel Cottage, as

I originally intended, I might have been able to prevent Joanie from being butchered. She might be alive now … I can't help feeling responsible for her death.'

'It's no good brooding over it. What's done can't be undone,' Payne said firmly. 'I've had regrets like that myself.'

'Have you? I always imagined you were the kind of chap who never put a foot wrong!'

'Kind of you to say so but I fear I am nothing of the sort. I am far from infallible.'

'If only I hadn't got cross with that fool of a cab driver!'

Payne looked at him. 'Did you ever give Joan a key to Philomel Cottage?'

'Key? Key? No. Never. Why? Oh, I see. Good lord. You said there was a key sticking out of the front door, didn't you? But what if the key had been left in the lock? What if it was there, when Joan arrived? Isn't that possible?'

'I believe it is.'

'Olga might have left the key in the lock. People do, you know, either by accident or design. Perhaps the key was there when Joanie arrived? Then all she had to do was push the door open – that was when she was stabbed, wasn't it? That's what you said. Well, I thought of going to Scotland Yard and having a word with whoever's in charge of the case, I mean tell them about the phone call, also that I suspect Bedaux of having made it, but I decided to talk to you first. I could do with some advice. So what do you say?'

'I think you should speak to the police about it, yes.'

Collingwood nodded. 'That, of course, is the right thing to do.'

There was a pause.

'Actually Bedaux did go to to Philomel Cottage,' Payne said slowly. 'He was seen outside the house some time after the murder, while the body was still lying on the doorstep.' Payne decided not to name Charlie as his informant.

Lord Collingwood's eyes bulged. 'He was seen? He was seen near the body? Good lord! But that clinches it then!'

'Perhaps it does. I don't know.'

'No "perhaps" about it! Good lord. Don't you see? Damn it, man, it all fits in! It was Deirdre's Svengali who killed Joanie! I mean Bedaux. Bedaux is the killer!'

'What motive could he possibly have had?' Payne asked. 'I know Joan Selwyn had been making a nuisance of herself over his master but would that have been enough for him to want to kill her?'

'No, of course not.' Lord Collingwood spoke impatiently. 'Bedaux had a much more serious motive for wishing Joanie dead. That's the other thing I wanted to talk to you about, Payne. You see, Joanie had been on Bedaux's spoor for some time. Ever since she laid eyes on those catering girlies of his. I mean that fatal engagement party. Joanie immediately knew what Bedaux was up to. She'd managed to collect evidence. She told me about it. She was incredibly efficient, I keep telling you. Fiercely efficient. As a matter of fact she'd been on the verge of going to the police and presenting them with her findings.'

'What findings?'

'All about his pimping activities of course.'

27

CABAL (1)

I stand beside the window of my room at the Holyrood Hotel and look across at the Brompton Oratory. In my hand I hold a copy of today's *Times*. There is a bit about the murder of Joan Selwyn. Not a lot. By a pure association of ideas I think of Olga. So that was Joan Selwyn, not Olga. Did Mr Eresby lie to me in order to put me off – or was he labouring under a genuine misapprehension?

I wonder how long it will be before the police manage to track me down. Though will they? Will they seriously think of me as a possible suspect?

I think back to the day before yesterday, the day of the murder, trying to retrace my movements as well as my thoughts. I had gone to Fulham with murder on my mind. I'd decided that Olga Klimt didn't deserve to live.

My eye falls on the Bible on the bedside table. The Holyrood is a traditional, old-fashioned kind of hotel. It is a Gideon Bible. I was brought up in the Catholic faith, but my God, as they say, died young. It was a Catholic priest called Father Lillie-Lysander who helped me see the light. Thanks to him I started finding Theolatry tedious, its central premise profoundly unsound. I started regarding the custom of preserving mystical relics as something sickening and generally repugnant.

Father Lillie died a few years ago. His body was found in a wishing well on an estate called Ospreys. There were a lot of stories in the papers about it at the time.

I remember that Father Lillie was rather fond of quoting to me the words Saul addressed to Elymas. 'You are a child of the devil and an enemy of everything that is right. You are full of all kinds of deceit and trickery.'

This strikes me as the perfect time for plotting revenge on Lord Collingwood. (I am sure I told you that I had been thinking of ways of 'getting' at him.) I believe it would not only take my mind off Olga Klimt, it would also channel and redirect all my frustrated desires, disappointments and pent-up resentments.

I take out my phone and call Lady Collingwood's number. She answers almost at once.

'It's Bedaux, m'lady.'

Lady Collingwood gives a delighted gasp. 'Bedaux! In the name of all that is marvellous! Bedaux!'

'I hope this is a convenient time, m'lady?'

'It most certainly is! I've been thinking about you, you know, so this must be another instance of the telepathic communication that exists between us.'

'Your ladyship is too kind.'

'I've been meaning to ring you. I don't want to be a bore, Bedaux, but things between me and Rupert have been really bad. I need a shoulder to cry on. Only you understand the impossible situation in which I find myself. There was a loathsome scene last night. It has left me devastated. Rupert is a beast.'

'I am sorry to hear that, m'lady.' Something tells me this is going to be easy.

'I haven't yet left my bedroom, Bedaux. I am a nervous wreck. Where on earth are you phoning from? Am I right in thinking you are no longer with Charlie?'

'That is correct, m'lady. I am no longer in Mr Eresby's employ.'

'Oh dear. Charlie can be temperamental, poor darling, and maybe the tiniest bit spoilt, but he's been going through a particularly stormy time. Something dreadful happened last night – you've probably read about it in the paper? Did he actually *sack* you?'

'Not exactly m'lady. I sacked myself.'

'How clever you make it sound. Can I do anything for you, Bedaux?'

'Perhaps you'll allow me to do something for *you*, m'lady?'

There is a pause, then she speaks. 'I have always prided myself on being the soul of serene self-sufficiency, but today I feel weak. The truth, Bedaux, is that I don't I want to see Rupert ever again. Not as long as I live. Or not as long as he lives. Does that make sense to you, Bedaux?'

'It makes perfect sense, m'lady. I would be honoured to aid you in any venture you might see fit to undertake.'

'Would you really? Do you mean it? Any venture?'

'I do mean it, m'lady. Any venture.'

She attempts a light laugh. 'Even if it's something in questionable taste?'

'Especially if it's something in questionable taste, m'lady,' I say gravely.

'Even if it's a matter of "aiding and abetting"?'

'Does your ladyship have anything definite in mind?'

'No. Goodness, no. Nothing *definite*. Not yet. But perhaps – perhaps you will be able to help me – how shall I put it? – reach a conclusion? You have such a *fertile* mind, Bedaux. I don't think you are ever short of ideas, are you?'

'Am I right in thinking the matter in question concerns Lord Collingwood, m'lady?'

'You are. But you haven't told me your whereabouts yet. Where *are* you?'

I tell her.

'The Holyrood Hotel? I don't think I know it. I bet it's horrid.'

'I find it perfectly serviceable, m'lady. I assume Lord Collingwood is not at home?'

'He is not. Thank God for small mercies. He went out. He is in deep mourning. If I have to be perfectly honest, Bedaux, I am at the end of my tether. I don't think I can go on.'

'This is by no means what your ladyship deserves.'

'That is one of the nicest thing anyone has ever said to me. Thank you, dear friend. You are one of the very few people who understand me, Bedaux.' Her voice shakes a little. 'Possibly the only one.'

'I remember your ladyship telling me once about the occasion on which Lord Collingwood spilled a drink over you. He pretended it was an accident but you felt sure he did it on purpose. He left you feeling like a tree that had been devoured by a swarm of locusts, I believe you said?'

'Fancy you remembering that! Well, there are few things in the whole universe of galaxies and nebulae that are as fearsome as Rupert in a bad mood.'

I decide to take the bull by the horns. 'Would you like to be free from Lord Collingwood, m'lady?'

'Depends on what you mean by "free from", Bedaux. I must admit I rather like the sound of it. I'd like to be free, yes – eternally, entirely free! Tyrannous yokes should be overthrown, shouldn't they?'

'Indeed they should, m'lady. By any means available.'

'Well, Bedaux, you have managed to persuade me. Once more you have cast your magic spell over me.'

'You are anxious to have Lord Collingwood removed?'

'I am, yes. But *how*? What do you propose to do? Have Rupert marmalised? Or vapourised?' She laughs a trifle hysterically.

'What would you say to having Lord Collingwood framed for murder, m'lady?'

'I would like to hear more about it, Bedaux. Whose murder?'

'Miss Selwyn's.'

'What an intriguing idea. He was most certainly not at home at the crucial time, which, I understand, was about five o'clock or a bit later. I came back home and he was not there,' she says thoughtfully.

'No alibi. That is excellent news!'

'I would certainly swear to it in a court of law, if it ever came to a trial. Though why in heaven's name would Rupert have wanted to kill Joan? What possible motive could he have had?'

I clear my throat. 'If I remember correctly, a month or so ago your ladyship confided in me that she suspected Lord Collingwood and Miss Selwyn of having an affair?'

'I did suspect them, yes. However –'

'It is not unusual for gentlemen in the autumn of their days to indulge in initially energising but ultimately catastrophic liaisons with persons much younger than themselves. Miss Selwyn might have been trying to persuade Lord Collingwood to divorce you and marry her? Perhaps she was exercising considerable pressure on him? Perhaps she was blackmailing him?'

'This is all most ingenious, Bedaux, but I am afraid it won't do. It's true that I did suspect Rupert of having an affair with Joan, but it seems I was wrong. You must think of something else.'

I find myself bristling. I don't like being contradicted. 'Why should your ladyship consider an affair between Lord Collingwood and Miss Selwyn such an unlikely proposition?'

'Well, I'll tell you but you must give me your word of honour that you won't breathe a word to anyone about it.'

'I give you my word of honour, m'lady.'

'Very well then. You see, it's like this. I found a letter and the draft of a new will in Rupert's desk —'

I listen in silence. Then I nod to myself.

That is the kind of story that opens a host of new possibilities.

28

THE PRIVATE WOUND

Lord Collingwood was speaking: 'It seems the villain has been grooming girlies from the former Eastern bloc. He is what in the old days they used to call a "procurer". Joan had been busy collecting evidence. She'd already interviewed one of the Lithuanian contingent. Girl called Inge, I believe, some such name. She is one of Olga's associates.'

'You think Bedaux got wind of it? He feared exposure?'

'That's what must have happened, yes. He must have become aware of Joan's activities and got in a blue funk. It's serious criminal business we are talking about, Payne. An escort service. An exclusive call-girl ring. He not only went about recruiting girls from run-down countries, but he forged papers, scouted for clients and so on and so forth. The villain also employed bribery and blackmail in equal measure. What did the Bard say, remember? "'Tis a knavish piece of work.'"

'When did Joan tell you about it? Was it at Richoux's?'

'Yes. She said she had gathered sufficient evidence to have Bedaux arrested. Apparently she had quite a file on him. Enough to persuade the police to start an investigation. Wouldn't you say her killing was a bit on the opportune side?' Lord Collingwood produced a cigar.

'I think you should tell the police about it, Collingwood.'

'Of course I shall. I am glad we are in agreement, Payne. Nothing will give me greater pleasure than to cook Bedaux's goose. Poor Joanie must be avenged. I can't begin to explain how much she meant to me. It's been a blow. A very private kind of wound.' He struck a match and held it to his cigar. 'I intend to spend some time at Collingwood. It would help me recuperate. Scotland agrees with me.'

Payne said, 'Scotland must look wonderful at this time of year.'

'It most certainly does. The best place to mourn the passing of a loved one. I am still extremely fond of Collingwood Castle. That, as it happens, is where I proposed to Deirdre. She was something quite exceptional in those days. If you could envisage the Holy Madonna crossed with the Whore of Babylon? An irresistible hybrid! I don't suppose you have ever made any wrong decisions, Payne, have you?'

'I have. Millions of times.'

'You do amaze me. But your marriage is in good shape? If you don't mind my prying?'

'My marriage is fine. As close to perfection as you'll ever get in an imperfect world.'

'That's splendid.' Lord Collingwood became wreathed in cigar smoke. 'Collingwood Castle, yes. My mother tells me the roof's leaking, the ghillies don't say much and the dogs keep howling, as though sensing some imminent calamity, but I can't wait to be reunited with my fishing rod and old Balmoral bonnet! Remember what a Balmoral bonnet looks like, Payne? Mine is festooned with dry-flies and battered old creed. Fond of trout fishing?'

'Used to be. Haven't done it for quite some time now.'

'Nothing like it! Perhaps you could join me at Collingwood when this awful business is over?' Lord Collingwood glanced at his watch. 'Must dash, if I'm to speak to someone at Scotland

Yard. Used to know all the chief commissioners at one time. I'll also have to convey my condolences to Joan's father, who of course wasn't –' Lord Collingwood broke off. He rose to his feet. 'Not a prospect I relish!'

'Have you by any chance a phone number for Joan Selwyn's new young man?' Major Payne asked. 'Or his address?'

'You'd like to speak to him? His name is Billy Selkirk. I haven't got his number but I learnt he shares a flat in Shepherds Market with a friend of his, a most decent chap called Mortimer, who happens to be the nephew of a great chum of mine.' Putting on a pair of half-moon glasses, Lord Collingwood produced a notebook and started leafing through it. 'Here it is – Sieg Mortimer – that's the chap's name – a terribly decent young fellow – much admired for his maturity and good sense – good address too –'

He dictated the address to Payne who wrote it down. Both of them rose to their feet at the same time.

'One more thing Collingwood. What was it you started to say but broke off? You are bound to think me a nosy parker but I can't stand the idea of loose ends. I am worse than Antonia in that respect. You started saying that Joan's father was not – what?'

Lord Collingwood looked at him steadily out of his bright china-blue eyes. 'You really want to know? Well, why not. You are a most trustworthy fellow. He was not her real father, Payne. *I* was.'

'Joan was your daughter? So that's what you meant by a "very private kind of wound" ...'

'Yes, Payne. I had no idea but her mother wrote to me about it some time ago. Came as a complete surprise. I was – well, appalled – I mean, delighted.' Lord Collingwood gave a little smile. 'It was a shock. I have no children, you know. I was glad to have found a daughter. And now I have lost her.' He shook his head. 'Makes everything appear so pointless, doesn't it?'

'I am sorry,' Payne said.

'I got Ada's letter a month ago. Ada de Ravigny. She seems to have reverted to her maiden name.'

'I knew a de Ravigny who was in the diplomatic corps.'

'Her brother, I believe. Well, Ada was my mistress for quite a while. Years ago. Poor Ada's in a hospice now. She is dying. Cancer. May be dead by now, I don't know. Her letter sounds like one of those deathbed outpourings. She never told Joan I was her father. It was up to me to tell her, if I thought it right. That's what she wrote.'

'Did you tell Joan?'

'Afraid not. Never got round to it.' Lord Collingwood sighed. 'But one thing I did do. I drew up a draft for a new will. I meant Joanie to have *everything*. All my earthly riches, including Collingwood Castle. I was going to take the draft to my solicitors next week … Now she is dead … The futility of it!'

They collected their coats.

'Does Lady Collingwood know that Joan is your daughter?' Payne asked.

'Deirdre? She is not supposed to know but I have reason to believe she does know, blast her. I strongly suspect that Deirdre's read Ada's letter – as well as the draft of the new will. Deirdre has the habit of ransacking my desk whenever the fancy takes her. She thinks I have no idea but I do. She always leaves everything in a mess.' He sighed. 'I should have been more careful. I should have changed the lock.'

'You said it was only the draft of a new will. Who is the main beneficiary according to your current will?'

'Deirdre of course, blast her, though I am not sure she deserves to be, do you?' Lord Collingwood put on his black homburg. 'Good grief, Payne, why are you staring at me like that? You don't think it was Deirdre who –?'

29

CABAL (2)

I clear my throat and say that the knowledge her ladyship has chosen to impart has given me an idea for a different and much more serious motive for murder that could be attributed to Lord Collingwood.

'Are you implying you've got another stellar plot up your sleeve, Bedaux?'

'More of a nouveau scenario, m'lady. I wonder what you will make of it. A gentleman of noble birth, the scion of a family of great distinction and antiquity, has an affair with his young secretary. He then learns that the girl is actually his daughter by a former mistress. He realises he has had an affair with his own daughter.'

'Ah, the incest motive. You mean it could be made to look as though Rupert's feelings of shame were so intense and devastating that he killed his daughter?'

'That's what I mean, yes. His mind suffered a lethal aberration which resulted in Lord Collingwood killing his daughter – before taking the honourable way out. A remorseful death. A kind of an *Oedipus Rex* in reverse. What does your ladyship think?'

'The honourable way out ... Yes ... I like that ... It's terribly clever ... I don't see why not.' She suddenly becomes brisk and business-like, 'It must be done *before* he gets the idea of changing his will once more. The draft I found in his desk remains just that, a draft. I phoned his solicitor who's an old flame of mine and asked some probing questions and he assures me the old will still stands, the one in which I am named as Rupert's principal legatee. But he and I are not on good terms and now that Joan's dead, he may decide to leave his fortune to – to some gardening society or heaven knows who else! So we must hurry. I can't bear the thought of being cheated out of what is rightfully mine, Bedaux.'

'An understandable sentiment, m'lady.'

'But I do so hate the idea of blood or any kind of mess!'

'There doesn't have to be a mess, m'lady.'

'Nothing too lurid or too sensational please. Can Rupert suffer a broken neck?'

'Indeed he can, m'lady.'

'Or take an overdose? He takes some absurd tablets for his Black Dog. He's a manic depressive.'

'Indeed he can, m'lady.'

'I feel rather inspired talking to you, Bedaux. I think that we should meet and work out the details as a matter of some urgency? It would be imprudent to try to do it over the phone. Any objection to a tête-à-tête?'

'No objection at all.'

She asks if I can come over at once.

I tell her I could be with her in less than an hour.

'There is a delightful little place just round the corner. A patisserie of a rather exclusive kind. Chez Charlus. It is authentic French. It boasts the best pastry-cook in Europe. It may sound a bit louche, to the cognoscenti, though it is a perfectly respectable place. I think it would be much safer for us to meet on neutral ground.'

It is forty minutes later and we are sitting in Chez Charlus, partaking of a selection of sugary concoctions, which I find I enjoy.

'Oh who would have thought it would come to this?' Lady Collingwood sighs wistfully over her cup of jasmine tea. 'When I married Rupert I didn't see how anything could possibly go wrong. Rupert was every young widow's dream. He had all the Bs, you know.'

'All the bees, m'lady?'

'Background, breeding, blue blood, bank balance … But he turned out to be a beast … And as they say, the beast must die … There is a novel of that name, isn't there?'

'We must prepare the ground for his suicide. Set the wheels in motion, if you'd permit the cliché, m'lady. I believe you said Lord Collingwood talked in his sleep?'

'He does. He shouts and screams. He is not a well man. He is prey to nightmares. I often hear him through the wall.'

'That would be perfect. You will say that you heard Lord Collingwood make a confession in his sleep: "Joan, my little girl, what have I done? I had no idea." Something on those lines.' Even though all the neighbouring tables are empty and no waiter is within earshot, I continue to speak sotto voce. 'He will also say that he can't possibly go on living with himself.'

She twists her face and moans in the manner of a soul tormented by toothache. '*Joan, Joan! My little girl! What have I done?*'

'You don't have to mimic Lord Collingwood's voice, m'lady. It is not as though you will ever be expected to impersonate him.'

'Who will be my "audience", Bedaux? Not Scotland Yard, I hope?'

'No, m'lady. There is no question of Scotland Yard being involved at this point. I have been giving the matter some serious consideration and I think you should approach Antonia Darcy, m'lady. In my opinion, Antonia Darcy will make the perfect witness. She is a detective-story writer and, according to one critic, she displays a fondness for "outlandish premises". I came across the phrase on the Internet. There is a great deal about her on the Internet. I am sure she'd want to listen to you. You said you knew her?'

'I only know her husband. How I wish I could have been married to someone like Hugh Payne! Rupert went on about how happily married Hugh and Antonia were. Their marriage seems to have been made in heaven, with angels as witnesses and St Peter as best man.'

'Do you think you could engineer a meeting with Antonia Darcy, m'lady?'

Lady Collingwood takes a delicate bite of a millefeuille, which is also known as the Napoleon of pastries and says, 'I'll do my best. I consider myself a good actress, you know. I excel at charades. Writers as a rule tend to be impractical and fanciful, don't they? They'd believe things ordinary mortals wouldn't. Six impossible things before breakfast and so on. Detective-story writers, someone said, are the worst. Their cleverness is of a particularly synthetic kind.'

'That strikes me as a fair assessment, m'lady. It of course applies exclusively to the purveyors of the more old-fashioned type of whodunit.'

'Of which Antonia Darcy is one!'

I glance around, at the purple peacock-patterned wallpaper, lotus-shaped tables and gilded chandeliers of Chez Charlus, then I watch Lady Collingwood swallow a tablet, which she informs me is one of her 'little Aconites'. She says it has no taste and is perfectly harmless. She never suffers any side effects. She might have been taking an aspirin, really. Then she swallows a *second* Aconite.

Suddenly I am filled with misgivings. My 'stellar plot' is a bit on the overcomplicated side. I have also remembered the way Antonia Darcy stood at the top of the stairs at the Sylvie & Bruno Nursery School looking down at me …

I clear my throat. 'May I suggest that you exercise caution, m'lady? Please, do *not* underestimate Antonia Darcy.'

30

SOMETHING HAPPENED

It was some time after two in the afternoon that Antonia received a phone call from Lady Collingwood.

'I don't think we have ever been properly introduced, Antonia, but I've been *dying* to meet you. I've heard so much about you. I don't think you were at the Peruvian embassy bash, were you? No, I thought not. I would have remembered. Hugh, of course, I remember vividly. I tend to think of Hugh as of one of the most remarkable men of his generation.'

'Do you really think so?'

'I most certainly do! Yes! But I need to thank you first. I'm so terribly grateful to both of you for what you did for Charlie the other night. That meant a lot to me. Do you think we could meet for coffee – or a drink? Would that be at all possible? It would give me tremendous pleasure.'

'Yes, of course. When?' Antonia was curious about Lady Collingwood.

'In the next hour or so? Or is that too soon? You'll prob-ably think me an awful bore but the fact is – all right, I'll put my cards on the table. The fact is I am at my wits' end, Antonia. I am absolutely frantic. I've been feeling terribly apprehensive. I need to consult you about something – *badly*.

It's extremely important. It concerns poor Joan – Charlie's former inamorata. You see, something happened – there's been a development, at least I think of it as a development.'

'What sort of development?'

'I can't talk about it over the phone. It's a very delicate matter – rather distasteful too – I may be completely wrong of course, in fact I hope I am wrong, but, you see, *something happened* – it concerns Joan and Rupert, my husband –' At this point Lady Collingwood became quite breathless and she started speaking very fast. 'A second opinion from someone like you would be most welcome. You have more than proved your credentials. I hold you in the highest regard, Antonia. I think you may be able to advise me. I haven't talked about it to anybody else –'

They arranged to meet at the cafe in Liberty's, of which Lady Collingwood said she had fond memories.

'I am sure I will recognise you,' Lady Collingwood said. 'I've managed to get hold of one of your books. Your photo is on the back flap.'

'I am afraid that looks nothing like me,' Antonia said.

'I never look right in photos either,' Lady Collingwood said. 'I am always taken for someone else. That's what people tell me. Sometimes I wonder if I lack reliable personal identity … I am sure I will recognise you.'

Lady Collingwood held out her left hand in a jet-black glove. She sported an indigo-coloured hat of the pillbox variety and a little tailored black jacket that managed to be at once sombre and severe, an effect somewhat spoilt by a provocatively plunging neckline and her preternaturally high heels. Lady Collingwood's hair was a curious silver-brown shade that reminded Antonia of the underwings of a moth. Her face was carefully made-up and she was wearing a very pale mauve lipstick. Her age was impossible to guess. Her mascara-ed eyes, Antonia noticed, did not quite focus.

'So good of you to agree to meet me. I don't know what I'd have done if you'd said no. It's an impossibly difficult situation, so I shall rely on your wisdom and discretion. But you must tell me something first.' Lady Collingwood lowered her voice. 'In reference to poor Joan – what's the latest news?'

'I'm afraid I don't know anything,' Antonia said apologetically. 'We are not in touch with the police.'

'You aren't?'

'No.'

Antonia noticed that there were little whitish crystals sticking to one of Lady Collingwood's lapels. Sugar? Had Lady Collingwood been eating cake?

'How perfectly extraordinary. I always imagined that you and Hugh had some very special contacts at Scotland Yard. I'd very much like to think the police are not as stupid and backward as most of us assume. We mustn't think poorly of the police, must we? I can't help thinking the killer is some maniac – and it's *got* to be a man. What do you think, Antonia? It's almost invariably a man, isn't it? Especially when the victim is a young woman.'

'That's what statistics tell us – but not invariably.' Antonia couldn't bring herself to address Lady Collingwood as 'Deirdre', though she had been urged to do so.

'There were no signs of – interference – of bruising? How terribly peculiar. You mean the killer could be a *woman*? How very interesting. Sorry – the little waitress has been trying to catch my eye. I hate making people wait, don't you? What will you have?'

'An espresso.'

'I will have a cup of China tea. I can't face anything else. Plain gunpowder, please.' Lady Collingwood leant back. 'You don't suppose the foreign girl who lives at the house may have done it after all? It occurs to me that she was probably brought up with a completely different set of values. I believe the slaughter of seals is a common practice in her part of Europe, isn't it?'

'Is it?'

'I admit I know next to nothing about her, nothing at all, only that her name is Olga and that she is "breathtakingly beautiful". That's what Charlie says. He's quite taken with her, poor darling. Is Olga "breathtakingly beautiful"?'

'She is beautiful, yes.'

'Not one of those primped-and-preened-Park-Avenue-princess types, is she? That look is so irredeemably *tacky*.'

'No, not at all. Olga is a natural beauty. She is sweet and charming as well.'

'Did Hugh think so too? I am so pleased. I wasn't at all sure. All love-struck young men tend to idealise the object of their affection. Charlie is terribly young and impressionable.' Lady Collingwood gave a wistful smile.

'Joan Selwyn was engaged to be married to him, wasn't she?'

'Only for a very short while. Charlie broke off the engagement. I never managed to make up my mind about Joan. She was awfully reserved. She was amiable enough, but there was never any question of our becoming "bosom friends". She was fearsomely efficient. I must admit I found her a little intimidating – even after she dyed her hair blonde. She was Rupert's secretary for a while. I had no idea then that – that –' Lady Collingwood broke off. She bit her lip.

'Yes?'

'As I told you on the phone, Antonia, I am anxious to talk to you about something that happened, but I can't. I'm finding it terribly difficult to come to the point. I am a coward.'

Lady Collingwood shook her head. She produced a slim silver cigarette case. 'I don't think I will be allowed to smoke here, will I? Actually, I don't feel like smoking.' She put the cigarette case back into her bag. 'What I really feel like doing is bursting into tears.'

'Is it so awful?' Antonia believed she could guess where this was heading – though would Lady Collingwood have made such a song and dance about a mere affair between her husband and his secretary? There was clearly more to it.

'Is it so awful?' Lady Collingwood echoed. 'It is, yes. It's perfectly hideous. No question about it. Unless I am *entirely wrong*. Well, you see – it is like this – No, I can't! Sorry but I can't.' Her voice shook. 'I need to calm down first ... Oh dear, do people still read Wodehouse? So passé, wouldn't you say?' Lady Collingwood had pointed to the book someone was reading at a neighbouring table. 'I've never been able to see the appeal of Wodehouse. Master of language he may be, but all that repetitive silliness! He never varied his plots, did he? Are you familiar with the Restoration dramatist Thomas Otway?'

'Otway? No, not very. Didn't he write *The Orphan*?'

'Yes. It is also known as *The Unhappy Marriage*. It was Charlie's valet who introduced me to him. Such a clever man. Thomas Otway wrote what became known as "she-tragedies" – plays about virtuous and afflicted heroines. And why am I telling you this? It's because at this very moment I see myself as one of those virtuous and afflicted women.' Lady Collingwood gave a self-deprecating laugh. 'Do you consider yourself virtuous, Antonia?'

'No, not particularly. Only moderately so.'

The waitress reappeared bearing a tray and placed it on their table.

Lady Collingwood closed her eyes and laid the tips of her fingers on the lids. 'Thank you, Antonia. Thank you for not losing patience with me. I'd have lost patience by now if I'd been confronted with me. I brought you here with the promise of a confession, didn't I? Well, there is a confession coming. I don't know why I keep putting it off. It's not fair on you.'

'Is it so awful?' Antonia said again.

'I do wish I had more courage,' Lady Collingwood whispered. She opened her eyes. 'You see, I want to believe Joan was killed by a maniac or even by Olga because the alternative is too horrible for words. I hope you will tell me I am imagining things. I can see that you are a sensible person. You've got your head screwed on. That's how I imagined you to be. That's why I wanted to see you. It's such a personal thing. It's about Rupert. I am extremely worried about Rupert. About his state of mind. You see, something happened and I don't know what to make of it and, honestly, I am terrified.'

'What happened?'

Lady Collingwood picked up her cup of tea and immediately put it down. Her hands, Antonia noticed, were shaking.

'It happened last night. I woke up suddenly. I could hear Rupert talking in a very loud voice in his bedroom, which is next door to mine. At first I thought he was on the phone but then I realised he was talking in his sleep. He has done it before. He has problems sleeping. I don't normally listen but this time I did listen. It was Joan's name that caught my attention –'

31

A TALENT TO ANNOY

'You *are* a policeman, aren't you? A plain-clothes detective?'

'I told you I wasn't.'

'A secret policeman would never admit to being a police-man,' Billy said.

'I used to work for the Secret Service, but that was quite a while ago. Light years ago. I am here in a private capacity. I am a friend of the Collingwoods. It was Lord Collingwood who asked me to look into the matter,' Payne improvised.

'Lord Collingwood actually asked you to investigate Joan's murder?'

'No, not investigate. Good lord, no. I wouldn't know where to begin!' Payne laughed self-deprecatingly. 'The police are already doing that. What Lord Collingwood wants me to do is – um – help clarify some points.'

'What sort of points?'

'You don't have to answer any of my questions if you don't feel like it.'

'Oh very well.' Billy sighed. 'Ask away.'

'When was the last time you saw Joan Selwyn?'

'Three days ago, the day before she died. She popped in to say hallo. She didn't stay long.'

The fair-haired young man sounded neutral but his eyes continued to be wary. How curious that all the young people in this affair should be blonde, Payne reflected idly. Even the victim – though she had owed her fairness to art rather than to nature.

'How would you describe Miss Selwyn's state of mind on that occasion?'

'Her state of mind? Perfectly normal. Joan was normality personified.'

'That wasn't always the case,' Payne said slowly. 'I understand she acted in a very strange manner when her former boyfriend broke up with her.'

'Did she? You do surprise me. I had no idea.' Billy shook his head. 'I must say I am astonished.'

'Can you think of anything – *anything* – that she said or did the last time you saw her that was perhaps a little out of the ordinary?'

'No, not really. She complained that one of her flatmates, can't remember which one, tended to use up all the hot water.' Billy frowned. 'She was also a bit annoyed with Lord Collingwood. He had wanted her to help him with something. As Lord Collingwood's friend, you probably know all about it.'

'As a matter of fact I don't.'

'It was something to do with Eresby's girlfriend, I think, that's the chap Joan used to go out with – and some other person.'

Payne pricked up his ears. 'It was to do with Olga?'

'Is that her name?'

'Yes … Miss Selwyn didn't give you any idea as to what it might have been about?'

'Um. No. Oh yes, it's coming back. Some rigmarole about an acquaintance of Lord Collingwood's – a highly respectable gentleman of advancing years, I think – who'd got into a spot of trouble with this girl – Olga? I am afraid I wasn't listening … What's this Olga – an escort or something?'

'Didn't Joan specify the nature of the trouble?'

'She did say something. Um. The elderly gentleman had been to Olga's house expecting favours, but she wasn't forthcoming? Something like that. Oh, and he seemed to have left something behind, which he wanted back, badly. Apparently, he phoned Olga and asked for it but she said she would only give it back on certain conditions. I got the idea it was something compromising.'

'What conditions?'

'No idea. It all sounded incredibly tedious. Joan had agreed to assist Lord Collingwood in getting the thing from the house. But she was annoyed about it. She found the whole business rather distasteful, actually.'

'How very curious. By "the house" you of course mean Philomel Cottage? That's where Miss Selwyn was killed ...'

There was a pause. Payne wondered whether he should believe this story or not. Lord Collingwood hadn't said anything about it. But then why should Joan Selwyn make up a story like that? It didn't quite fit in at all with the anonymous phone call she had received at Richoux's either – or did it? She had told Lord Collingwood someone had asked her to go to Philomel Cottage. But she was already going to Philomel Cottage! There was something wrong. He believed someone was lying. He glanced across at Billy.

'I got the idea this girl – Olga – was blackmailing the old fellow,' Billy said.

'I wouldn't have said Olga was the blackmailing type.'

'Do you *know* Olga?' Billy's eyes opened wide.

'I have met her. The impression she made on me was almost entirely positive,' Payne said firmly. He pointed to a mobile phone that lay on the coffee table. 'That's not your Blackberry, is it?'

'No – how – how did you know?'

'It's got the initials "JS" on it.'

'Has it? Where?' Billy blinked. He looked down at the mobile phone. 'Oh, are those letters? I thought that was part of the design – had no idea they were *letters*!'

'What did you think they were?'

'Two snakes, one standing on its head, the other preparing to strike! That's what it looks like, doesn't it? Can't you see the snakes? Yes, it's Joan's Blackberry. I had no idea she'd had it personalised. I have had it ready to give to the police – or to Joan's father.'

'Has Joan's father been in touch with you?'

'No. I doubt whether Joan's father is aware of my existence. I don't think he and Joan were ever close.'

'I see.' Payne wondered as to the reason for the estrangement – could old Selwyn have been made aware of the fact that Joan was not his real daughter? Something stirred at the back of his mind. 'How long have you had Joan's phone?'

'Um. I think she left it behind the day before she died. I meant to give it to her but, as it happened, I never had the chance.'

'You said you were going to have dinner together. Weren't you at all worried when she failed to turn up?'

'I was. Of course I was.' The chap sounds defensive, Payne decided. He saw Billy cast a glance at the door, as though expecting it to open at any moment. Billy didn't appear to be particularly grief-stricken. 'I sat and waited and then I rang her but there was no answer – it was about ten o'clock, I think.'

'She couldn't have answered as her mobile was here,' Payne said.

'Yes, quite. But I'd completely forgotten that she'd left it here!'

'Unless she had a second phone?'

'I don't think so – not that she'd have been able to answer even if she'd had a second phone – I assume she was dead by then – I mean, by ten?' Billy swallowed. 'When was she killed exactly?'

'At about five-thirty,' said Payne.

The door opened. It was the young man called Sieg Mortimer, to whom the elegant flat belonged. 'Sorry to intrude but I was wondering whether Major Payne would like a cup of coffee? Or perhaps a drink? How about some whisky? As you are *not* a policeman, you can have a drink with impunity, can't you?'

He must have been standing outside the sitting-room door, listening to their conversation.

'Indeed I can. A whisky and soda would be very acceptable,' Payne said amiably.

'You can relax, Selkirk. Major Payne is not a real policeman. This proves it. The police don't drink while performing their duties. Major Payne is what is known as an "independent agent", isn't that so, Major Payne?'

'Something like that.'

'Unless this is a ploy to put us at our ease, so that he can have his evil way with us. The thing to remember, Selkirk, is not to make any statements that would be considered unwelcome by learned counsel on either side … What will you have, Selkirk?'

'Nothing, thanks, Mortimer. Nothing for me.'

It was Mortimer who had opened the front door to Major Payne, though he had then made himself scarce. Payne didn't care for Mortimer's sneering mouth and facetious manner. Mortimer was blonde too – like Billy, like Charlie, like Olga! How funny. Was that another coincidence – or could it be a conspiracy? Payne smiled at the thought and for a moment or two he gave full rein to his imagination.

Joan Selwyn was killed because she was not a real blonde. She had dyed her hair blonde in order to infiltrate a sinister secret society that consisted exclusively of blondes. Some bizarre ring of fanatical neo-Aryans? Yes. The solution to the affair would turn out to be one of those rather outlandish sub-Dan-Brown ones … The luminous league … The band of blondes … The fair hair affair …

All very silly, yes, but people did cause harm to others for the oddest of reasons imaginable sometimes. Like the old chap in the news who had laced his wife's tea with mercury – he wanted to make her ill, so that he could nurse her back to health – he hadn't meant her to die – he had seen it as a way of winning back her love and affection – or so he claimed – they'd been at loggerheads over something – he described her death as a 'tragic accident' – he swore that he never meant to kill her –

Payne's eyes remained fixed on Joan Selwyn's mobile. Once more he was aware of something stirring at the back of his mind. What was it? The mobile shouldn't be here, he suddenly thought, though he didn't quite know what he meant by that. And then another thought floated into his mind. It was a thought he'd had earlier on: lies. Rather, one particular lie …

He asked, 'Were there any messages on Joan's mobile?'

'Yes, several, but I am afraid they were deleted.' Billy seemed to regret the words as soon as they were out of his mouth. If there had been such an invention as a 'word-eraser', he would have applied it at once, of that Major Payne was certain. Billy went very red. 'It was an accident.'

'You deleted Joan's messages by accident?'

'Well, actually –'

'There is a disapproving glint in your eye, Major Payne, and I don't blame you. You clearly think that one or more of the deleted messages contained some kind of clue to Joan's murder, am I right?' The young man called Mortimer had re-entered the sitting room. He was holding a small tray with two glasses, one of which he handed to Payne, the other he kept for himself. 'In fact, it wasn't Selkirk who deleted the messages. I did. *Mea culpa*. No sinister reason for it, I assure you. I was fooling around.'

'Fooling around?'

'Yes. Fooling around. I was fooling around. I always do when I try to relieve my *taedium vitae*. Stop looking so bloody sheepish, Selkirk. One might be excused for thinking you'd been caught cartwheeling on the grounds of Buckingham Palace or some such inexcusable transgression. Fooling, yes. Fooling with other people's mobiles is to me what cocaine and the violin were to Sherlock Holmes. Incidentally, I am a great aficionado of the Sherlock Holmes stories – are you?'

'Didn't you think Joan would mind?' Payne asked.

'It was unprincipled of me, I admit. I partly did it to annoy her, I think. I didn't really like her.'

'So it wasn't an accident. You deleted the messages on purpose. To annoy her.'

'She deserved it, you know. She never laughed at my jokes. Besides, I didn't really approve of her association with Selkirk. She reciprocated by disapproving of my association with Selkirk. That's often the way, isn't it? She actually had the gall to tell Selkirk that I was a phase. How would you feel if someone described you as a phase? What a life, ye screeching cockatoos, what a life!' Mortimer threw up his hands. 'No point saying sorry to *you*, is there, Major Payne? I would have most certainly apologised to her but I can't as she is dead.'

'Did you by any chance listen to her messages before you deleted them?'

Sieg Mortimer assumed an expression of thoughtful concentration. 'You don't think Conan Doyle ever meant to kill Sherlock Holmes off at the Reichenbach Falls, do you? The fact that no body is ever recovered at the end of *The Final Problem* is extremely suggestive, I always thought. No dead body, as every self-respecting aficionado of the genre knows, means one thing only — *no murder*.'

'You are probably right,' Payne conceded. 'But I asked you a question —'

'Honestly and truly, I don't believe Holmes' miraculous escape idea was the afterthought it was taken to be later on. It was a ruse. I am sure that all along old Doyle intended to resurrect his lucrative creation, which he eventually did do, to the delight of millions. Oh how I wish I could have been able to see all those gentlemen sporting black armbands, marching in the Strand, swinging their brollies and clamouring for Sherlock Holmes' return!'

'Did you by any chance listen to the messages on Joan's phone before deleting them?' Payne asked patiently. It wouldn't do for him to show irritation. Neither of the two young men, he reminded himself, was under any obligation to answer his questions.

'Did I listen to the messages? As a matter of fact I did. Yes. I was fooling around, I told you. It was part of the fooling.'

'Weren't you afraid she might mind your deleting her messages?'

'No, not really. I am never afraid. I told you I wanted to annoy her. I was rather hoping she would blame Selkirk for it. I was hoping it might cause a rift between them ... Sorry, Selkirk. I thought I was acting for the best.'

'You couldn't have known she was dead when you deleted her messages, could you?' Payne said.

'No, of course not. I have the feeling you are trying to catch me out. You do pride yourself on solving puzzles, don't you, Major Payne? No, no use denying it. I have heard stories about you.'

'What were the messages about? Do you remember?'

'How good are you, really? I mean, at solving puzzles? I hope you don't mind being put to the test? Please listen carefully – I've got a puzzle for you … A man goes into a restaurant and orders an albatross. He cuts it with his knife and fork, takes a mouthful, then another, then another. A couple of moments later he produces a gun and shoots himself. *Why?*'

'They don't serve albatross at restaurants,' Billy pointed out.

'In Fiji and such-like barbaric places they do, Selkirk. Kindly do not interrupt. Well, Major Payne? Why did the man shoot himself?'

Losing his temper with these annoying young men would be fatal, Major Payne reminded himself. If he wanted to learn more about the messages on Joan Selwyn's Blackberry, he might as well accept Mortimer's terms and play along. For some reason he was convinced now that Joan Selwyn's mobile phone was central to the solution of her murder.

'Why did the man shoot himself? Well, that's pretty obvious, isn't it?' Payne gave a little smile. 'He loved his wife too much and couldn't imagine life without her. You see, he had found his wife's wedding ring among the bird's *dejecta membra*. He realised that his wife – who had been mountaineering in the Himalayas – had been killed in an accident and that nobody was aware of it yet. He had worked out that an albatross had pecked at his wife's flesh and swallowed her ring – before being caught, killed, sent to the restaurant, grilled and served?'

'Not at all bad, Major Payne. Not at all bad.' Mortimer nodded. 'Your answer is gruesome enough for my taste, though perhaps not as gruesome as the official solution.'

'I have a solution,' Billy Selkirk said. 'The man suddenly realises that this is his pet albatross, which he reared from a chick and that he released into the wild only a couple of days before. He has recognised the ring on the albatross's leg, which he himself put there. He loved his pet albatross more than anything in the world, he can't imagine life without his beloved bird, so he shoots himself.'

'Too damned feeble, Selkirk! Too damned feeble! Beloved bird indeed. We need to do work on your lateral thinking. Now don't interrupt and listen to the official solution.' Mortimer paused. 'The man, his wife and a second man were shipwrecked on a desert island. The man's wife died in the wreck. The two men went looking for food but couldn't find anything edible, but then the second man went searching on his own and he brought what he said was an albatross but was in actual fact – can you guess?'

'A part of the dead wife,' Payne murmured.

'Yes! So they made a fire by rubbing together two dry sticks, grilled the piece of meat and ate it. Later they were rescued; life returns to normal and, at some point, the bereaved husband decides to order albatross at a restaurant. Of course it tastes nothing like what he was told was albatross on the island, which makes him realise that what he had eaten was his dead wife. The shock is too great for him, consequently he suffers a form of derangement and shoots himself!'

'Ingenious,' Payne nodded. 'Though a bit on the elaborate side. You see, my wife maintains – and I tend to agree with her – that the less explanation a denouement involves, the more effective it is. My wife writes detective stories,' Payne explained.

'I read a French detective novel once where all the clues were given in italics,' Billy Selkirk said.

'Your wife writes detective stories? How terribly interesting,' Mortimer said. 'She is not beaten or done, I hope?'

'Beaten or done? What on earth do you mean? Oh. No, no, no, no – she is not Beaton or Dunn, no! I am married to Antonia Darcy.'

'I am very glad to hear it. I'm no fan of those two. I've heard of Antonia Darcy but so far I haven't read any of her books.

Does Antonia Darcy produce *textes de désir* or *textes de plaisir?*' Mortimer raised the glass of whisky to his lips.

'Let me see. If I remember correctly,' said Payne, 'in *textes de désir* what matters is the reader's desire to reach the denouement and discover whodunit, correct? In *textes de plaisir*, on the other hand, it is wit, style and interesting characters that matter?'

'That is correct, Major Payne. So which one is it? *Désir* or *plaisir?*'

'Wouldn't it be wrong to separate *désir* from *plaisir?*' Billy said. 'They always go together, don't they?'

'In our experience, Selkirk, they do, invariably, you are quite right, but it is detective stories we are talking about,' Mortimer said. 'Well, Major Payne?'

'I would describe Antonia's books as a blend of both … I am biased of course … But I believe you were about to tell me about Joan Selwyn's phone messages, weren't you?'

'I was about to do no such thing. Why do you keep harping on those messages? They weren't of the slightest interest or importance, I assure you. They were extremely boring. The first one was from one of Joan's flatmates, a girl called Minerva – Selkirk admires her immensely – something about an unpaid electricity bill, to which Joan was expected to contribute. Another message was from Joan's MP boss – something about completing a research task he'd set her, I think. He sounds a severe taskmaster. I told you they were boring. I did warn you, didn't I?'

'Were those the only messages?'

'Yes. There were only two. Sorry to disappoint you.'

Major Payne took his leave soon after.

As he drove away from Shepherds Market, Payne found himself wondering about Lord Collingwood's mysterious friend and his connection with Olga Klimt. Lord Collingwood did say Joan had been helping him with something but why didn't he ever mention the fact that it was to do with Olga and Philomel Cottage? How very odd ... Who *was* the mysterious friend?

On an impulse he took out his mobile and rang Lord Collingwood's home number.

'Ah, good to hear from you, Payne. Any progress with the untangling? As a matter of fact I got a call from Mortimer only a minute ago. He asked me whether you'd been acting on my behalf. I said no. That was naughty of you, you know, quizzing those boys under false colours! What's that? What friend? My friend? But I have no friends, Payne. Not a single one. All Deirdre's fault, I fear ... Oh you mean that old fool and Olga? Oh yes, yes. But I wouldn't call him a *friend*. I'll explain everything, though not now, if you don't mind frightfully.' Lord Collingwood lowered his voice. 'Deirdre has come back home, I can hear her and I suspect she is up to something. I'll have to ring off now. Au revoir.'

Outside it had begun to drizzle. Payne turned on the wipers.

Suddenly he had the absolute certainty that he had been presented with every fact necessary for the solving of Joan Selwyn's murder. All he needed to do was produce one of those brilliant pieces of sustained explication for which he was famous –

Only he couldn't. His mind had gone blank!

Certainty my foot, he murmured. As a matter of fact, he had absolutely no idea who killed Joan Selwyn – or why. No idea at all.

No, that wasn't true –

That mobile phone ... Yes ... It held the key to the mystery ...

32

L'HEURE MALICIOSE

Lord Collingwood was having another harrowing dream, only this time it was mainly aural.

He heard his wife's voice say, 'Unless God performed some kind of miracle, your darling mama would be unable to bear any more children. Her womb must be entirely shrivelled up by now. And if a miracle happened and she did procreate, it is God, *via* the Holy Spirit, who will be the child's father, *not* a Collingwood. That's good news for civilisation, isn't it?'

To which Lord Collingwood said, 'Turgid carp, tail-walking like a sketch by Tenniel.'

He woke up with a start. He was sitting in the swivel chair at his desk. He heard the chiming of the grandfather clock downstairs.

Midnight?

Lord Collingwood rose. He was wearing his smoking jacket. He felt as stiff as a board and a little nauseous. For some reason he remembered the time when he had eaten a dog biscuit by accident and how ill it had made him feel. The funny thing was that he had rather enjoyed it and felt ill only *after* he realised it had been a dog biscuit and not one fit for human consumption, which showed what an infernal machine the human mind was.

He hadn't meant to fall asleep. As a matter of fact he had been urging himself to stay awake.

If one had to have dreams, why couldn't they be of pleasanter things, such as of glitter, for example? Lord Collingwood liked glitter. There was nothing like the glitter of a military parade, compounded of frosted brocade, blades of ceremonial swords, bright buttons and decorations on uniformed chests ...

He noticed a large white cup standing on his desk. It contained some purplish liquid with an invasive smell. Strong, sweet, herbal. Then he remembered. It was a tisane that Deirdre had brought him. Some supposedly miraculous concoction, she had described it as, an elixir of youthful vitality, which, she insisted, *everybody* – including the Duchess of Cornwall, Joan Collins, the Prince of Wales *and* the prime minister – was mad about.

Well, Deirdre was wrong if she imagined he would drink it!

He felt exhausted. Why did he feel exhausted? It was as though he had come back from a ten-mile trek over wild and snowbound country ...

The next moment he heard voices. They were coming through the wall. He had been feeling depressed – the Black Dog again – but now his mood changed to one of alertness and suspicion. He might have been a fox lifting his head at the first notes of the hunt.

He heard conspiratorial whispering ... Deirdre and someone else – a man? They were next door, in Deirdre's boudoir.

He could hear their voices because of the hole in the wall which was covered by a picture – a Spy cartoon of one of his Victorian ancestors.

Lord Collingwood tiptoed up to the wall and carefully took off the picture. There was a spyhole in the wall. That had been his little joke; Spy shielding the spy in the wall. A gag that was visual as well as verbal. Jolly clever! He did things like that in an effort to keep his spirits up.

He had drilled the hole himself. He had thought it would be interesting to watch Deirdre undress when she thought no one was watching her. He had an idea that she would do it *differently* than on those occasions on which they were 'together'. They hadn't been 'together' for a long time and he no longer cared about the way she undressed. He had lost interest in such matters. It was one of those things, he supposed.

It occurred to him that the situation might have been different, better, if he had been a *proper* writer and not just an occasional scribbler, if he'd been somebody who churned out a book or two every year. Writers got whatever it was that troubled them, even the most idiotic idea, out of their systems, by the simple expedient of putting it down on paper.

Lord Collingwood brought his eye to the hole in the wall.

He saw Deirdre and – and – no, impossible! It couldn't be Charlie's man, could it? That villain Bedaux! No, impossible! He blinked. Well, it *was* Bedaux! No mistake about it. That blasted flunkey! Not that he disapproved of servants as a class – he didn't! The ghillies at Collingwood were a delight, faithful old dogs to a man! Why, his mother had had the same ghillie sleeping outside her bedroom door for the past sixty-five years. But they never said a word and their expressions remained deferential at all times. They knew their place.

He remembered that earlier on that evening he had heard his wife talking to someone on the phone. Deirdre hadn't used any names but she had referred, rather obliquely, to 'the arrangement'. He knew now that she had been talking to Bedaux.

It was outrageous. Bedaux under his roof! The blighter should be in jail, not in Deirdre's boudoir. Lord Collingwood had already phoned the police and informed them that Bedaux had been spotted outside Philomel Cottage in the aftermath of Joan Selwyn's murder. He'd also told them about Bedaux's pimping activities and that Joanie had been investigating the matter. He'd also told them about the phone call Joanie had received on the morning of the murder – from someone who'd actually asked her to go to Philomel Cottage. He had said he strongly suspected the caller had been Bedaux … Should he ring the police now and tell them Bedaux was at his house? No, he felt exhausted. He couldn't face any visitors.

Deirdre couldn't be having an affair with Bedaux, could she? She wouldn't stoop that low, would she? Such a grotesque idea, a woman of Deirdre's standing having an affair with her son's valet. But he wouldn't put anything past Deirdre. She might be seeing herself as *la nouvelle* Lady Chatterley or something.

Deirdre and Bedaux looked so cosy together, ensconced on the sofa, heads together, whispering. They had an air of absolute agreement about them. But why couldn't he hear a word of what they were saying? He saw their lips move but not a sound came out. It felt as though he were watching the box and someone had turned off the sound. Perhaps they were aware of him observing them and doing it to annoy him? Or had his hearing suddenly gone? He tapped his right ear, then his left.

As a matter of fact he didn't think there was anything amorous or sensual about their pose. They were not canoodling, merely conferring. It looked as though they were waiting for something. The next moment he knew – the tisane! A pill or a powder had been slipped into the tisane, some doping agent, some powerful soporific, most likely, and now they were waiting for him to pass out.

Well, he'd already decided he wouldn't touch the tisane. They were planning to dispose of him in some way or another, yes. They looked as thick as thieves! Well, Deirdre had had an odd air about her when she brought him the tisane. She had been dressed in one of her flowing golden draperies that made her contours sway and she was wearing her high heels and she had put her hair up in the way that, once upon a time, he used to find terribly alluring.

The most likely explanation was that they wanted to bump him off, so that they could share his fortune.

He stood very still, deep in thought. He rubbed at his eyes. When he looked through the spy hole again, he saw that the boudoir was empty. In a nanosecond Deirdre and Bedaux seemed to have vanished into thin air! The cushions on the sofa were plumped and prettily arranged. The sofa bore no signs of having been disturbed in any way. How was that possible? Had they ever been there? Were they playing games with him? Or was there a more sinister reason for it? It wasn't another one of his lapses, was it?

'I've had enough,' Lord Collingwood said aloud. 'I am sick and tired of it all.'

Then suddenly he saw them again. They had reappeared and were now standing in his room! There they were, by his book-shelves, blast them, pretending to be admiring his collection of first editions while watching him covertly out of the corner of their eyes ... It seemed they still expected him to drink the tisane ... They were *willing* him to drink it ... They were trying to hasten him to his doom!

But how had they entered the room? His door was not only locked but bolted! By some process of transubstantiation? They probably had demonic powers ...

Then Lord Collingwood had his idea. He'd make them look foolish! He knew exactly how. He would steal a march on them! A little giggle escaped his lips, though of course he was far from happy. No, happiness didn't come into it at all.

He sat down at his desk and glanced at his copy of Audubon's *Flowers and Birds*, at the silver scissors and the strips of paper, then at the framed photograph of his father. He nodded.

Well, it *had* to be done. His world was crumbling all round him. He took a sheet of thick cream-coloured writing paper and picked up his pen. His hand, he was glad to see, was perfectly steady.

He started writing.

When he finished, he signed it: Collingwood. One might as well observe the proprieties. He sat scowling at his signature for a full minute. The flourish underneath was like the tail of a comet and the three dots brought to mind stars.

33

EYES WIDE OPEN

Although it was getting late, Antonia and Major Payne sat in the drawing room at their house in Hampstead, drinking coffee and comparing notes.

'Deirdre Collingwood suggested that her husband had been having an affair with Joan Selwyn who was his daughter and whom he subsequently killed. She said she feared he was completely unhinged and might be contemplating suicide. Lord Collingwood had been talking in his sleep and some of his words could be interpreted as pointing that way.' Antonia paused. 'She was extremely interesting to watch.'

'I am sure she was. I don't think an affair between Collingwood and Joan Selwyn terribly likely, do you? Wrong psychology,' said Payne. 'Joan was plain and appears to have had a somewhat stern if not harshly dominant personality whereas Collingwood's amorous tastes incline towards luminous beauties and whores of Babylon crossed with holy virgins.'

'Deirdre gave a magnificent performance, real masterclass ... She played the ditzy dowager to perfection, though at one point I caught her looking at me from under her eyelids, as though watching for my reaction ... I think she was acting on someone's instructions.'

'What gave you that idea?'

'She had already been at some café or tea rooms. I mean before our meeting. There were tiny granules of sugar on her left lapel. She had been eating a pastry or something. I know it was sugar because she picked one up with her forefinger and licked it. She did it quite unconsciously. She then gave a little smile – reminiscent – pleased – sly.'

'She was remembering the person she had been with, you think? Someone she respects and admires? You think it was an accomplice?'

'I do. And I have an idea as to who that person might be,' Antonia said. 'You see, there was a man at a neighbouring table reading Wodehouse, one of the Blandings novels, but then he left the book behind on the table. When we were about to leave, Lady Collingwood reached out and picked it up. The cover showed Beach the butler, I think, next to Lord Emsworth's pig. Deirdre shook her head and said, "The idea of the portly butler is so passé. Butlers can be slim and saturnine and distinguished looking. They can have a full head of hair and they can be dark." And again I saw the reminiscent look.'

'How fascinating.'

'Then she asked me if I thought valets could ever be butlers. I said I didn't see why not. My answer seemed to please her. Again she smiled and nodded and she picked up another sugar granule off her lapel and put it in her mouth. Well, the next moment I had my brainwave. I *knew*. And I don't think I was letting my wondrously prolific imagination get the better of me. I knew who her partner in crime was. A bit obvious, really.'

'Bedaux?'

'Yes. She was thinking of Bedaux. Who is a valet on the loose …'

'The sugar granule was Deirdre's madeleine moment, eh? I salute thee most heartily for a supremely ingenious piece of deduction! Well, it all makes perfect sense.' Payne nodded.

'Collingwood did refer to Bedaux as "Deirdre's Svengali". Deirdre was put in mind of the person she had been with earlier on at some patisserie, prior to meeting you, and then she made a connection with the illustration on the book cover.'

'Yes. Bedaux's is tall, dark, saturnine and quite distinguished looking. She's clearly considering making him her butler.'

'Which she can only do *after* her husband's death,' Payne said slowly. 'Collingwood told me Deirdre had been pestering him to get a butler and he said, "Over my dead body." Well, well, well. It all adds up. It seems they have been busy plotting Collingwood's murder, eh?'

'Yes.'

'They have been over-egging the pudding a bit, haven't they? I mean, an incestuous affair followed by murder followed by suicide ... Too rococo ... Most rococo schemes are doomed to failure ...'

'Bedaux is the evil puppetmaster operating behind the scenes. I also suspect it was Bedaux who recommended me as a possible patsy,' said Antonia.

'They underestimated you!'

'What was a "patsy" originally, do you remember? Not some sort of cake?'

'No, not a cake. Patsy Bolivar was the brainchild of vaude-villian Billy B. Van ... Early twentieth century, I think. Patsy Bolivar was an ingénue who became the victim of some unscrupulous or nefarious characters.'

'They are planning to get rid of Lord Collingwood. They are setting the scene for a suicide. I was being used as a possible witness – someone who, when the time comes, will be able to say yes, poor Lady Collingwood was terribly worried about her husband's state of mind. Her husband had been talking in his sleep and he came up with a shocking confession.'

'Collingwood said Deirdre had been eating out of Bedaux's hand. You yourself had him marked down as a Machiavel when you ran into him at that nursery place, didn't you?'

'I most certainly did. I didn't like his eyes.'

'Their motive is of course money. Collingwood is a very rich man. Lady Collingwood is afraid that he is going change his will and leave his fortune to someone other than her. She is still the current beneficiary,' Payne went on in a thoughtful voice. 'He told me about it. He also said he didn't think Deirdre deserved a penny. He had been planning to leave his fortune to Joan ... Yes, it all fits in perfectly ... Incidentally, my love, why didn't you tell me you were going to meet Deirdre?'

'Sorry, I was in a rush.'

'You could have phoned or sent a message. I was worried. I kept trying to ring you.'

'Oh I am so sorry but I'd left my mobile at home. Were you really worried?' She reached out for his hand. 'Sweet of you to worry.'

Payne picked up a sheet. 'I have made more jottings. This is how the case stands at the moment. Joan Selwyn meets Lord Collingwood at Richoux's in Piccadilly for morning coffee. She gets a phone call. She tells Lord Collingwood that someone has asked her to go to Philomel Cottage at five-thirty that same afternoon. She says she has no idea who the caller is. Lord Collingwood tells her it's probably a trap and begs her not to go. She promises she won't, but she does go. She is killed as she is about to enter the house. She is stabbed in the back. Olga Klimt is not at the house at the time.'

'We still believe Olga is innocent, don't we?'

'We most certainly do. Olga's story is that she received a call from a stranger who told her to go to Dr Bishop's clinic in Bayswater as Charlie wanted to see her.' Payne looked up.

'Well, I strongly believe that the person who phoned Olga is the killer. What do you think?'

'Phone calls can be tracked down, can't they?'

'They can – but I suspect that particular call was made from a public phone or from a disposable mobile that has since been dropped into the Thames.'

'Is Olga's caller the same person who rang Joan Selwyn?' Antonia frowned. 'I am getting a bit confused. It must be the same one. Yes. It's the killer.'

'Here's a theory.' Payne leant back. 'The killer gets Olga out of the way. He tells her to go to Dr Bishop's clinic. He – or she – sets the stage for Joan Selwyn's murder. The killer wants Joan to die at Philomel Cottage, to make it look as though Joan was taken for Olga and that her murder was a mistake. Both girls are of a similar height and built and they have fair hair. Easy to mistake one for the other in the growing darkness, especially from the back.'

'Bedaux had a motive for wanting to kill both Olga *and* Joan,' Antonia said. 'The former out of jealous revenge – the latter, because she happened to be on his pimping trail. But it could also have been Lady Collingwood. She also had a motive. Deirdre had read the draft of her husband's new will. She saw Joan as her financial rival …'

'Talking of rivals, we should also perhaps consider Sieg Mortimer. He clearly regarded Joan as his rival for Billy Selkirk's affections,' said Payne. 'He wouldn't have liked it if Billy Selkirk had married Joan. He was infuriatingly flippant on the subject of Joan's mobile phone and the messages that he'd deleted –' Payne broke off. His hand went up to his forehead. 'Why, oh why, do I keep thinking that Joan's mobile phone is the key to the puzzle? For some reason I am convinced that Joan's mobile should *not* have been at Sieg Mortimer's flat!'

'Where should it have been?'

'I don't know. Let me try again. I seem to feel it was impossible for something to have taken place – because of Joan Selwyn's mobile. That doesn't make much sense either, does it? Well, I also seem to believe that someone – one of the people involved in the case – told a particular lie that in some way is of the greatest significance …'

'What about Lord Collingwood's mysterious friend?' Antonia asked suddenly. 'Where does he come in?'

Payne shook his head. 'I have absolutely no idea. Collingwood said he would explain but I am not sure I want to hear it as it will only add to the chaos. You don't think the mysterious friend will turn out to be the killer, do you? It makes no sense … What's the matter?'

Antonia had opened her eyes wide. 'I believe it does make sense. Yes, it does. Oh, my God – Hugh, it does!'

'What does? Don't tell me you've worked it out. You couldn't have.'

'Yes, I have. It's all there. The mobile – the particular lie – the lie is of paramount importance, exactly as you said. But – but if so – if so – it turns the whole case on its head!'

'Who is the mysterious friend then?'

'There is no mysterious friend,' Antonia said. 'The mysterious friend does not exist. Oh my God, Hugh, it's so simple. You will want to kick yourself when I tell you –'

'No, don't tell me!' Payne raised his hand. 'I believe in making the old cerebellum work. All right. I know with absolute certainty that there is an event that couldn't have happened. It's something to do with those deleted messages, isn't it?'

'No, not really. It's to do with Joan's mobile phone all right, but *not* with the messages.'

'It can't be Billy, can it? No, too stupid. Must be Billy's evil avatar then. Mortimer is the kind of chap who luxuriates in his own transgressive badness. He hated Joan. He and Billy look uncannily alike. D'you remember Bros, the singing twins that were such a hit with teenage girls in the eighties? Mortimer and Selkirk reminded me of them, though I very much doubt they have much time for girls. Perhaps they did it together? I mean the murder.'

'It's nothing to do with Sieg Mortimer or with Billy Selkirk. Sorry to disappoint you. You are running out of time now.' Antonia glanced at her watch. 'Shall I tell you?'

'No, wait. I think it's coming ... You said there was no mysterious friend? That means Collingwood told a lie.'

'Yes –'

Suddenly Payne leant forward. 'What was it you said earlier on? You couldn't let me know you were going out to meet Deirdre because you'd left your mobile phone behind.' He slapped his forehead with his hand. 'Good lord, I've got it! That's what happened with Joan Selwyn, isn't it? *She had left her mobile phone behind!*'

'Yes,' Antonia said quietly.

'Joan Selwyn couldn't have been phoned and told to go to Philomel Cottage for the simple reason that she didn't have her mobile with her. She couldn't have received that call at Richoux's. Her mobile was at Sieg Mortimer's flat. She didn't have a second mobile. *That phone call never took place.* Therefore, the question is, why did Collingwood need to invent a phone call and an anonymous caller?'

'There is only one obvious answer.'

'Yes. The obvious answer is that Collingwood wanted to distract attention from himself since it was he – *he* – who asked Joan Selwyn to go to Philomel Cottage. Collingwood invented a mysterious friend who'd left something behind and urgently needed to retrieve it. Collingwood wasn't aware of the fact that Joan didn't have her mobile with her –'

Antonia said, 'Some killers try to be *too* clever and that in the end proves to be their undoing.'

Sieg Mortimer was giving Billy Selkirk a short lecture on the art of writing a certain type of detective story.

'Imagine one counter, the killer, advancing slowly, capriciously, moving here, halting there, along a zigzag path traced upon a multi-coloured board, while another counter, the detective, follows, also moving at intervals, until, suddenly, and should chance and logical deduction will it so, the second counter overtakes the first, and then the two, the pursued and the pursuer, meet on the final square –'

34

TERROR BY NIGHT

I get a perturbing message from the manager of the Holyrood Hotel and I am compelled to leave Lady Collingwood with undignified haste. She is disappointed that we can't go through with the plan after all. Some other time, I tell her, or perhaps she could do it without me? Is she capable of acting solo? She is sure she is, so long as I remain with her 'in spirit'. She reminds me of the telepathic communication that exists between us. As we part she clutches my hand and begs me to remain with her 'in spirit'.

I arrive back at the Holyrood Hotel and the manager tells me there has been a visit from the police. They have been making enquiries about me. There were three of them and they clearly meant business. They showed him a photo of me. They also showed him a search warrant, then went up to my room and ransacked it. They left a message for me – would I get in touch with them as soon as I returned?

Well, I do not intend to get in touch with the police.

I have known the manager of the Holyrood Hotel for some time now. As a matter of fact Mr Ibrahim is one of my most ardent clients. He is also a man who sets great store by discretion. He has two wives and a considerable number of children but seems to find family life uninspiring. He has always been pleased with the girls I send him, which is why he is sympathetic to my predicament, though, naturally, he resents the notion of him or his hotel being embroiled in a scandal.

Well, there will be no scandal. The situation is serious but not desperate. At the moment I have no plan for action ready, but I am seriously considering the idea of a false passport.

I will need to change my appearance. I intend to dye my hair blonde. I seem to be one of the very people involved in this peculiar affair that is not blonde. Blonde men tend to be less noticeable than dark ones. And I shall wear a pair of blue contact lenses. A complete change of identity may be a little difficult these days of hysterically heightened security, but not, I imagine, impossible.

It is a great shame that I should be in danger of being apprehended just as I have been so busy putting the final touches to the disposal of Lord Collingwood. I am not convinced that Lady Collingwood will be able to manage without me but I may be underestimating her. She needs to stop taking dope.

It is a pity that I shall not be able to enter Lady Collingwood's employment in the capacity of her butler. Or maybe I can still do it, at some later point in time – *as someone else*?

'We must go to Park Lane,' Payne said briskly. 'Before something happens. Before it's too late.'

'It's nearly midnight, Hugh.'

'The witching hour, eh? So what?' He shrugged. He then stood up and checked if his car keys were in his pocket. 'Let's go. The game's afoot.'

'Aren't we getting a bit too old for such nocturnal adventures?'

'We are not. Think of the boxer who loses speed but learns new tactics? That's us.'

'What about calling the police?'

'Later. We'll call the police later. When we are absolutely sure.'

'But what in heaven's name was his motive?' Antonia asked as they got into the car. 'Why kill his own daughter?'

'I believe I can guess,' Payne said grimly. He told her his theory.

'That's one of the craziest things I have ever heard!'

'Well, since madness does come into it, "craziest" strikes me as the *mot juste*.'

Lady Collingwood stared at them in a puzzled manner. 'It's the maid's night out and I am afraid we haven't got a butler – yet,' she said, as though either Hugh or Antonia had challenged her about her opening the front door herself.

'Can we come in?' Payne said.

'This is most unexpected. I believe it is nearly quarter-to-one in the morning, some such unearthly hour. Oh. *Hugh*?' Her eyes didn't quite focus. She was wearing high heels. 'It *is* Hugh, isn't it? Hugh Payne? I am so sorry. And is that ... Antonia?'

'Yes, it's me.'

'Do forgive me. The light here is awful. Of course you must come in. I happen to be in an unaccountably wakeful state tonight.'

'Is Collingwood in?' Payne asked as they stood in the sumptuous hall.

'Rupert was in his study half an hour ago, but he may have gone to bed. It's late, you know. I am not sure. I am rarely sure about anything these days.' She sighed. 'Did you want to see him?'

'Very much.'

'I had a visitor earlier on but, sadly, he left. It's been a very disappointing evening.' Deirdre started leading the way up a grand staircase. 'I don't suppose your unexpected visit has anything to do with that terrible murder?'

'As a matter of fact, it has.'

'If I have to be perfectly honest, Rupert has been acting rather peculiarly for quite some time. He hasn't been himself, though it would be impossible for me to say what he is like when he is himself.'

Lord Collingwood was not in his study.

Major Payne's eyes rested on the desk and took in the porcelain cup with some dark liquid in it, the silver scissors, the strips of paper and the framed photograph that showed a middle-aged gentleman wearing a tailcoat, pale spats just visible at the end of black-and-white striped trousers and a moustache trimmed to a nicety.

'My late father-in-law,' Deirdre Collingwood said. 'The fifteenth earl.'

'What's in the cup?' Payne asked.

'The miracle drink everybody's talking about. The Chancellor of the Exchequer swears by it. The new elixir of life. I see Rupert hasn't touched it,' Lady Collingwood said with an air of regret.

'What's happened to your father-in-law's head?' Antonia asked. She stood peering down at the photograph.

'The top of his head is missing. It wasn't always like that, I assure you.'

'It's been cut off.' Payne said.

'Rupert's performed a trepanation, I think. He's been having trepanation dreams.'

Payne's eyes went back to the scissors and strips of paper. He picked up one strip at random. 'What's this? "William Collingwood m. Mariah Carr 1567 ..."'

'Rupert's family tree. He's mutilated his family tree. When we first got married Rupert was incredibly proud of his ancestors, but some time ago he discovered that one of his great-great uncles had supported Cromwell. That perhaps has something to do with the current state of affairs, wouldn't you say?'

'What's the current state of affairs exactly?'

'Rupert has convinced himself his blood is tainted. It's been bothering him. He has very strong views on the subject. Some time ago he started giving family portraits away, his father's relatives, mainly, to charity shops, to jumble sales, awful things like that. When I suggested Christie's or Bonhams, he said he didn't want to profit from what he wanted to forget. His mother let him do it; they are that sort of family. But what a terribly peculiar conversation to have at one in the morning!'

'Where is he?' Payne asked.

'Perhaps in his bedroom? He wouldn't thank us for waking him, I warn you. He values his beauty sleep.'

But Lord Collingwood was not in his bedroom. His bed showed no signs of having been slept in.

'How perfectly extraordinary,' Lady Collingwood said. 'I have no idea where he could possibly be. We lead practically separate lives these days.'

'What was that noise? Was that the front door?'

'It sounded like the back door – to the garden – there appears to be a draught. Nights are getting chillier, have you noticed? Summer's *definitely* over.'

Major Payne turned back and walked out of the room. They followed him down the stairs.

Once more they stood in the hall. 'Which way?'

Lady Collingwood pointed to the left. They passed by a great ormolu console, its marble slab supported on the outstretched wings of a gilded eagle.

The back door was open and swinging on its hinges in the wind.

'What's that light?' Payne asked.

'The conservatory. Rupert takes great pride in his orchids. He sometimes feeds them with lobster thermidor and he claims he can hear them sigh with pleasure. He must be in the conservatory.' She glanced up at the sky. 'Wasn't there a poem about moonlight and orchids being as pale as the flesh of a dead girl? What was it orchids stood for in the Lexicon of Flowers? I await your favours?'

'Treachery and misrepresentation, more likely.' Major Payne gave Deirdre a sideways glance.

'Oh, I thought that was dahlias!'

They had started crossing the garden. Lady Collingwood's progress was somewhat hampered by her high heels.

The conservatory door was closed but not locked.

Inside it was warm and humid and the smell of fresh earth pervaded the air.

The neatness of the plants and the flowers was almost oppressive, Antonia thought. Some of the plants looked as if they had been not only washed but ironed as well, while others gave the impression of being made of wax. Perhaps they *were* made of wax?

Half hidden among the palms and the rhododendrons stood a black marble sculpture: a tall angel, with stark staring glass eyes, which were as bright as the bleached blue of an ancient mariner's eyes. The angel's gaze was turned heavenwards. A flock of brilliantly coloured butterflies fluttered above the angel's head, purple and turquoise, vermilion and fuchsia pink …

'Are they *real*?' Antonia asked.

'Oh yes. Rupert cultivates them. Rupert prides himself on his aesthetic sense. He has them specially ordered – he raises them from cocoons, you know.'

236

The next moment Lady Collingwood gave a little cry and pointed.

It was a gruesome sight that met their eyes.

'I always knew something like this would happen,' she said.

Lord Collingwood was hanging from a palm tree. His face was blue. He appeared to have used his red silk braces to form a hangman's noose. A garden chair lay on the ground where he had kicked it away.

A line of poetry floated into Antonia's head.

His hanging face, like a devil's,
sick of sin –

Payne proceeded to cut the body down with shears he found on a garden table. He attempted artificial respiration, but it was too late.

There was a letter sticking out of the breast pocket of Lord Collingwood's smoking jacket.

It was addressed to Major Payne.

35

THE FINAL SOLUTION

I am arrested as I leave the Holyrood Hotel. It appears my movements have been monitored. Rather imprudently I resist. I struggle and my nose gets bloodied in the process. For a moment mist and darkness come over me. My arms get twisted behind my back and I am handcuffed, then the brutes caution me.

The whole distressing episode takes place only moments after Lady Collingwood has rung me to say that she has managed to bump off her husband and that she has been so clever about it that no one will ever think of suspecting her. I believe she is only showing off, trying to impress me. She said she had felt my presence beside her all along.

I wonder if Lady Collingwood can provide me with a good solicitor …

Antonia stood looking over Hugh's shoulder.

The letter rustled between his fingers.

How unsatisfactory this would be as a murder motive in a book, she thought. One could explain anything and everything with madness. Which, in her opinion, wasn't exactly fair play.

Well, life sometimes was stranger than fiction.

My dear Payne,

You may have been able to work things out for yourself, I don't know. But, in case you haven't, here in short is the 'Final Solution'. (Pun intended.)

Joan was planning to have children with her new man, which would have meant extending the Collingwood line into the next generation. I couldn't possibly allow that. I am sure you are the only person in the world who will understand.

There is madness in our family. An inexorable rust gnawing at the gilded structure. Bad blood, if you prefer simple English. I have had little peace, thinking about it. I have been aware of the problem for quite some time now and I have been through hell.

I am also afflicted. There have been all sorts of signs and manifestations. I am given to bouts of irrational introspection, to melancholy meanderings followed either by great anger or by the deepest stupefaction. I hear voices. I see visions. I have time lapses. I experience states of confusion, what I believe are called 'fugues'? A woman who is Deirdre's spitting image keeps appearing to me in a dream.

Joan displayed some of the signs of my family's madness. I could see it in her eyes, in the way she frowned, in the way she held her head, in her smile – not that she smiled often. Even if Joan had become conscious of the fact, there would have been absolutely nothing she could have done about it. Like me, she was doomed. She had my blood running through her veins. She was after all my daughter.

I have no doubt in my mind that what I did was the right thing. I released Joan from the burden she would inevitably have had to bear.

Most of my people were mad, I realise now. All sorts of small things, seemingly insignificant details come back to me, like the way my father sometimes wore his kilt – back to front. Nobody seemed to mind, it was deemed little more than an endearing eccentricity. I didn't think anything of it myself when I was a boy. It is only recently that my eyes have been 'opened'.

You see, don't you, Payne? The Collingwood line simply has to disappear. The police would have got me sooner or later – my movements must have been 'captured' on all those blasted CCTV cameras you see everywhere in London these days. I would have been arrested, then 'assessed' and then shut away. That's the fate of mental defectives. I can't possibly allow that. I am a proud man. When I die, there will be no more Collingwoods. I have quite an *idée fixe* about the whole thing, which is perhaps further evidence of my deteriorating mind? I am mad and yet I also seem able to stand outside of myself and view my actions with a degree of detachment, which only adds to my torment.

What about doctors, you may ask, what about the miracles of modern medicine? Well, modern medicine has been unable to help me. As a matter of fact, I have already undergone a trepanation. Nobody knows about it. I wouldn't want it bandied about, so, please, keep this particular piece of information under your hat.

The operation was conducted not such a long time ago by that damned woman who looks like Deirdre. She took something out of my head. She assured me the operation had been an unqualified success. She said I would be 'fine'.

Did I become more normal than I had been? I don't think so. As a matter of fact, I have been feeling much worse since. Which only proves my point about the inadequacy of medical science.

But you will want to know more about the murder. Well, this is how I set about it. I told Joan I wanted her to help me retrieve a compromising paper from Olga Klimt's house. I said we might have to search for it. I invented a friend and said the paper belonged to him. I said he had been a client of Olga Klimt's and that I was keen on saving his reputation. She demurred, but I managed to persuade her to go to Philomel Cottage. I gave her a front-door key. As it happens, I am in possession of several keys.

I was after all the previous owner. I told her to go first and unlock the door.

I caught up with her as she was about to enter the hall. I meant to stab her after we'd got inside but she happened to glance over her shoulder and she saw the knife. I was compelled to do it on the spot, you see.

I wish I could have explained I was doing her a favour, that she should be grateful to me, but of course it was quite impossible in the circumstances. I don't suppose she would have understood anyhow.

What did I feel when I saw my daughter pitch forward? A sense of fulfilment, that's what. The ecstasy of achievement that is only realised in dreams. A kind of an apotheosis.

I didn't look back. I hailed a cab and went home.

The knife is actually an ancient Venetian stiletto that I had been using as a paper knife. Its blade is deadly and it is slim enough to fit inside my brolly. You can find it buried among the orchids.

What else is there? You said you hated the idea of loose ends. Oh yes. That draft. The new will. Once I made up my mind that Joan should die, I produced a draft for a new will and made it look as though I intended to leave all my money and property to her. That was my way of ensuring that I wouldn't become a suspect. I mean, what kind of a papa kills his daughter after making her his sole legatee? That was clever of me, you must admit. I knew Deirdre would get to see the draft sooner or later. Deirdre, as I believe I told you, is notorious for her forays into my study.

Choosing Philomel Cottage was part of the smokescreen I set out to create. I wanted to give the impression Olga Klimt was the intended victim and that Joan was killed by mistake. Joan had dyed her hair blond for some reason, to make herself more alluring to Billy, if not to Charlie, I suppose. That's what gave me the idea.

I wonder if you have managed to work out that Joan couldn't have received a phone call while we sat at Richoux's? That was my one slip but then I couldn't have known she had left her mobile at Sieg Mortimer's flat. He told me you took special interest in the damned thing. No one rang her. There was no mysterious caller. No one asked her to go to Philomel Cottage at five-thirty – apart from me, that is.

I contacted Olga Klimt and told her to go to see Charlie. I rang her on the Philomel Cottage landline since I had no idea what her mobile number was. I knew she would immediately try to call Charlie, as I'd got her worried, so I immediately rang him on his mobile and pretended I was someone from his bank. I muffled my voice. I kept his phone busy for a couple of minutes – till Olga got to the Tube where I knew there would be no network.

As I sit writing this, I am convinced that Deirdre and Bedaux are plotting my demise. Earlier on they were next door, in Deirdre's boudoir. It is outrageous that she should have let that villain into the house. Well, they won't be able to bump me off now, I won't give them the pleasure as I intend to do it myself, so there.

I have actually left all my money to you and Collingwood Castle to the National Trust. I have already contacted my solicitors, the will's been witnessed, so this time the whole legal side of it is as it should be.

If, for some reason, you are not happy about this arrangement, perhaps you could choose to use the money to have our old beloved haunt, the Military Club, restored to its former glory? To the days when it stood – in the words of those bloody Socialists – for 'everything reactionary and establishmentarian'? Please, have the dilatory waiter sacked. And make sure the coffee continues excellent. I would be most grateful.

It is time for me to go. My only regret is that my trip to Scotland will have to be postponed indefinitely.

Goodbye, Payne. *Ave Caesar* – and all that kind of rot.

Yours, Collingwood.

ABOUT
THE AUTHOR

R.T. RAICHEV is a writer and researcher who grew up in Bulgaria and wrote his university dissertation on English crime fiction. He has lived in London since 1989, and *The Killing of Olga Klimt* is the ninth book in his popular Antonia Darcy and Major Payne mystery series.

ALSO IN THE ANTONIA DARCY AND MAJOR PAYNE MYSTERY SERIES

PRAISE FOR R.T. RAICHEV

'Fascinating ... recalls the best from the Golden Age of Detective Fiction.'

Lady Antonia Fraser

'I have read all of Raichev's books. They are very clever. I really am a fan.'

R.L. Stine

'Most original and intriguing ... An England of club and country house, with a delicious shot of bitters!'

Emma Tennant

'Raichev clearly has a great deal of fun writing the Antonia and Major Payne series, giving these modern stories almost an Edwardian feel, and we're rewarded with finely drawn characters, clever murder mysteries, and dialogue that sparkles. Best recommended to fans of golden age authors (Christie, Sayers, et al.) who can tolerate a little modernity!'

Booklist

'A most intriguing yarn of mystery, imagination, observation and splendidly old-fashioned sleuthery which skilfully probes the surface smoothness of clubland and country house. I couldn't put it down.'

Hugh Massingberd

'Deftly mixes dark humour and psychological suspense, its genteel surface masking delicious deviancy.'

Kirkus Reviews (Starred Review)

'Greed, jealousy, rampant emotions and a killer lurk in the wings of this tale that mixes Henry James' psychological insight with Agatha Christie's whodunnit plotting skills ... a diabolically clever story line.'

Library Journal (Starred Review)

'An ominous feel, reminiscent of Hitchcock.'

Mystery Morgue

'Recommended for any mystery fan who likes surprises.'

New Mystery Reader Magazine

'Murder is fun again! Each chapter parcels out just a bit more of the story, just enough, drawing open the curtain to reveal the picture behind ... A mystery that harkens back to the thirties and forties, but pays respect to modernity ... Definitely a keeper.'

Suspense Magazine

'Intricate and inventive ... very witty dialogue and a cast of gloriously eccentric characters.'

Francis Wyndham

'Stylish ... deft use of literary allusion and well-drawn characterisation.'

Publishers Weekly

'The kind of old-school mysteries that fans of Christie and Sayers love ... but this will be pleasing to more than traditionalists, because it adds a P.D. Jamesian subtlety to the comfortable formula. Antonia Darcy is a terrific sleuth and Raichev is a very clever writer, indeed.'

Booklist

'Liberal doses of imagination, experimentation, intelligence and sprinklings of irony, satire and fun ... the riveting attention of a game of Cluedo.'

The Hidden Staircase Mystery Books

'A whodunnit with more twists than a snake in a basket!'
Robert Barnard, CWA Diamond Dagger Winner

'Superbly plotted ... Raichev delivers this classic with the perfect panache one expects from an author who wrote his doctoral dissertation on English crime fiction ... Excellent series!'

Toronto Globe & Mail

'A dazzling tour de force, as ingeniously plotted as anything Agatha Christie ever wrote but wittier and more sophisticated.'

The Denver Post on The Death of Corinne: An Antonia Darcy and Major Payne Investigation

'Clever … Raichev's series has attitude, like a mash-up of
Evelyn Waugh, P.G. Wodehouse and P.D. James …'
Milwaukee Journal-Sentinel on Murder at the Villa Byzantine:
An Antonia Darcy and Major Payne Investigation

'With plenty of unexpected twists and a good ending,
The Murder of Gonzago is pure fun!'
www.gumshoereview.com on Murder of Gonzago:
An Antonia Darcy and Major Payne Investigation

'A grand whodunnit in the great tradition of English crime
writing.'
www.crimesquad.com on The Riddle of Sphinx Island:
An Antonia Darcy and Major Payne Mystery

'Another baffling case … A risky romp in pursuit of the
truth … Raichev's page-turner captures the tart elegance of
classic cozies but adds an appealing modern edge.'
Kirkus Review

Also from The History Press

We are proud to present our history crime fiction imprint, The Mystery Press, featuring a dynamic and growing list of titles written by diverse and respected authors, united by the distinctiveness and excellence of their writing. From a collection of thrilling tales by the CWA Short Story Dagger award-winning Murder Squad, to a Victorian lady detective determined to solve some sinister cases of murder in London, these books will appeal to serious crime fiction enthusiasts as well as those who simply fancy a rousing read.

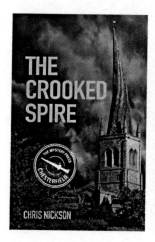

Find these titles and more at
www.thehistorypress.co.uk

Lightning Source UK Ltd.
Milton Keynes UK
UKOW03f0012110714

234894UK00001B/1/P